Quest for Light – Adventure of the Magi

Quest for Light – Adventure of the Magi

Byron Anderson

Quest for Light – Adventure of the Magi

© Byron Anderson 2012

This book is a work of fiction. Named locations are used fictitiously, and characters and incidents are the product of the author's imagination. Any resemblance to actual events or places or persons, living or dead, is entirely coincidental.

All rights reserved. Without limiting the rights under copyright reserved above, no part of this publication may be reproduced, stored in a retrieval system, or transmitted, in any form or by any means (electronic, mechanical, photocopying, recording or otherwise), without the prior written permission of the copyright owner of this book.

Published by
Lighthouse Christian Publishing
SAN 257-4330
5531 Dufferin Drive
Savage, Minnesota, 55378
United States of America

www.lighthousechristianpublishing.com

Chapter I – A Star Shines on Persia

Winter's first storm brought stillness to the village. The brisk wind swept the remaining storm clouds from view as wisps of pink and purple clouds flashed softly before revealing a clear sky. Drifting down from the palace anchored high on the nearby hill, faint sounds were all that were heard. The palace home of Balthasar, the High Priest of Asdin, was the most superior structure in the region, a fortress of great grey stones commanding an expansive view of the valley. A panorama unfolded from the palace roof where sky and horizon melded heaven to Earth. But instead of fading into the expansive darkness, the lingering sounds were soon transformed into a chorus of shouts as torches appeared on the palace roof, illuminating the silhouettes of rooftop gatherers.

Although it was not unusual to hear Balthasar shout instructions to his servants on the palace roof, tonight brought more torches and more people, while Balthasar's boisterous shouts seemed to carry more meaning than usual. Over supper, many curious villagers below the palace walls speculated as to what might have been the cause of such excitement.

    Balthasar positioned himself on the roof, fixing his sight on the western horizon. After many anxious days, he hoped the sky would once again reveal the fantastic star he had glimpsed a few days earlier. In the many years he had studied the heavens, he had never seen such a star. Although he only briefly saw the star before the clouds obscured his view, this encounter dominated his thoughts and imagination. Each day he grew more anxious, while frustration impaired his emotions as his family and servants suffered from their encounters with him. His mood shifted from excitement and wonder to confusion and despair, all within a matter of seconds.

    As he contemplated whether this incredible star signified something magnificent, he wondered: Would he see it again? Was it a onetime event? Perhaps he never saw the star; perhaps he only imagined it. After all, no one was with him on the roof that night; perhaps he was going mad. Balthasar positioned himself on the roof, fixing his sight on the western horizon as the last of the clouds disappeared behind the mountains.

    Holding his breath in anticipation, Balthasar froze in place until that exhilarating moment when he shouted, "Fantastic! There it is! It is brighter and larger than before. In the midst of the setting sun it shines!"

    The quiet of the evening was shattered by Balthasar's bellow echoing through the valley, as listeners near and far tried to make sense of his excitement.

    As darkness fell, the radiance of the star suspended just above the western horizon dominated the heavens in the moonless sky. Balthasar's shouts and laughter soon attracted a crowd of family and servants.

Upon their arrival, he addressed them in his usual loud voice, but this time in the form of instruction, saying, "Unlike heaven's other lights, this star shines bright and steady. See how the other stars shimmer as rocks in a creek? But this great star, observe its light… it is a mighty torch… a piece of the sun has taken its place in the night sky!"

Balthasar watched the star until the cold had him shivering beneath his heavy wool robe. He was unaware that only one lit torch remained and that his companions had long since departed for the warmth of the palace. He kept to his watch, pondering the star's significance. It appeared in an instant… would its departure be as sudden? His mind raced as he wondered why the star appeared at all and for how long it would remain.

A few others on the roof shared Balthasar's sense of awe and wonder over this extraordinary star, including his wife, Dinbanu, and his servant, Ainairya, who were amazed by the star and believed it to be a sign from heaven. Others, however, did not consider the star unusual. And a few people said they could not see the star at all. For them, the real mystery was why there was so much excitement, as one person was overheard saying that all the stars looked the same to him and perhaps Balthasar had spent too much time alone in the night air.

As Balthasar remained alone outside in the cool night air, Dinbanu returned to check on him just as the last torch flickered out.

Tapping him softly on the shoulder, she said, "Come inside before you freeze to death."

"Oh! I did not see you… where is everyone?" asked a startled Balthasar.

"We left you hours ago… before your lips turned blue!" said Dinbanu, shaking her head.

"Has it been that long? I cannot pull myself away from it. Is it not amazing?" Balthasar explained to his wife without ever taking his eyes off the star.

"Yes, it is wonderful, but if you want to live to see it tomorrow, you should come inside now," scolded Dinbanu.

Dinbanu took Balthasar by the arm and led him to the door. But before leaving the roof, Balthasar turned one last time to look at the star and said, "Dinbanu, I do not have the answer to this."

"You will find the answer," Dinbanu replied as she tugged on Balthasar's arm, pulling him further inside.

"I have more questions than answers. It appears for a reason and I must know why," Balthasar replied quietly as he followed his wife inside the palace.

What brought Balthasar to the roof this evening, however, was something more than just his curiosity of nature. There was a far deeper meaning to his fascination with unusual occurrences in the night sky, one that was part of a larger quest for truth and the meaning of life that was rooted deeply in his soul. He would seek advice from others who studied the stars, he decided, people whom he trusted and respected. His life-long friend, Gaspar, for example, was familiar with the many prophecies attributed to celestial wonders. If the weather cooperated, as Balthasar hoped it would, he would send for his friend at first light.

Before dawn, Balthasar's servants, Stipay, Nanarasti and Thrita, prepared for the trip to Shahnaz to summon Gaspar. They were among the best riders in the village and had made this trip many times. They retrieved their horses from the crudely hewn stable and, once packed, began their ride into the valley towards Shahnaz. If all went as planned, they were expected to report back to Balthasar in Asdin within twelve days.

The men paused for a moment to take a last look at the village, briefly savoring the sweet aroma of breakfast cooking over wood fires, but their only well wishers this cold morning were a few horses huddled together to keep warm. Steam rising from the horses, which produced a small vapor cloud that quickly evaporated, was the only movement in the frigid air this morning.

The journey to Shahnaz, although not a great distance, would be difficult now that snow covered much of the road. Winter's arrival in the mountains halted travel along the merchant's road several weeks ago, preventing caravans from returning to Asdin until the spring thaw relieved the mountain passes from their burden of snow. Even more, the sun's time in the sky had grown short, signaling that the harshest weather was yet to come. Balthasar's men hoped, however, that this harsh weather would deter robbers and unfriendly militia bands that might have threatened them.

Back in the village, for those not faced with the challenge of travel, winter was appreciated for its peacefulness and isolation. This was a time for family and friends, a season to reflect on days past and to give thanks for life, health and prosperity. It was also a time to tend to the things that needed attention, such as planning the next year's crops and making sure the animals were fed well enough to survive the dramatic drop in temperature.

This was not the time of year to set out on a trip, but Balthasar had given the order, and his riders knew that such a request would not be made of them unless it was a critical matter, given the asks of their journey.

Chapter II – The Magi Way of Life

Balthasar and his people were descendents of Persians known as Medes. For many generations, Medes lived in this great valley where the vast Hamedian Plain rose to meet the Zagros Mountains. Medes living in this rugged area benefitted from access to the merchant road that connected Persia with the rest of the world. Babylonia, Assyria, Amernia and the Great Sea lied to the west. Parthia, Aria, Bactria, Sogdia and the Asian kingdoms were to the north and east. The trade road was the source of life for Asdin; its endless supply of travelers brought prosperity and news from afar.

Medes were known for their generosity and treated visitors with respect, usually extending more patience and tolerance to foreigners than they did to each other. Although visitors were welcome, they were watched closely to ensure that they did not pose a threat.

Many years ago, Persia boasted great and ambitious military leaders, who ruthlessly conquered neighboring lands, and the Medes established a reputation as Persia's fiercest warriors. Their neighbors learned that it was unwise to provoke the Medes because their response would be quick and deadly. Balthasar's Persia, however, no longer sought conflict and the Medes engaged in battle only when under threat. Such reputations of the past, however, did not fade quickly. Recognizing the benefits of their warrior image, the villagers perpetuated that reputation by training horses and practicing battle skills when visitors were nearby.

Balthasar's people were also known throughout the region and beyond as breeders of exceptional horses. Beautiful and fast, the horses were bred for strength and stamina, the perfect horse to serve a soldier in battle. Their horses were not particularly tall, but they were bred to produce large heads, strong necks and powerful haunches. The Medes clipped the manes of their horses, keeping them short so they would not interfere with the archers who shot from them as they rode. They also tied the tails of the horses so they could not be grabbed by the enemy in battle.

 Most of the horses were dark in color, usually brown or black, although there were horses of a golden chestnut color and a few golden bays with black manes, tails, lower legs and ear tips. A small number of white horses, which were viewed as a sign of wealth, were also bred and reserved for generals and kings. Balthasar had a herd of these rare white horses and kept them separate from the other horses to ensure the integrity of the breed.

 Several generations of Medes prospered by trading horses to militia groups and merchants in exchange for silk, jade, medicine and other valuable items. While Asdin benefitted from its proximity to the trade road, its location also availed it to close inspection by potential foes. Driven by the need to defend themselves, Balthasar's people were quite proficient in warfare, and training for battle was conducted in public view to help discourage potential attackers. These public displays also provided a good showcase for their finely trained horses, so every effort was made to feature the best of the breed for these public training exercises.

 Balthasar was an expert horseman and had trained many villagers in defending themselves from invaders. Balthasar and other young men were taught these skills at an early age by the men who were responsible for protecting their community. One of Balthasar's childhood friends, Gaspar, also received this special training. The two boys grew up together, fending off bandits and invaders who threatened their families.

Gaspar was a close friend of many years who shared Balthasar's beliefs and knowledge. Both men commanded respect because of special training passed to them through many generations of scholars. This training developed their skills as philosophers, astronomers, breeders of fine horses and, most importantly, priests. They were the chief priests of their regions, commanding influence extending far beyond their kingdoms. They were the spiritual leaders of their people and, as Mede priests, trusted by all Persians.

Persians knew Balthasar and Gaspar as Magi, those who led their people in spiritual matters, the most important aspect of Mede life. Magi were the only authorities called upon to settle religious disputes and perform public religious rites. They were also often sought out by the wealthy and powerful to educate and train their families. They were so well respected that royalty often sent Magi to represent them before foreign leaders. Many Medes considered the Magi to be their kings.

Possessors of many talents, the Magi had a particular reputation for their astronomy skills. For generations, Magi recorded their observations and studies of important celestial events. While Balthasar possessed much knowledge of the heavens, he would need help from other Magi if he was to discover the meaning of this most unusual star and thus, he sent his most trusted men to bring Gaspar to his side for advice.

The Magi shared a philosophy of life with its roots planted centuries before by a Persian known as Zoroaster.

Zoroaster started a religion based on the principle that man should "do only good and should hate all evil." He preached that there was only one God, Ahura Mazda, which meant "The Wise Lord." Ahura Mazda was the good force in the world and was represented by fire and water, nature's purifiers.

It was said that when Zoroaster was born, his laugh scattered the evil spirits. Legend claimed that he grew up with a love of wisdom and righteousness. When Zoroaster was thirty years old, he immersed himself in water during a spring religious festival. When he emerged in a state of purity, he had a vision of a being of light who introduced himself as Good Purpose.

According to the legend, Good Purpose took Zoroaster up a mountain to the great god, Ahura Mazda. Zoroaster returned from the mountain to preach that Ahura Mazda was all wise and the source of all justice and goodness. Angra Mainyu, however, was the enemy of Ahura Mazda and sought to bring pain and suffering to the world. Ahura Mazda was goodness, while Angra Mainyu was the ruler of all that was dark, wicked and cruel. In the great battle between Ahura Mazda and Angra Mainyu, people were responsible for choosing between right and wrong. Zoroaster called people to a rigid discipline to support Ahura Mazda's goodness.

Followers of Zoroaster adhered strictly to their religious traditions, integrating prayer deeply into their lives. There were five daily prayer watches observed by Medes: Ushahin, Hawan, Rapithwin, Uzerin and the Aiwisruthrem. Their religious rituals included a sacramental fire, or Adar, which symbolized purification. The greatest sacred fire was Adar Burzin, while the lesser of the fires were Adar Farnbag and Adar Gushasp. It was

believed that these sacred fires kept Angra Mainyu's demons away.
While most Magi used their knowledge wisely, there were a small number of Magi who pursued darkness instead of light. These dark Magi turned away from Zoroaster to engage in divination, interpreting dreams and predicting the future. The Magi religion, however, forbade sorcery and Balthasar and Gaspar were obedient to Ahura Mazda, and used their knowledge wisely; never for self gain.

Balthasar's fascination with the heavens and the meaning they held was an interest developed over a lifetime. His knowledge of the stars, his code of conduct and his spiritual beliefs were shared by his father and other Magi. Magi observed the heavens and respected all nature because they believed it would help them know and understand Ahura Mazda, the creator of all things good. They believed that Ahura Mazda communicated his desires and intentions to all people each evening through the signs, comets and stars he placed in the sky.

Much of Balthasar's childhood was spent traveling with his parents. His father served as an emissary to a Persian prince and once traveled beyond Persia's western border to the Great Sea, which led to Greece and Rome. As a young man, Balthasar made many trips with his father delivering horses to traders and soldiers. It was during these occasions that he gained experience in warfare, fending-off robbers along the road. While the skirmishes were few, the threat was constant.

That was many years ago and Balthasar now kept closer to home. Advancing years may have slowed his pace, but his enthusiasm for life and his quest for truth remained strong. He was passionate about his beliefs and enjoyed a good challenge. While his beard showed some white, his body benefitted from the work of breaking horses, chopping wood and training men for warfare. Balthasar longed for adventure, but he came to accept his role as leader of his people.

Like Balthasar, Gaspar spent his younger years traveling, visiting many lands. Gaspar was born in Greece and most of his childhood was spent in that part of the world where he learned many different languages and customs. At times, Gaspar could be impatient and hot-tempered, but he had a great zest for life and strived to be thoughtful and cautious in his affairs.

As Balthasar awaited Gaspar's arrival, he used the time to review his celestial charts and manuscripts. Over the years, Balthasar recorded many of his observations of the night sky. As he studied, he was reminded that unusual celestial events often signaled the occurrence of a significant event on earth. He had read of signs appearing in the heavens that forewarned of earthquakes and famines, and often these signs corresponded to well known prophecies. But Balthasar understood that deciphering these events required much knowledge and wisdom. While explanations of celestial events often differed among Magi, Balthasar was certain that there had never been an event in the heavens that compared to this magnificent star. It must have had an important meaning.

It was eleven days since Balthasar dispatched his servants to Shahnaz. A clear sky kept the trails free of new snow. A generation or two ago, travel was more difficult in this area of Persia. Now, however, the growing supply of horses was making travel easier. It was not that long ago when horses were only used to pull carts, but riding on horseback was becoming a common sight, although it was also a cause of much worry. Groups of people could now travel great distances on horseback and not all of the travelers were friendly, especially groups of armed nomads on horseback whose intentions were never certain. Asdin and other kingdoms were vulnerable to the presence of these large groups of nomads, who appeared one day and were gone the next. On the occasions when armed warriors appeared outside the village gates, Balthasar's men could not be certain if they had friendly or hostile intentions.

It was just after the noon hour when the village bell sounded. It was not a rapid tolling of the bell that warned of danger, but a rhythm signaling something less urgent. The bell might have been welcoming the return of Stipay, Nanarasti and Thrita or, just as likely, it could have been a casual alert that a goat escaped from its pen. Balthasar made his way to the palace roof and strode quickly to the southwest corner where he had the best view of the valley. He saw four riders on horseback and one pack horse approaching the village. Surely this must have been his servants returning with Gaspar. Balthasar hurried from the roof and, seconds later, bolted out of the palace as the heavy wooden doors banged shut behind him. In too much of a hurry to grab his coat, Balthasar made his way down the hill as quickly as he could negotiate the loose stones and ruts that served as the road. He did not want to lose any time in welcoming his servants and Gaspar.

As Balthasar approached the riders, Gaspar greeted him in a loud voice, "Brother Balthasar, is life so hard that you no longer own a horse?"

Before the laughter subsided, Balthasar replied, "I would rather walk than sit upon a shabby beast as you do.

How did such an old and broken animal survive the trip? You must have carried it on your back!"

It was obvious that the Magi were good friends. This was not a typical Persian greeting and certainly not the manner in which Magi were addressed. As Gaspar dismounted his horse, the two greeted each other with the traditional embrace and kiss.

Persians were aware of how their behavior was viewed by others and matters of etiquette were important to them. It was common for Persians holding superior positions in society to offer their cheeks to be kissed by those of a lower status. Persians of equal status often embraced and kissed each other on the lips. Gaspar was kissed on his cheeks by several of Balthasar's servants, who greeted him with warm words and a jug of fresh water.

As the crowd dispersed, the two friends walked slowly up the hill with arms locked and with Gaspar's pack horse trailing close behind.

In a soft voice, Balthasar whispered, "Old friend, we have much to discuss."

Gaspar smiled and said, "I knew that I would hear from you. I would have come sooner, but the weather has not been good for travel, especially with an old, broken down horse like mine."

"You would have come sooner? So you have seen it?" asked an excited Balthasar.

"Of course I have seen it! How could I miss it? There is no star its equal," Gaspar replied.

As they walked the hill, Balthasar placed his arm on Gaspar's shoulder and said, "I sent for you because I feared you would not find your way without help, given your many years."

"My many years? I heard that you left this world a long time ago. Will you survive the walk up this hill or shall I carry you as I carry my horse?" Gaspar asked with a laugh.

Laughter followed the two as they made their way to the palace.

Balthasar's family and servants were waiting at the palace door to greet Gaspar.

As the door closed behind them, Gaspar turned to Balthasar and said in a firm voice, "Friend, we must go to this star. Ahura Mazda hung it there for a purpose... it waits for us!"

Balthasar grew quiet, his mouth lost its smile and he looked troubled as he joined Gaspar on a bench next to the fire pit.

"Waiting for us where?" Balthasar asked in a quiet voice.

Gaspar jumped to his feet and shouted, "Ispaghol!" which meant "my horse's ear." Pointing to the west, Gaspar said firmly, "It hangs over the land of the Hebrews, of course! Is it not clear? Have you consulted the Hebrew Scriptures? The star is Balaam's scepter!" Gaspar stood motionless, staring at Balthasar, waiting for his reaction.

Balthasar slowly rose to his feet and with his eyes fixed on Gaspar, he asked, "How can we be sure that the star is not the sign of the Persian messiah, the one who will return Persia to greatness? The one whom we were taught is the Saoshyant and Astavatereta, the victorious benefactor and world-renovator. I have read the prophecy many times and Zoroaster teaches that the messiah will be the benefactor because he will benefit the entire physical world, and he will be the world-renovator because he will establish a permanent physical life for all believers."

Balthasar was now standing close to Gaspar, studying his friend's face for some reaction. Contemplating Balthasar's words, Gaspar's expression remained unchanged, except for a raised eyebrow.

Believing that Gaspar may have been coming around to his point of view, Balthasar continued in a serious tone, "I see that the star may lie beyond Persia, but my heart pounds and my soul stirs when I see it! It is placed there for us as much as it is for any man. If Zoroaster tells us that our messiah is for the entire world, perhaps he will not make his appearance in Persia. Do you not agree? Does the star speak to you?"

"I also am drawn to the star. I cannot explain the power it has over me," Gaspar replied as he sat and kicked off his boots. Gaspar stretched his legs, placing his feet close to the fire, and said, "I have read the scrolls countless times, searching for some hint of prophesy that can be connected to the star. Does Zoroaster's prophecy of a messiah have meaning to us now? I do not know. I suppose that we cannot rule out anything as a possibility, but I am growing more certain each day that this star is a sign of the Hebrew messiah!"

After taking a moment to think about Gaspar's comments, Balthasar responded, "There are many ideas about nature and religion that differ from Zoroaster. In the years that I traveled, I saw many who have different beliefs about life, nature and God. We cannot be certain if the star is a sign of a messiah, or a warning of a calamity that is about to come upon us!"

Gaspar nodded in agreement and was about to speak when Balthasar interrupted, "Good friend, please excuse my rudeness. After such a long and tiring trip, you must want to rest."

Gaspar smiled as he stretched his legs, but he wanted to continue the conversation. He said, "When I first saw the star, I was reminded of Zoroaster's teaching that Ahura Mazda's message will be carried throughout the world and that those who follow Angra Mainyu's lies will dwell in darkness and misery. The final days of man will end with the pronouncement of a last judgment and the destruction of Angra Mainyu."

Gaspar paused as the two men contemplated the significance of what was being discussed.

After a moment, Gaspar asked, "Is it possible that the star is a sign that the last judgment is upon us? Is that great resurrection about to come to all good people who will cross the bridge into Ahura Mazda's kingdom, free of decay, old age and death?"

"Who can say? I do not know if Ahura Mazda's message has been carried to the entire world. Zoroaster is not followed outside of Persia and many in our own land have strayed from his teachings. Many people believe in a prophecy of a messiah. No prophecy is better known to us than the one in the Hebrew Scriptures. Their numbers may be small in Persia, but much is known about Hebrew beliefs. Since their days as captives more than 500 years ago, they continue to be faithful to their god, Yahweh," Balthasar added.

Gaspar glanced toward the sky and said, "We cannot be certain what the star holds. If it is heralding a messiah, it may be an event that changes the lives of all men. If the star warns of disaster, it must be a warning to all who witness the star's brilliance. Surely a god who sends such a sign will not conceal its meaning!"

"When I first saw the star, I knew that it would require much investigation. I suspect that there is much speculation about it. We often receive praise for solving such mysteries, but we do not hold the answer for the star," Balthasar replied.

"We may not know everything about the star, but we are in agreement that it hangs over Jerusalem and that it is consistent with the Hebrew prophecies," answered Gaspar.

Balthasar became quiet and stared into the fire. He picked up a piece of wood and used it to gently push an ember back into the fire. After a few minutes of contemplation, Balthasar dropped the piece of wood and jumped to his feet. With an excited voice, he responded to Gaspar, "Yes, of course, this must be correct. The star, the scepter, the Hebrew messiah... it is as easy to see as the nose on my face."

"Then we must go to where the star rests… Jerusalem! It is the only way we will learn its true meaning!" Gaspar shouted as he slapped Balthasar on the back.

Too excited to sit, the men paced about the room and discussed their next steps.

"Such a quest will be difficult. It will take time to plan. This will be the adventure of our lives, perhaps our last if we do not properly prepare. We will need others to join us. Good men, men we can trust!" offered Gaspar.

"With some prodding, I believe I can convince a few men to join us. It will be a long journey and a great sacrifice for the men to be away from their families, but this is a journey that must be undertaken," Balthasar replied with a trace of concern in his voice.

Over the next several days, the Magi planned the details of their trip. Their route, their provisions and their companions were discussed. They reminisced about the days of their youth and shared news about family and friends. It didn't take long, however, for these conversations to lead back to the matter at hand. While they were committed to their journey, they had some doubts about their ability to reach their destination and return home safely.

Occasionally, they heard the ring of doubt in each other's voices, but neither Magi raised the subject. But, one evening when they were on the palace roof, Gaspar asked, "Balthasar, good friend, neither of us has ever contemplated such a trip. We cannot even imagine the trouble we could find ourselves in. Can we do this? Do you believe we have the men, the discipline and the experience necessary to keep ourselves alive long enough to reach Jerusalem?"

"I also have doubts about this trip. But when I look over there, I remember that we are not alone," a smiling Balthasar replied as he nodded in the direction of the star.

The concern in Gaspar's face disappeared as the two men fixed their gazes on the star that provided them with the inspiration to undertake such a long and treacherous journey.

Chapter III – Preparing for the Journey

The Magi reviewed their scrolls and charts to consider routes of travel. After much discussion, Balthasar tossed a chart onto the table in frustration.

"Impossible! How can we make decisions with so little information? We put everyone at risk if we do not choose safe routes!" complained Balthasar.

"I understand. There is much we do not know about the roads beyond our region. I suggest we prepare for the worst so we can overcome any problems," Gaspar responded.

"There is so much uncertainty! We know there will be problems, but how do we determine the number of men necessary to keep us safe? How do we ensure that we will have enough food and water to get us through the wilderness?" asked a frustrated Balthasar.

"Friend, do not worry. If we take our time and proceed cautiously, much will be made known to us once we are on the main road. The caravan drivers will be helpful to us," Gaspar replied confidently.

"Help from caravan drivers? They cannot be trusted. You know their lying ways. They tell of the great distances they travel and the danger they encounter, but we know that most drivers keep their travel within a boundary of only a few days. They only complain of danger and distance to increase their prices. Each time their goods change hands, the value increases! I would not trust information from any driver," an irritated Balthasar said.

"You speak the truth," laughed Gaspar. After a moment, Gaspar appealed to Balthasar, "Yet some drivers are trustworthy and much can be learned from piecing together what we are told by many of them."

"I pray that you are right, but we should still be cautious about what they tell us. We know how protective they are of their information. I have heard of neighboring villages unaware of the other's existence because the traders have kept that information to themselves!" warned Balthasar.

The Magi reviewed their charts and discussed possible routes of travel well into the evening, unable to reach an agreement on which roads they would follow.

The following morning, Balthasar paced the room where he kept his scrolls and charts. When his wife, Dinbanu, entered the room, he asked, "Have you seen Gaspar this morning?"

"He woke early and left before dawn," Dinbanu replied as she placed some wood on the fire.

"Did he say anything?"

"He said nothing. He grabbed his coat and hurried out the door. He did not even notice me tending the fire," answered Dinbanu as she placed a pot next to the blazing fire.

"Most unusual," murmured Balthasar as he lifted his cup, motioning for Dinbanu to fill it.

As Dinbanu poured, she told Balthasar, "He is much like you. He has a mind of his own and he cannot keep still!"

Balthasar smiled, briefly nodding in agreement, and then softly replied, "Sit with me," as he gently kissed Dinbanu's forehead.

Dinbanu and Balthasar had been married for many years and known each other since they were children. Dinbanu's dark hair was thick and shiny, flowing to the floor. Her face was round like the moon and her eyes were as blue as the summer sky. Balthasar loved her deeply. Her name meant "Lady of Faith" and it suited her well. She shared Balthasar's strong spiritual beliefs and honored his role as chief priest. She was obedient to Balthasar, but not in a way that compromised her personality or expression. Dinbanu knew that Balthasar had much on his mind, and as she sat next to her husband, she tried to comfort him.

"Balthasar, remember how uncertain life seemed for us at the time of our marriage?" Dinbanu asked in a soothing voice.

"I suppose I remember some unsettledness in our lives then, but why do you think of such things now?" asked a puzzled Balthasar.

Dinbanu gently rested her head on Balthasar's shoulder and replied, "Life brings changes to everyone and those changes bring challenges. We have faced many challenges over the years and we have always overcome them, but not without some difficulty. The journey you and Gaspar plan is also a difficult challenge, but I know your journey will be a successful one."

Balthasar was silent for a moment as he considered his wife's encouraging words. He then asked, "And why are you so certain that our journey will be successful?"

Kissing her husband softly, Dinbanu confidently replied, "Because yours is a journey of the heart, inspired by God's star."

Balthasar placed his arm around his wife and gently brought her closer to him. His spirit comforted, he was once again reminded of the insight and wisdom that she was able to impart in only a few words.

Dinbanu was a special woman, but she shared many qualities of other Mede women. The Medes made no distinction between the status of men and women. Zoroaster taught that women were equal to men and should be treated with respect. Mede women chose their spouses and were free to learn and teach in the same manner as men. This freedom enjoyed by Mede women, however, did not extend to other parts of Persia. Foreigners traveling through Mede regions were quite surprised to see the women expressing themselves freely, and performing roles usually reserved for men.

Zoroaster taught that men and women were to live according to the principles of good mind and love, and should try to surpass each other in truth and righteousness so that each reaped the rewards of joy and happiness. This is the principle that fueled Balthasar and Dinbanu's enduring love for each other.

Medes treated everyone with respect. Balthasar's servants served in that capacity out of respect for Balthasar as chief priest and they were rewarded for their service. They were free to leave their roles as servants, but these positions were highly prized.

As Balthasar and Dinbanu waited for Gaspar, the tea pot sitting next to the fire began to steep. Tea was served with meals and was drunk at all times during the day. Balthasar's tea, or "tu" as it was called, was grown in Han China and purchased from traders on the Silk Road. It was a simple pleasure, but not one that was always available. Balthasar used the tu as a beverage, but some ate it as a vegetable and took it as a medicine.

When purchased, the tu was in the form of a hard cake. To prepare his drink, Balthasar ground chunks of the cake in a stone mortar, then placed it in a kettle filled with boiling water. The tu, however, could be bitter and harsh, so Balthasar often added a spice or two to the mixture. What Balthasar enjoyed most about drinking tu on a cold morning was that it was served hot.

Balthasar finished his tu and began gathering his documents when Gaspar reentered the palace with a bang of the doors and a loud shout.

"Balthasar, are you up from your bed or do you still slumber?"

"We are in here, friend! I thought you changed your mind and had gone home," answered Balthasar.

Gaspar entered the room and removed his coat, his breathing fast and his face red.

"Has the cold turned your skin red or did you run up the hill?" asked Balthasar with a laugh.

"It is some of both. It is terribly cold this morning, so cold that nothing moves. The birds have no song, their beaks must be frozen. And yes, I did run up the hill," gasped Gaspar.

Still laughing, Balthasar asked, "Was something chasing you?"

"No, I was in a hurry to get back so we could continue our planning," Gaspar said while catching his breath. "And running is the only way I could get my blood flowing again. Terrible cold! Is what you are drinking hot?" asked Gaspar with outstretched hands.

"No, not hot, warm, but there is plenty and breakfast will soon follow," answered Balthasar as he handed his friend a cup.

Balthasar carefully poured the tu into a cup as Gaspar took a seat close to the fire, dangling his feet above the flames.

Balthasar handed the cup of tu to Gaspar and cautioned, "Good friend, please be careful. If you get any closer to the fire, I'm afraid that you will be cooked." Gaspar grabbed the cup with both hands so he could warm them and slowly sipped the tu.

Still shivering, he muttered, "terribly cold," a few times as he sipped his tu.

"This drink is almost good... what gives it flavor?" chuckled a warming Gaspar.

"Oh, I throw whatever I can find into the pot. This time of year, there is not much to choose from, but I always seem to find something sweet near the stables," Balthasar answered with a grin. There was silence for a moment until both men broke into laughter.

Servants entered the room to deliver their breakfast; freshly baked grain cakes, warm from the pot, dipped into sweet syrup mixed with dried fruit. The cakes, which could be dry, were filling and quite tasty once they soaked up enough syrup.

"Shall we discuss our plans as we have our meal?" asked Balthasar.

"As long as those cakes don't get cold," Gaspar replied as he inspected their breakfast feast. Dinbanu took her seat at the table and the three bowed their heads as Balthasar offered the prayer.

He began, "Ahura Mazda, we praise you and we are grateful to you for providing us with this food and for the warmth and comfort of this shelter." He paused briefly and then continued, "As we begin our journey in search of your magnificent star, we ask you to provide us with wisdom, strength, courage and good health to overcome the challenges we will encounter."

"Well said, friend," Gaspar softly responded.

Balthasar pulled a folded piece of parchment from the top of his stack of documents. It was a well worn map that he unfolded and placed on the table. He set bowls on the corners of the map to keep it in place.

Studying the map, Balthasar asked, "Now then, are we certain about our course?" He continued before Gaspar has a chance to respond, "We make our way south to Nishapur and then take the trade road west to Ecbatana. Is that what we agreed?"

"Yes, but I worry that the mountain passes will not be clear for us. We could ride east towards Merv and then south to meet the road. Of course, it is a greater distance, but the trail is more manageable, the slope not as steep and we are less likely to get stranded," Gaspar suggested as he peered at the charts.

"We do have another option. We could wait for a few weeks until the sun is higher in the sky."

Before Balthasar could continue, he was interrupted by Gaspar. "Brother! We will take many risks on this journey, but the threat of a little snow is the least of them. I say that we proceed with haste." In a softer voice and with a smile, Gaspar added, "Besides, by the time we are underway, it will probably be too hot for travel."

Balthasar smiled and nodded his approval to Gaspar.

"In two days we can check the skies and make a decision on Merv or Nishapur. Either way, the preparations will be the same. Provided that we do not encounter any serious problems, how long do you estimate our journey?" asked Balthasar.

"Jerusalem? A year, perhaps longer. Plan on two years before you see Asdin again."

Dinbanu, who had been quietly listening to the conversation, gasped when she heard Gaspar say two years. She began to stand to express her disapproval of the journey until she saw that Balthasar had turned his eyes to her, desiring to know her reaction.

Dinbanu slowly settled back into her chair and said to Balthasar in a comforting tone, "I know how important this journey is to you. We will miss you every moment you are away from us, but we will manage just fine until you return."

Balthasar did not respond, but the concern that was showing in his face soon relaxed to an expression of contentment.

"It is a long ride, but one worth the hardship. We will be miserable for the rest of our lives if we pass on this adventure," Gaspar reminded his old friend.

As the servants cleared the table, Balthasar readied another piece of parchment to make a list. He sorted through his collection of writing reeds, a common tool of hollowed marsh grasses. Using his knife blade, Balthasar carefully trimmed an end of a reed into a point. He removed the wax from the top of a jar filled with writing fluid and poured a small amount into the stem. By gently squeezing the reed, fluid was forced to the point.

Balthasar's writing fluid, another product of the Silk Road, was from Han China and was made from a mixture of pine smoke soot, lamp oil and gelatin from animal skins.

As the two men continued discussing plans for the journey, Balthasar asked Gaspar about the men they would try to persuade to join them. He began, "As we consider provisions, let us think about the companions we will require and what work will be expected of them.

Once that is settled, we can discuss those who might be best suited for these roles. Shall we proceed in that order?"

"Reliable and capable companions are essential, but there may be few volunteers," answered Gaspar.

"Ah, but remember my friend, by a sweet tongue and kindness, you can drag an elephant with a hair. If they truly understand what we seek, there will be enough volunteers with willing hearts," Balthasar replied in an encouraging tone. Then Balthasar asked, "How many men shall accompany us? Many of the caravans that pass through Asdin are escorted by militia. Many warriors lead a single caravan."

Gaspar paused for a moment and then said, "We could follow a friendly militia if we come upon one moving in our direction, or we could hire such men if necessary. Our men are capable warriors, but we do not want to lead a large number of them across Persia."

"Remember, we will be carrying valuable cargo," Balthasar cautioned.

"Yes, but we do not want to be burdened with the requirements of a large number of men for the next two years. We may need to place our trust in hired militia," suggested Gaspar.

"Trust? Trust makes way for treachery. It is difficult to trust strangers when riches are involved," warned Balthasar.

Nodding in agreement Gaspar replied, "Let us agree on a modest number of our own men. If we need more protection, we will follow a militia. Perhaps we will find a Persian militia in Merv that we can follow west."

"We need proficient archers and two bowers and a fletcher to supply us with bows and arrows. As we travel, our archers should be visible to discourage attackers. They will be our first line of defense, so they need to be experienced men," added Balthasar.

"Yes and the archers can also hunt game. We will need a steady supply of fresh meat to keep everyone fed, so I suggest we take two fletchers. If we have a plentiful supply of arrows, we can use them for trade. We will also need jade, gold, perfume, silk and spices," replied Gaspar.

"I agree. Not many of our items will be returning with us. We must be prepared to trade for provisions along the way. We must take along a few replacement items, such as extra wheels for our carts. It will be difficult to find what we require along much of the road. It is impossible to know all of the things we may need," said Balthasar.

The two Magi began compiling their list of items and things to be done in preparation for the journey. Gaspar started the list by saying, "We will need our best tents, those with strong material and stitching. We need to select the ones in the best condition. But not those that are too heavy; they will burden our animals."

In considering which items to bring, Balthasar offered, "Everything I have is available for your inspection. Consider the condition of your items and compare them to mine. I will rely on your judgment. When will you return to Shahnaz to organize your belongings? Shall we commence the journey from here and make our first stop Shahnaz?"

"No, that will slow us down... we will lose twenty days. Let us meet at Meherzad. Send one of your men to my village to alert my servants to begin organizing my items. When I arrive home, I will be ready to go. Then I will travel northwest to meet you at Meherzad. With the help of Ahura Mazda, we should reach Meherzad at the same time," suggested Gaspar.

"That is an expedient way to proceed, but we still need to consider our starting date. I am as anxious as you to get underway, but we may have many weeks of bad weather, particularly at higher elevations. We run the risk of getting stranded, but I suppose we can turn south if we get into trouble," replied Balthasar.

The next morning, a group of men gathered at the stables. Two of Balthasar's men were selected to make the trip to Shahnaz to deliver packing and preparation instructions to Gaspar's servants. Their horses were packed as the riders discussed the route and conditions with the men who made the trip to retrieve Gaspar. The men would ride swiftly, so they packed only essential provisions. In a day or two, Gaspar would begin his own return trip to Shahnaz.

After sending the riders on their way, the Magi walked together toward the center of the village, but there was not much conversation. They were both deep in thought, contemplating the task before them. They were beginning to realize that their remarkable idea for a journey was underway, set into motion a few moments ago when the riders departed for Shahnaz.

As they approached the bottom of the hill leading to the palace, Gaspar surveyed the sky and said in a confident voice, "This morning is warmer, the sky is clear and the air is calm. Hopefully this weather will stay with us. A good time to travel, don't you agree?"

"Do not be surprised if we wake up tomorrow to mounds of snow," answered Balthasar, his voice filled with caution.

"Yes, anything is possible this time of year. We will hope for the best and prepare for the worst," Gaspar nodded in agreement.

Balthasar placed his hand on Gaspar's shoulder. "I believe that we have planned well. We will take our time, we will be cautious and we will avoid unnecessary risks. No matter how well we have planned, we can be sure that there will be problems and there will be danger."

The remainder of the day was spent organizing their supplies and meeting with villagers who may have made suitable traveling companions. Balthasar's first conversation was with Ethan, one of the few villagers who was not Persian.

Ethan was Hebrew and his ancestors were among the Hebrews taken captive to Persia many generations ago. Ethan, whose name in Hebrew meant one who is always strong and firm, had deep roots in this region and was loyal to Balthasar. Balthasar had great respect for Ethan and benefitted from their discussions of the Hebrew Scriptures.

When Balthasar found Ethan, he began, "Ethan, my friend, you know of our journey and of the difficulties we will encounter. You are under no obligation, but it would mean a great deal to me if you would consider joining us."

Ethan, who also had deep respect for Balthasar, replied without hesitation, "Yes, most certainly I will join you. The star speaks to me as it speaks to you. I have dreamed of seeing Jerusalem, but, until now, it was always beyond my reach. I have been praying that I would be permitted to join you."

Ethan's response provided Balthasar with encouragement. He was enthusiastic in his appeal to potential companions, but he wanted to ensure that everyone understood the danger and the expected duration of their travel. Their companions had to be willing and their commitment voluntary. The Magi could not have men depart the caravan once they were underway.

Another man whom Balthasar was intent on persuading to join them was Hutan. Hutan, which meant well-bodied in Persian, was a large man with exceptional strength. He was a trusted servant, a skilled craftsman, an exceptional horseman and afraid of nothing. More importantly, Hutan was one of the few servants who could see the star. He did not share Balthasar's excitement, but he could see it and recognized it as unusual. Balthasar was careful in choosing his words when he spoke to Hutan; if he was unsuccessful in persuading him, it would be difficult to convince others to commit to the journey. Hutan had been organizing the supplies for Balthasar, so he was aware of the journey and what it would entail. Balthasar found Hutan and asked him if they could talk about preparations.

Amid talks of supplies, Balthasar said, "You know, friend, this will be a difficult trip. The road will be dangerous in places and the weather and bandits will add to our burden, but these challenges are nothing when compared to the adventure and excitement in store for us. Best of all, the satisfaction upon reaching our destination will make it all worthwhile."

Before he could continue, Hutan interrupted. "Are you asking me to join you?"

"Well, I was about to ask you," Balthasar responded.

"As your humble servant, you know there is no place you could go where I would not follow. I committed to this trip when you did," Hutan quickly replied as he resumed his preparation of supplies.

"Ah, that comforts me greatly. Will you help me invite others to join us?" requested a relieved Balthasar.

"That will not be difficult, as long as you brought your purse," Hutan replied with a smile.

"I was afraid of that," Balthasar replied with a laugh as the two men made their way to the stack of supplies assembled near the stables.

As their priest, Balthasar commanded everyone's respect. Any villager would be reluctant to refuse his request, but committing to a long and dangerous journey was a different matter. There was careful consideration of one's health and family before committing to such a trip. While no one talked openly about the risks, there was an understanding that lives could be lost.

As the preparations continued into the afternoon, talk of the journey and their appeal for volunteers spread throughout the valley. The activity of the past few days and this morning's departure of riders to Shahnaz captured everyone's attention and imagination. Unfortunately, by the day's end, only a few men had committed to the trip. With Hutan's help, three servants volunteered and several others requested time to make a decision. Balthasar's oldest son, Nekdel, Persian for "good-hearted," and Nekdel's cousin, Rushad, Persian for "one whose soul is joyous," wanted to make the journey. The boys were young, with Nekdel twelve years of age and Rushad only one year older, but Balthasar was excited for their company.

When this day came to a close, the Magi sat next to the fire inside the Palace.

Gaspar asked Balthasar, "You are quiet this evening. Are you changing your mind about our journey?"

"No, but much work remains to convince others to join us," Balthasar replied as he looked for Gaspar's reaction to his words.

"Friend, every journey begins with a first step. You have done quite well today. I hope I have such success in Shanaz. I know you are disappointed that your offers of adventure and excitement were not met with shouts of joy. But many with whom you spoke were hearing of this trip for the first time. When you are ready to depart the village, you will be turning men away," replied an enthusiastic Gaspar.

Balthasar, however, had a heavy heart because he realized the difficulty of such a decision. Family was an important part of Persian life and it was painful to desert one's family, even for the most noble of causes.

Gaspar moved closer to the fire and told Balthasar, "I do not believe that there is anything more I can do here. With your approval, I will begin the trip back to Shahnaz tomorrow. As soon as my affairs are in order, I will be able to join you in Meherzad."

"I suppose you are right. We will meet you in Meherzad three weeks from tomorrow. Does that sound reasonable?" asked Balthasar.

"Both of us will need to move with haste, but I believe we can keep to that schedule. If I am going to leave tomorrow, I will need a good night's sleep and a generous breakfast of your sweet cakes," replied Gaspar with a grin.

"Let us check on our star before we find our beds," whispered Balthasar.

The two Magi made their way to the palace roof without a torch to light their way. Once on the roof, they marveled at the brightness of the star, which illuminated the roof.

Gaspar placed his hand on his friend's shoulder and said, "If we ever need a reminder as to why we are undertaking such a difficult journey, we only need to glance in God's direction."

In the morning, Balthasar and Dinbanu accompanied Gaspar to the stables, where several villagers had already gathered and the riders who would be accompanying Gaspar were carefully packing the horses for their trip to Shahnaz.

Gaspar embraced Balthasar and Dinbanu, and, with his arms around both of them, he said, "These have been enjoyable and exciting days. Thank you for sharing your home with me and filling me with delicious food. My poor horse will have a much heavier burden on the trip home."

Gaspar kissed Dinbanu's cheek and said, "We will miss you greatly on our journey, but your spirit will be with our every step. You can be sure that I will watch out for Nekdel and his father!" Turning to Balthasar, Gaspar continued, "Help me onto my horse. My pockets are so loaded down with cakes that I can barely move."

Both men laughed as Gaspar got comfortable on his horse. Pulling the reins slightly, Gaspar gave his horse a gentle kick to move him away from the stable. "I will see you in Meherzad!" he shouted as his horse carried him away.

As the caravan began to move, Balthasar quickly inspected the packs on the horses as they passed to make sure they were securely tied.

"May Ahura Mazda keep you safe!" he shouted.

The rising sun warmed the backs of the riders as they departed the village and Balthasar silently noted that he would see them again in only three short weeks.

Over the next several days, Balthasar organized, packed and rechecked his lists. He met with the twelve men who would be joining him and visited with their families to discuss the journey and to reassure that every effort would be made to bring their men home safely. Much of his time, however, was spent consoling Dinbanu, who was about to lose her husband and son for what would surely seem like a lifetime.

One evening, Balthasar and Dinbanu were sitting quietly by the fire, enjoying each other's company, when Balthasar says confidently, "We will pass many on the road who will be traveling in this direction. We should have no trouble passing along notes that will find their way to you."

Dinbanu smiled, shook her head in disapproval, and then responded, "Dear husband, you know that your notes will have no privacy in the hands of strangers. Would you trust travelers unknown to you with information about your travel plans? Please do not put your caravan at risk by relying on strangers. If you spend your time worrying about me and Asdin, you will only make your journey more difficult."

Once again, Balthasar was reminded of his wife's wisdom and good judgment, but he could not help but feel that he would be abandoning his responsibilities by leaving behind those he loved.

He nodded in recognition of Dinbanu's wise words and replied, "Yes, I suppose you are right. But there is the chance that we may pass trustworthy travelers on the road, perhaps even Magi. So please know that if I can get word to you, without placing ourselves at risk, of course, then I will do so."

A smile filled Dinbanu's round face as she responded, "Take comfort in knowing, my dear Balthasar, that whether we learn of your progress or not, Asdin and I will survive in your absence."

Neither knew how they would be able to cope without the other for such a long time, but they were comforted in knowing that each of them had a strong will and confidence that they would find their way through the next two years.

Similar conversations were taking place throughout Asdin and most villagers were busy preparing for the journey. New clothing was made for the travelers and other garments were mended. All items for travel had been sorted and arranged in homes near the stables for easy packing and the villagers worked at a fever pitch until the day before travel. There was much excitement, many tears and a great many embraces. While there was sadness over the separation of families, there was also much joy because of the spiritual nature of this journey, led by the highest of their spiritual leaders.

To commemorate this occasion, Balthasar announced that there would be an Afrinagan, a religious ceremony of blessings, hymns and prayers, held in the temple where a sacred fire was burned.

To prepare, Balthasar performed the Padan, the ritual washing of himself, which was symbolic of purification. After washing, he put on the sacred shirt and girdle, known as the Sudre-Kusti, over his robe and he placed the Kusti around him. The Kusti was the sacred cord that was worn around the waist of the Magi. When the Kusti was put on, a brief ritual occurred where the Magi untied and retied the Kusti several times.

Once properly dressed, Balthasar joined other worshippers gathered outside the temple, the Agiary, or "place of fire," which held the sacred fire. Sacred fires, important to the spiritual lives of Zoroaster's followers, provided purification and the sacred fires of the Agiary took many forms. Atash Dadgah was the lowest of the consecrated fires and was followed by Atash Adaran and Atash Bahram, the victorious fire. On this afternoon, Balthasar would prepare the Atash Bahram, the highest form of consecrated fire. When Balthasar entered the Agiary, he went before the altar to start the fire. He retrieved a Barsom, a tied bundle of twigs, which, once lit, would elicit an offering of incense in which sandalwood and frankincense were used to consecrate the fire.

On occasion, an animal was sacrificed during the highest of these ceremonies. The animal was not slaughtered by the Magi, but by someone assisting him. Foreigners who witnessed these sacrifices were often shocked by the manner in which the animal was killed. The man performing the sacrifice may have strangled a bird with his bare hands or slit the throat of an animal for a slow, brutal death. This ritual added to the perception shared by some onlookers that the Medes were warriors who took delight in killing. There was structure to the sacrifice and rules in which all participants abided. During the ceremony, no one was permitted to pray for any personal or private blessing. Only blessings for the king or for the village were permitted.

A pattern was followed for the Afrinagan with two bells tolling at certain intervals. As the ceremony began, several hundred villagers had gathered at the Agiary, but only a small number of them would be able to enter because it was not of great size. Those who waited outside the Agiary would be able to join in the singing of the Gatha, the five sacred hymns. The words of the hymns came from the Avesta, the sacred book, and were attributed to Zoroaster.

This was a joyous occasion and the people of Asdin came together in one voice to praise Ahura Mazda and seek his blessing. Everyone sang because the songs were easy and the harmony was derived from a cadence that closely followed their speech. Balthasar's singing voice was more of a shout than a song and not of a pleasant tone. Either no one noticed, or no one wanted to speak to him about it.

This day, Balthasar blessed a goat that was being sacrificed and offered a prayer for a safe journey to Jerusalem and the protection of Asdin. Once killed, the goat's meat was cut into pieces and cooked. After the ceremony, Balthasar permitted the villagers to eat a piece of the offering. This would serve as a reminder to the villagers that they participated in the ceremony to commemorate the journey to Jerusalem.

In spite of the cold, most of the villagers remained when the Afrinagan concluded to say goodbye to those who would be leaving in the morning. As evening arrived, light snow turned to heavy snow blown by a strong wind in only a matter of minutes.

Balthasar's heart sank as he walked up the slippery hill to the palace. It was not good to have snow fall on the eve of their journey.

Dinbanu, seeing Balthasar's worried face, took him by the arm and said, "Do not worry, Ahura Mazda will guide you. Remember, it is he who hung the star to light your way."

Balthasar smiled as he pulled Dinbanu, who was always comforting him, close into his thick robes of wool.

They would miss each other dearly and both knew their separation would be difficult. As Balthasar held Dinbanu in his arms, he searched for the words to comfort her. But, as he was about to speak, she placed her finger on his lips and whispered, "Shh, do not speak. It will only cause my heart more pain. I know how you feel, do not forget we are one."

At dawn, Balthasar was awakened by Dinbanu as she shouted, "Good news! Come and look, come and look!"

Balthasar, still not fully awake, made his way to the window, although he was unable to focus his eyes.

"What is it?" he mumbled.

"The air became warm overnight and the snow turned to rain. The snow is gone! The road is wet, but there is no ice. I told you all would be well this morning, that Ahura Mazda would help you!" shared an excited Dinbanu.

"Yes you did! It is a beautiful morning. I cannot yet see, but I know already it is a beautiful morning!" answered a smiling Balthasar as he embraced and kissed his wife.

After sharing breakfast with Dinbanu, Balthasar walked to the roof with his youngest son, Tizran, which meant "one who is quick moving." Balthasar, carrying a crate covered with a blanket, placed the crate on the floor and covered his arm with the blanket. He reached into the box with both hands and brought out the falcon he had spent a year training, placing it on his arm. Balthasar gave a short, sharp whistle and the bird flapped its large wings, lifting itself into the morning air. Balthasar and Tizran watched as the bird climbed the air above them before soaring beyond view into the valley. After a few minutes, Balthasar gave another whistle and the falcon soon returned to his arm.

Balthasar placed the bird on Tizran's covered arm and said, "Son, he is yours now. Take good care of him. Feed him well and let him fly when the weather is fair. I expect to see you both in good health upon my return. Now let me hear your whistle."

Tizran was missing his front teeth so he was unable to produce a whistle. After a few attempts, Balthasar gently stopped Tizran and said, "Perhaps the whistle will come with your teeth. Until then, train the bird to respond to your water buffalo horn."

Chapter IV – The Quest Begins

As Balthasar arrived at the stables, he found that his men had already prepared his horse and packed the carts. The caravan got off to an early start and emotions were running high as the men departed the village, with family members calling out their farewells and waving goodbye to their husbands, sons and brothers.

"We are on our way!" Balthasar shouted as he turned to see the procession behind him. But they had only been travelling for half of an hour when Balthasar stopped the caravan, cupping his hand around his ear as he strained to hear the faint sound of Tizran's horn echoing through the valley. With a smile, Balthasar motioned the caravan to continue.

Over the next two weeks, travel for Balthasar's caravan progressed smoothly. The air was cold and snow occasionally fell, but only in harmless small amounts. On most nights, the caravan rested in a remote area unless a village was nearby. Although a considerable distance from Asdin, the caravan was still within the area of Balthasar's domain as chief priest. These brief visits to neighboring villages provided Balthasar's men with the opportunity to get reacquainted with some of their more distant friends.

When they arrived in a village, Balthasar performed a religious ceremony known as a Jashan. On each stop, Balthasar shared the purpose of his journey with his host. Not many understood the significance of the star, but if Balthasar believed it to be important, then it must have been so.

As they traveled, Balthasar and his men prayed that they would not encounter a hostile militia. While they were well trained and more than willing to defend themselves, their group was modest in size compared to the typical armed militia. All understood that they were to avoid conflict unless their lives were threatened.

As each day's travel came to an end, Balthasar looked for a suitable place to spend the night. Ideally, he sought a location with a supply of water and enough visibility to spot unexpected visitors. On this evening, Balthasar was unable to find an appropriate site for his caravan and he was apprehensive about stopping in this area of tree covered hills. It was difficult to see into the thick forest, so it was somewhat unnerving to be spending the night there. But Balthasar, having seen no signs of travelers this day, believed it unlikely that others were nearby. As a precaution, he posted an extra guard, Vanghav, near the tents, with another, Kanuka, guarding the horses.

This night was moonless and the steady wind whistled through the tall pine trees, making it difficult to hear much of anything. The men slept soundly until they were awakened by a terrifying scream. Expecting the worst, the men stumbled around in the darkness, searching for their swords and the openings to their tents. They gathered outside in the darkness with swords raised, ready to battle. Expecting intruders, they found only their guards. One of the men pulled a stick from the ashes of the cook fire and blew on it to produce a flame. He held it high to reveal a visibly shaken Vanghav and his companion, Kanuka, who was trying to hold back his laughter.

"What happened?" demanded Balthasar.

"We were attacked by a beast and I screamed to scare it off," replied Vanghav.

"You were attacked?"

Vanghav paused for a moment, then replied, "I woke up to see an enormous beast at my feet. I screamed to scare it off."

Kanuka added, "I got a good look at him; a Caspian Tiger, a big one. I think he was making his way to the horses before he stopped to lick Vanghav."

Balthasar shook his head and said to his guards, "Your shift is over!" Then, speaking loud enough for all to hear, Balthasar continued, "Let this be a lesson to everyone. Stand guard as if our lives depend on it… because it just may. Keep awake!"

The men returned to their tents and put their swords away. They were relieved that Vanghav was not hurt, but troubled to learn how vulnerable they would be to an attack by a militia. No one slept much more, especially Vanghav, who was still shaking when the sun rose. Half awake, everyone mumbled through their breakfast and worked slowly at packing their carts. More than one "meow" could be heard whenever Vanghav came near.

There were many dangerous animals in this part of Persia: tigers, cheetahs, panthers, leopards and bears among them, also with possible threats from lions. There was plenty of food for these meat eaters to prey upon, like wild sheep, goats, gazelles, wild asses, pigs, foxes and deer. Like the wild animals of Persia, Balthasar's men also hunted for fresh meat. Red deer had been supplying the men with many of their meals and when the archers were lucky, there may have even been a few pheasants or partridges to eat.

As the men organized the caravan the next morning, Balthasar stood on top of a cart to speak.

"Friends, if we make good time today, we should arrive in Meherzad this evening. Let us press forward and keep our stops brief."

The weather was fair and the trail in good condition. As the sun set, Meherzad was in sight. They had kept to their schedule and, if Gaspar has kept to his, he may have already been in Meherzad.

Meherzad was not a large village, but it received many visitors because it was intersected by several roads. From Meherzad, it was possible to continue south to Nishapur or take the road east to Merv. As Balthasar's caravan approached the village, they met an old man leading goats to the Village.

Balthasar called out, "Friend, direct me to the stables!"

"Just ahead… a caravan rests there, but you will find enough room for your horses and plenty of water," answered the old man.

"Thank you, friend," Balthasar replied as he kicks his horse and shouted for his men to follow him. Balthasar turned to Hutan and said, "Gaspar may already be here. I can't imagine anyone else traveling through here this time of year."

As they approached the stable area, they saw two large tents with several packed carts alongside. Balthasar dismounted, handed his reins to Hutan and walked toward the tents. Just as he was about to call out Gaspar's name, Gaspar emerged from one of the tents. "Welcome to Meherzad!" shouted Gaspar.

After the two embraced, Balthasar surveyed the tents and fire and asked, "Your travel must have gone well. When did you arrive?"

"We have been here for two days," Gaspar replied with a smile.

"Two days? How is that possible?" asked a puzzled Balthasar.

"When I arrived home in Shahnaz, everything was packed and ready to go. We left the next morning. Have your men come join us for dinner? Everything is ready," Gaspar replied.

"Not just now, we need to assemble our tents while we still have some light," Balthasar replied as he turned to give instructions to his men.

"There is no need for your tents. We can make do with my tents tonight. Come, sit, relax… we have much to discuss," replied Gaspar as he waved his hand for Balthasar's men to join them.

Balthasar smiled as an acceptance of Gaspar's offer and the men tended to the horses before joining the others in the tent. Once all were together, Balthasar and Gaspar introduced their men. Several had known each other for many years, while others were meeting for the first time.

After the introductions, Gaspar announced, "Now that you have been introduced, I suggest that you get to know each other. You will have to live with the sight of these ugly faces for the next two years."

There were many groans and laughs until Balthasar motioned for quiet with his hands, as if pushing the air down in front of him. The Magi offered an Afrin, a prayer of blessing on their food, their men and their journey.

As they enjoyed their dinner, Balthasar asked Gaspar, "How was your travel, any problems?"

"No problems. We had some snow, but not enough to slow us down. Two days from here we saw a Seres militia. They kept their distance, so I'm not sure where they were going, but that was the only group we saw. We stopped in the villages along the way, which were very quiet and friendly. It has gone well for us. How has it been for you?" replied Gaspar as he munched on a piece of bread.

"It was much the same for us. Not many people on the trail, except for a few moving between villages. Steady and quiet. We have a horse with a bad leg and I was hoping we could buy another one here. How do they look? Old and worn?" asked Balthasar.

"There are a few healthy ones I am sure will do. Let us see about them at first light," Gaspar responded.

After days of traveling, Balthasar's men were tired. Their evening ended early to ensure that they were rested for travel in the morning. By day break, all were anxious to get the caravan moving, but organizing this larger group took more time than expected. Some of the carts needed to be reorganized and the men needed to be instructed on their roles as part of this larger caravan. Two men were selected to ride ahead of the caravan to serve as scouts, as a large caravan would draw attention, necessitating riders on the lookout for trouble. Two more men were instructed to trail the caravan at a distance for additional protection. The Magi took every precaution to protect the valuable items carried in their carts.

There was not much caravan travel in the winter months, particularly away from the main trade road, so caravans moving through remote areas could be easy targets for unfriendly militia and other armed groups. Han militias were frequent visitors in this region and their behavior was unpredictable. It was not uncommon to see them as far west as the Caspian Sea in search of horses or serving as escorts to a caravan. On occasion, they would even venture into Persia in search of their enemies who sought refuge inside Persia. It was best to steer clear of these Seres when possible and accommodate them when an encounter was unavoidable.

The horses and carts forming the caravan departed Meherzad at mid-morning, heading east into the sun, toward Merv. After assessing the total amount of cargo and the more than two dozen riders, the Magi believed it would be safer to avoid the rugged terrain to the south and decided on a more manageable route east to Merv. It may have added a few extra weeks to the trip, but getting stranded in the mountains could have brought the caravan to a halt for an extended time. In a few days, the caravan would enter the desert and enjoy warmer weather as they neared the oasis of Merv.

On the third morning of travel from Meherzad, the wind grew quite strong. By midday, the sand was stinging everyone's skin and eyes, making it necessary for the men to cover their heads. Seeing that the horses also struggled in the blinding sand, Balthasar pulled his horse out of line, rode to the end of the caravan and shouted, "Gaspar, we should get our tents in place before it gets any worse!"

Balthasar quickly turned his horse and shouted to each rider as he rode to the front of the caravan, "Move to the right. Bring the tents to the front. Quickly!"

Within minutes, the horses were unpacked and the men were raising the tents. They had become quite proficient at setting up and breaking down the tents, but it was a struggle to work with sand stinging their faces.

Several men stood on one end of a tent to anchor it as the other end was unrolled and stretched.

Gaspar dropped the blanket covering his face just long enough to shout to Balthasar, "Will our tents hold in this?"

"As long as the wind is no stronger!" Balthasar shouted in response.

The tent, made from tightly woven goat hair, was of a tough material that held up well in inclement weather. It was airy enough to let the air escape in hot weather, yet, when wet, the hair swelled to keep the water from seeping through. Once wet, however, it became heavy and bulky, making it difficult to handle.

Once the first tent was assembled, it served as a wind break for the men as they worked to erect the second tent. They could accommodate all the men in two tents, but several of the men insisted on a third tent for their horses. The three tents, forming a triangle, provided the remaining horses huddled between them with protection from the worst of the blowing sand. Inside the tents, the men shook the sand from their clothes, hair and boots, and helped each other get the sand out of their eyes. It seemed like everyone was spitting sand out of their mouths and drinking water to relieve their throats.

Then Hutan shouted to Balthasar, "A tent has collapsed!"

But before Balthasar could respond, several men covered their faces and ran outside to help those who were trapped underneath.

As the men began to erect the tent once more, Gaspar said to Balthasar, "If we had waited much longer, we would be huddled under the carts."

"The wind came upon us quickly and just when I thought it was slowing, I was nearly blown off my horse," replied Balthasar.

Sitting on a crate to remove his boots, Gaspar added, "The storm may be over in a few minutes... or it could last for several days. No way of knowing about these storms. Several years ago, I was returning from Merv in the spring when our beautiful day was overtaken by a horrible storm. Three days it lasted. Three days in a tent with our horses! To this day, I remember our fear... and the smell. If the storm had lasted much longer, we may have eaten one of our horses."

At that moment, one of the horses whinnied, generating a laugh from the men in the tent.

"I speak too loud!" shouted Gaspar above the laughter.

During the night, the wind grew in strength and the men took turns checking on the tent and the stakes that held it in place. All of the horses were now inside the tents, the men not wanting to risk the horses' health with so much travel left before the journey's end. The tents were withstanding the storm, but some of the seams were beginning to tear, so much mending would be needed when the storm subsided. Ushtra, one of the volunteers from Asdin, was a tent maker and was assigned the task of keeping the tents in good condition. It seemed that with every strong burst of wind, Ushtra could be heard asking, "Was that a tear? Did that sound like seams coming apart?"

By daybreak, the wind had slowed, but it remained too strong to travel. The Magi were anxious to get to Merv, but they would have to wait for better weather. This morning was spent inside the tent, with the Magi further discussing the meaning of the Hebrew Scriptures and their possible reference to the star.

Balthasar asked Ethan to share his scriptures with the men. As a Jew, Ethan understood the Hebrew Scriptures and traditions. Like his ancestors, Ethan remained true to his beliefs, but he was reluctant to discuss such matters with Persians. Hebrews believed that their god, Yahweh, was superior to all other gods; Ethan was quite aware that this idea was not well received by followers of Zoroaster. Balthasar discussed the Hebrew Scriptures with Ethan many times, but did not challenge Ethan's beliefs. While Balthasar was always courteous to Ethan during these discussions, he was troubled when Ethan showed him certain passages, such as the one where Yahweh proclaimed, 'There is no other God besides me." Over time, Balthasar came to accept these words as a belief held by another people and not as a threat to followers of Zoroaster, but he was nonetheless intrigued by the stories in Hebrew Scriptures and he found many similarities between them and the teaching of Zoroaster. Since the star they followed dominated the thoughts of all the men, Balthasar saw this as a good opportunity to raise the subject.

Surrounded by men and horses, Balthasar now asked Ethan, "Do your scriptures prophesize about the star that hangs over Jerusalem?"

Ethan thought for a moment before replying, "Jews pray for a messiah, a king like our King David who ruled with power and strength, a messiah who can deliver the Jews from their suffering."

Balthasar nodded and responded, "Please continue." As the wind raged on, the men squeezed in around Ethan so they could hear.

Speaking loudly so he could be heard over the wind, Ethan continued, "Many generations of Jews have struggled for freedom. God's promise of a messiah is what has sustained the Jews. Some of you may have heard of the prophecies of Balaam. His words have a special meaning for the Jews and I believe it brings meaning to the star that we seek."

Gaspar interrupted, "Ethan, tell us of Balaam's message. Some of the men do not know of Balaam."

"When my people, the Israelites, were freed from Egypt hundreds of years ago, God led them on a journey for many years. They faced many enemies, but, with God's help, the Israelites defeated them. While on this journey, God led them to a place known as Moab. Balak, the King of Moab, saw the more than two million Israelites who came into his land and he began to tremble with fear, because of their large number."

Ethan paused, as a gust of wind briefly sent the horses into mayhem. When control and order were restored, he continued, "Balak had heard how God delivered Israel by parting the Red Sea and destroying all the mighty Egyptian warriors. Balak also heard how the well-trained Amalekites were defeated by the Israelites, so the terrified Balak called upon Balaam for help. Balaam, a Syrian who lived in the town of Pethor, near the great Euphrates River, was not a good man. Like others in his family, he was a baru, a dark priest, a diviner and soothsayer who used dreams and omens to predict the future. His family was known for placing curses on people. In fact, the name 'Balaam' means 'devourer of people,' so you can see that he came from a family of evil doers."

Ethan paused again for a moment, this time he stopped to drink from his sheep skin. As he drank, he glanced at the faces of the men to see if they continued to listen. He knew that the star they followed may not have held the same meaning for everyone and he was not anxious to create any hard feelings with his friends. Once he determined that he still had the attention of the men, he continued.

"Balaam claimed to know our God, but he was not obedient to him. King Balak wanted Balaam to curse the Israelites, to weaken them, so the King could then defeat them. On three occasions, the King sent his men to get Balaam so Balaam could curse the Israelites. King Balak promised Balaam great riches for his curses. When God came to Balaam in a dream and told him not to curse the Israelites, because they were blessed people, the evil Balaam ignored Him. In spite of God's warning, Balaam climbed upon his donkey and rode toward King Balak. On the way, one of God's angels tried to stop Balaam, but Balaam could not see the angel and he continued on. Balaam's donkey, however, saw the angel and tried to stop, but Balaam beat that poor donkey until God gave Balaam's donkey the ability to speak as a man."

Some of the men were surprised to hear that Ethan's god gave the donkey speech. One of the men interrupted Ethan to ask, "A donkey speaks as a man? How is this possible?"

In a confident tone, Ethan smiled and replied, "It is possible because my God chose to make it possible."

The men were eager for Ethan to finish the story, so he continued, "When Balaam heard the donkey speak, his eyes were finally opened so he could see the angel."

Ethan now had their full attention and continued, "God told Balaam that he could continue on to King Balak, but Balaam would only speak the words that God commanded. When Balaam reached the King, he ignored God's words and attempted to conjure up God so he could curse the Israelites. Balaam attempted to curse the Israelites three times, but each time, God took control of his mouth so he blessed the Israelites."

"How marvelous," replied one of the men. "I wonder if that would work on a woman I know."

There was some laughter, but Balthasar quickly quieted the men and asked Ethan to continue. The men were fascinated by this story of angels and talking donkeys, so Ethan now stood to make sure he was heard.

"Balaam could only speak what God commanded. Three times he tried to curse the Israelites, but Balaam could only bless them. More than that, God also gave Balaam the words that foretold of the destruction of King Balak and of the coming of the star. Balaam prophesized, 'I see him, but not now; I behold him, but not nigh: There shall come forth a star out of Jacob, and a scepter shall rise out of Israel, and shall smite through the corners of Moab, and break down all the sons of tumult.'"

Ethan took another drink of water and continued, "Much to his own dismay, Balaam was forced to prophesize the coming of the Hebrew Messiah. Balaam proclaimed that a scepter shall rise out of Israel. In our scriptures, scepter and star are one in the same."

Balthasar interrupted, "What do you mean that they are one in the same?"

"The writers of our Scriptures often use poetry to tell God's story. The poetry in Balaam's prophecy tells of a scepter, which is a symbol of royalty, and of a star that would come out of Jacob. This scepter and this star refer to the same thing. The Jews believe that this star is not one that will hang in the sky, but is instead a man who will rise up like a star and become a great king."

"If the star points to the great king, does it signal that he now rules over his kingdom or that he will rule in the future? Will we find this king in power when we reach Jerusalem?" asked Gaspar.

"The Hebrew prophet Daniel made a prophecy about the many events that would occur before the Messiah's arrival. Many Jews interpret his prophecy to mean that the time for the Messiah is upon us," replied Ethan.

Ethan turned to Balthasar and said, "Many of our prophets speak of the Messiah, but there are none who speak as clearly as our prophet Isaiah. Our scriptures record Isaiah as saying that God will give a sign and then the virgin will give birth to a son who will be called Immanuel, Wonderful Counselor, Mighty God, Everlasting Father and Prince of Peace."

Balthasar placed his hand on Ethan's shoulder and said, "Isaiah prophesizes that a virgin will give birth to a child? Do I understand that this child is the Messiah… and it is his star that we seek?"

"That is what my Scriptures speak to me," Ethan replied.

Balthasar looked at Gaspar and asked, "A virgin gives birth and her child is the Messiah?"

"Is that any more of a miracle than a star that we can see, yet others cannot?" asked Gaspar.

Balthasar smiled and nodded. "Thank you, Ethan. Your scriptures speak to all of us."

One of the men, still skeptical, said to Ethan, "Many religions wait for a messiah. Confucius told of a Teacher who will come in the west and Zoroaster speaks of a prophet who will come from the heavens. Are these prophecies not true?'

Ethan responded, "I cannot say whether these prophecies are true, or if they point to the same messiah or to a different one. But when I see the star shining bright in the western sky, my heart tells me that God has given his star as a sign to the Jews. It is as if Heaven has come to Earth."

"The Messiah, a child, born of a virgin… God's own child, imagine that!" Gaspar replied.

"By the word of our prophets, the Messiah will come as a child," Ethan replied.

"Amazing!" added Balthasar.

While some of the men believed they now had a clearer understanding of the purpose of their journey, a few men were confused or disappointed in hearing the Hebrew prophecies. One such man, Hutan, reminded his friends, "What does it matter if the Hebrew messiah is a child, a man, or a great warrior. He is not our messiah! We follow Ahura Mazda's star! Whatever we find when we reach Jerusalem, so be it!"

Not all of the men shared Hutan's viewpoint, but no one wanted to challenge him, at least not at this moment. The men had much to contemplate and it would take some time for them to consider all of the implications of what they heard. Hutan took exception to the idea that the Hebrew god was responsible for the star. But the men were very aware that the Magi did not object to Ethan's stories, or to his interpretation of the Hebrew Scriptures.

It was midday when Balthasar next addressed the men. "Begin packing. The wind slows and the sky brightens. We will be back on the road within the hour."

Conditions improved enough to take down the tents and pack the carts, but the damaged tents would need repairs when the caravan stopped for the evening. Several men were already busy digging out carts that were partially buried in sand. Once the caravan took form, the scouts took their positions in advance and behind the carts. Sand covered much of the trail and the lead driver proceeded with caution, relying on reports from the scouts ahead of soft, deep sand and other problems along the trail.

As they traveled, the men discussed Ethan's stories of Balaam and Daniel. Some men were troubled about the prophecies because they did not know the Hebrew god.

They asked each other, "Is this god Ahura Mazda? Did this god speak to Zoroaster as he spoke to Balaam and Daniel?"

There is much discussion and Ethan answered questions until his voice grew weak.

Balthasar asked Gaspar, "Should we stop the men from discussing Ethan's lesson? Should I not have called upon Ethan?"

"No, these conversations are good for all of us. The thoughts running through their minds are the same ones that trouble us. We do not know the Hebrew god. Is he Ahura Mazda? Does he speak to Zoroaster? If it is the will of Ahura Mazda, we shall learn the answers together," Gaspar responded as he contemplated what had been discussed.

Balthasar could sense from the tone of Gaspar's voice and the concern registered in his eyes that Gaspar was troubled by the question of God's identity.

Chapter V: Seres, Friend or Foe?

When the caravan rested that evening, the air was calm, the sky was clear and the star shone brightly in the western sky. Depending on the weather and the condition of the trail, they would be in Merv within a few days. The men were tired and looked forward to relaxing in Merv, an oasis and trading center on the southern edge of the Murgap River, which was abundant with water in the midst of the dry Garagum desert. The oasis provided a route linking the northern highlands to the desert, where traders, militia and marauders were among those who passed through in search of silk and exotic spices. Salt, pepper and spices used to preserve and improve the flavor of food were also among the things traded in Merv. Most of Balthasar's men had never been to Merv and this evening's discussion turned to the city's markets, visitors and women.

There was much laughter and loud talk until Balthasar interrupted, "I know that we all look forward to Merv, but I caution everyone: do not become careless in your work! The closer we get to Merv, the more likely we will encounter marauders. Beginning tomorrow, we will post extra scouts."

Hutan tapped the sword strapped to his side and replied, "We are ready for trouble, but we have not seen a militia or bandits since we left Asdin."

"We will not have to look far for trouble. We are in the area where bandits hide along the trail waiting for travelers. To the bandits, we are just another small merchant caravan," Balthasar warned.

The men did not need a reminder about the possibility of attack. The many altars they passed along the trail served as reminders of the danger. Travelers built altars where they offered prayers for deliverance from the weather, bandit attacks and evil spirits. The men had seen such altars before, but never in such great numbers. The harsh terrain and few inhabitants provided the marauders with a strategic advantage. The unpredictable weather in this region also claimed the lives of many travelers; it was not unusual to encounter powerful winds that could knock a man off his feet.

 Once the caravan moved into the warmer area of the desert, the men took extra steps in preparing their camp. Before the tents were erected, rocks and wood were overturned in search of snakes and other crawling things. Flying insects were also their targets. These forms of life were found and killed because the men associated them with evil things. This practice was a tradition among the Medes, but the Magi had no interest in it.

 Balthasar's men were cautious and kept alert for trouble as they approached Merv, but were distracted by the quickly changing landscape. The desert gave way to grasses and other vegetation and, soon, prickly pistachios could be seen. They passed many streams and great numbers of birds, and other animals appeared, including a herd of wild asses grazing on clumps of grass. The streams soon widened into canals where thick reeds swayed gently in the breeze. Herons, storks and pelicans were a strange sight after weeks of travel where life was so sparse.

 As the outline of Merv came into view, Balthasar asked Gaspar, "Is it the time of year, good fortune, or the protection of Ahura Mazda that has kept us safe?"

"We are fortunate. A short sand storm and a curious tiger, if only the remainder of our trip would go so well," Gaspar replied.

Soon, the great wall that encompassed Merv was within view. Many years ago, Alexander the Great conquered this region. After his death, Caesar Antioch constructed a great stone wall around the oasis.

As the caravan approached the gates of Merv, the smoke of a nearby smelting oven could be seen. Magnificent sword blades were forged there and sold to militias and traders. Just outside the city's walls, the caravan's men marveled at the sight of grapevines grown from stalks so huge that they appeared to be growing from tree trunks. Merv was a fascinating place with many strange people passing through its gates. Lining its streets were merchants trading local food and exotic items from distant lands. Taking advantage of the water, farmers within the oasis produced an abundance of food. The mountain people traded their timber, limestone, gold, silver and copper for the wheat and barley grown in the oasis. People living in the river valleys grew flax, which was then woven into cloth. Great amounts of flax, cloth and wool were traded in Merv.

As they moved through the city, Gaspar was troubled by the presence of a large Seres militia and said, "Such a large group of warriors, what can be their purpose? There are too many to serve as escorts!"

"I have seen Seres in Merv, but never in such numbers in the winter," Balthasar replied.

The Magi and their men were uneasy as they passed dozens of armed Seres. Some of the Seres were on foot, while others rode fine Caspian horses. Balthasar's men took notice of the Seres and their crossbows.

Upon seeing their bows, Hutan rode forward to speak with the Magi and said, "We have never seen so many warriors! And those bows… deadly accurate!"

"They are of no concern to us," Balthasar replied as he gave his horse a kick, trying to hurry along.

After several minutes of riding past the militia, Gaspar asked Balthasar, "Where shall we set our tents?"

"Not anywhere close to here, let us keep riding," Balthasar replied.

Gaspar leaned toward Balthasar and in a loud whisper said, "See that large man? He looks to be their leader and appears to have taken an interest in your horse."

"Keep riding, friend," Balthasar replied without turning to look.

The Seres and other foreigners who valued fine horses considered the Persian horses the most desirable mount. Superior in size, strength and stamina, these magnificent animals were sought in all colors. Traders from Han China and as far away as Rome would pay a premium for these exceptional animals. It was said that Wu-ti, a former emperor of Han China, thought so highly of the great Persian horses that he gave them the name of "Heavenly Horses". A Seres legend held that these horses were descendents of dragons. The Seres gave Persian horses the name of Soulun, which meant "the vegetarian dragon."

As the caravan passed the Seres, Pulan returned to Balthasar from his position in advance of the caravan.

"We have found a good clearing with shade and water. Just a few minutes more," Pulan reported.

"I trust it is beyond the sight of our neighbors!" Balthasar replied.

As Pulan led them to the clearing, Balthasar's son, Nekdel, rode to join Balthasar. Nekdel's assignment was to ride in the center of the caravan, alongside the carts with his cousin, Rushad.

"Father, are we in Han China?" asked Nekdel.

"No, son, Han China is many days from here," Balthasar answered.

"Then why are there so many of their warriors in this place?" Nekdel asked as he looked at the Seres militia lining the road.

"They probably have an assignment here, son. The Seres do much business on the trade road," Balthasar explained.

"What is their business, Father?"

"They come to trade. You have seen the silk and jade that comes from their land. They trade for things they need and often travel far into Persia looking for horses. The Seres have many enemies that come into their land, so their militia is always seeking good horses," Balthasar replied with his eyes fixed on the road.

"I see, Father. I suppose everyone needs horses," Balthasar's son replied, young, but eager to learn the trading secrets as Balthasar learned from his father.

Once Balthasar's men were settled, they made repairs, tended to their horses and purchased provisions. Balthasar spoke with several other travelers to learn about the condition of the road to the south and west, but the visitors had not traveled a great distance. The trade road, a vast network of strategically located trading posts, was traveled only a short distance between two posts by most caravans. From what Balthasar could gather, the Seres militias came from the northeast and had been in the area for a few weeks. Even if Balthasar dared speak with the militia, it was doubtful that they held useful information.

    Years ago, when caravans began appearing on the road, travel was sporadic and much was unknown about travel beyond their region. Over time, the road's span had grown to a length beyond comprehension, providing traders with a route leading to Rome in the west with Han China to the east. Although little was known about Han China, its name had become popular because of a covering produced there, which was called "silk." Soft and beautiful, silk was in great demand and had become the most popular trade item along the road. Silk was said to be produced through a strange process involving worms. It had become so closely associated with the road that it had taken on its name and was known in many places as the "silk road." Within a generation or two, it grew to encompass a network of many roads. People from Han China were often referred to as "Seres," meaning "silk people."

    After three days in Merv, the Magi instructed their men to prepare for departure. Although the Magi planned to stay longer, they were uneasy about being around such a large foreign militia with no sign of the militia's departure.

    As the Magi observed their men pack the caravan, Balthasar spoke to Gaspar. "I would have preferred to wait here long enough to join a reliable militia traveling in our direction."

    Nodding, Gaspar agrees. "Yes, an escort would give us comfort, particularly as we travel through this area. Our men may be tested on this journey, but I pray it is not anywhere near this place."

It was not unusual for caravans to receive protection from the authorities for part of their travel, but the availability of an escort was never certain. The time of year and the location were important considerations in securing an escort. Traders who traveled a specific route with some regularity were better known to the militia serving in that area and were more likely to receive an escort. In the remote areas where militias did not often venture, travel was riskier. Some aggressive mountain tribes in Persia had been fighting each other for many years, so travel through those areas was particularly dangerous. In search of horses, myrrh, frankincense and aloes wood, Seres militias often visited this region of Persia, which lied close to Han China. Persian tribesman and the bandits would not usually bother Seres militia. Persian militia, on the other hand, may have challenged Seres if they considered them a threat. Travel was safer near the settled areas such as Merv, where bridges and paved roads were already in place. The Magi had limited options for escorts in this less-occupied area. Seres militias were frequent visitors in Merv, but they did not often venture further west.

As the carts were being packed, Hutan found Balthasar inspecting the caravan and reported that men had been asking about their horses.

"That is not unusual; traders always want our horses," Balthasar replied without averting his eyes from the horses.

"These men do not appear to be militia or traders, as they travel too lightly. We are concerned because they offer very little of value for our horses, yet they are persistent in their requests. They appear to be testing us," explained Hutan.

"What has been your response?" asked Balthasar.

"At first, we told them that our horses were not for sale. After continued requests, we began ignoring them. The right answer to a fool is silence! I would like your permission to drive them away from us," pleaded Hutan.

"That will not be necessary. We will be leaving soon," Balthasar replied sharply.

"What if they follow us?" asked Hutan.

"We will watch for them," Balthasar answered.

"Oh, there is another matter. Several of these strange men were seen studying our carts," Hutan reported.

Looking up from his cart, Balthasar responded, "Studying our carts? That should have been your first news to report."

Fearing that he had disappointed his leader, Hutan dropped his head and turned away. But when Balthasar finished packing his cart, he gently slapped Hutan on the back and said, "Do not worry. They are of no concern to us because we will soon be on our way."

After the carts were packed, the Magi performed a Jashan for the men and prayed for Ahura Mazda's continued protection. When the prayers were finished, the caravan began moving south. Their next destination was Nishapur and then on to Rhagae; a journey of many months. The trade road should have provided for better travel conditions than the trail they took to Merv, but there was no way of knowing what other dangers awaited them.

Once Balthasar's caravan was moving at a comfortable pace, he instructed Hutan, "Check on our scouts and archers. Make sure they are properly equipped and remind them to keep alert for the militia or any others that come upon us."

The double curved bows, an ideal weapon for horseback, were checked by Hutan to ensure they were in good condition. Hutan also quickly looked over the single curved bows in the carts, which were used by the archers on foot.

Balthasar's men, although skilled horsemen and well trained in warfare, were a modest party wanting to avoid conflict. Hutan reported to Balthasar that all was in good order, and the caravan continued moving, making only brief stops to water the horses. Several of the men asked about taking a longer break, but Balthasar wanted to push on, putting as much distance as possible between them and Merv, and thus, the Seres militia.

It was mid-afternoon of their first day of travel from Merv when one of the men positioned at the end of the caravan swiftly rode up the line to Balthasar. In a loud voice, Nekmard, meaning "a good man," said, "Riders coming fast in our direction. They will be on us in a few minutes."

"How many riders?" Balthasar asked, as he motioned with his hand for the caravan to stop.

"I cannot be certain. From the dust of their horses, they may be few in number, but they ride at full speed."

Balthasar turned to Gaspar and said, "It cannot be good if they are riding at such a pace. What reason is there to run their horses? The closest place of any consequence is several days journey from here."

"If they have been riding hard since leaving Merv, their horses must be close to dead," Gaspar replied.

"No one has passed us since we departed Merv. They must be coming for us. If they have come for our horses, they will not mind if their horses die from exhaustion. I could be wrong, who knows. Perhaps they come to say goodbye. After all, we did leave in a hurry!" Balthasar answered.

The caravan now at rest, the Magi sat upon their horses in silence, contemplating their situation and their response. "Is it possible that these riders believe us to be a militia?" asked Balthasar.

"Not likely. We carry no armor. We wear the same caps, but does that make us look like a militia? Could we pose a threat to anyone?" Gaspar replied.

"No, I suppose we do not appear threatening. We do not wear helmets or armor. Our horses wear no armor, even our saddles are different from those of Persian militia," Balthasar replied as he considered how his men might have appeared to other travelers.

This area of Persia was frequented by many foreign travelers, many of whom possessed distinctive clothing and armor. Some Persian militia used chest armor and helmets made of steel or brass that was hammered into shape. They also used saddles that were curved to protect their thighs. Their horses wore a leather and metal apron to protect their breasts and a bronze plate was used to protect the horse's head. Often these Persian riders carried light shields made of leather or wicker. Balthasar's men did not wear armor or helmets, but they did wear similar clothing decorated with elaborate designs. Most of the men also wore the traditional yellow cap of the Medes.

Still troubled over the identity and intentions of the approaching riders, Balthasar ruled out the possibility that his caravan contributed in any way to the situation at hand. "We ride fine horses and we carry swords and bows, but we have not given any indication that we pose a threat. Nothing we wear or carry could confuse us with a militia," offered Balthasar.

Balthasar turned to Hutan and directed him to take Nekmard and two others of Hutan's choice to meet the riders. In doing so, Balthasar hoped this would give the Magi and their men time to prepare for a possible threat.

Hutan agreed with few words and then left to carry through his orders. Riding toward the lead scouts, Zinawar, which meant "having weapons," and Pulan, which meant "having steel," Hutan shouted, "We will ride to them, but we will not get too close!"

Meanwhile, Gaspar returned to the caravan and shouted for Balthasar.

Balthasar looked to Gaspar as he pointed ahead to a grove of small trees. "Let us take cover between them!" Gaspar shouted.

"That will do!" answered Balthasar, who motioned for the rest of his men to follow. In a forested area of rolling hills separated by meadows of high grass, it was difficult for the men to see. The grass was even tall enough to conceal a man on horseback and Balthasar knew that the trees would provide protection for now, but may not have been a safe place to spend the night.

Balthasar pointed and shouted instructions to his men as they approached the grove of trees. "This group, take your carts to the back of the trees! This group, pull in here, in front of the trees. Tie the horses toward the center of the trees! Tie them securely; we do not want them running away!"

Cupping his hands over his mouth so he could be heard, Balthasar shouted, "Gaspar, take the first group!"

"We are on our way! Our bows will cover the east and south," Gaspar shouted.

"Good! I will place archers on the other side of the road," Balthasar answered.

It was quite hectic as the men whipped their animals so they could quickly position their carts as instructed. One cart overturned as it left the road and its horse was quickly untied and led away. Meanwhile, Hutan and his men were riding four horses toward the approaching riders. Hutan motioned to his men to slow their pace by raising his arm. As their horses came to a stop, each man released a bow strapped to his leg and pulled two arrows from his quiver. Placing one arrow in the bow string, ready to shoot, the men held the second arrow against the bow with the other hand so it could quickly replace the first after it was shot. As Hutan and his men waited for the riders, they checked their bows and horses. If any of the men were frightened, it did not show.

Hutan gave the men instructions and said to them, "We do not want to encourage a fight if none is intended, so keep your bows low. If their bows and swords are at the ready, or if they do not break their speed, we will shoot. We need to slow them down so our caravan has time to take cover."

Zinawar broke the silence. "A good fight is definitely what we needed to get our blood flowing!"

The men laughed, then quickly focused their eyes on the road. The dust cloud got closer and in a moment, the riders appeared over the hump in the road.

Covering his brow with his hand to block the blazing sun from his eyes, Pulan said, "Here they come and it looks like there are eight!"

"No! Ten riders!" shouted Hutan. "They wear armor, but not that of Seres. They must see us, but they do not slow their horses."

"No, they are gaining speed and I see a raised sword in the hand of one rider!" shouted Nekmard.

Zinawar added, "I see bows at the ready. Crossbows!" The mention of crossbows sent a shiver down the men's spines. In the hands of a skilled rider, such bows would make Hutan and his companion's easy targets.

"We will be cut to pieces if we sit here," Hutan said calmly as he watched the approaching riders. Hutan paused for a moment and then said, "We will begin riding toward our caravan, as if we are in retreat. Nekmard, you and Zinawar lead. Pulan and I will follow. Let us trot at first. Let them get closer to us."

"Closer? They already have a running start!" responded an excited, but nervous Nekmard.

"Listen to me! They will be on us quickly. We will trot and, on my shout, we will break into a full gallop. When they are in range, I will shout to Pulan, 'Ready… and… Shoot!' Pulan and I will turn and shoot at the lead riders. You know this maneuver! After we release our arrows, we will move ahead for your turn to shoot! Remember, once we begin to gallop, do not break stride!" shouted Hutan.

"Will this work?" Pulan asked Hutan.

"If they have not seen this before, we may catch them off guard. They expect us to retreat to our caravan, not to turn and shoot," Hutan replied.

Turning to look back briefly at the riders, Hutan yelled, "Gallop! Gallop!" to his men. The four riders gave their horses a kick and a yell, and in a few short seconds, they were riding at full speed. Hutan turned his head for another quick look back and saw that the riders were now within range for their arrows.

"Ready… and… Shoot!" Hutan shouted as he and Pulan turned to release their arrows. Nekmard and Zinawar slowed their pace to let Hutan and Pulan pass.

Seconds later Nekmard shouted, "Ready… Shoot!" as he and Zinawar turned to let their arrows fly.

Hutan turned to see the approaching riders slow their pace. Two of their arrows hit their mark, but the riders remained on their horses. Before calling for the next flight of arrows, Hutan looked back again to see that the riders were out of range. He did not want to risk his men being injured by one of the riders getting off a lucky shot with their crossbows, so they continued at their pace.

Hutan shouted to his men, "Keep your heads down and ride for the caravan."

At that moment, several of the enemies' short arrows hit the road, falling just short of Hutan's men and their horses.

As they neared the caravan, Hutan looked back again at the riders and saw that they had stopped on the road, some of them standing next to their horses.

Hutan shouted for his men to stop and then directed Pulan to stay and watch the bandits closely. "If they get off the road, see where they go. We do not want them surprising us. If they ride toward you, return to us quickly." Looking at Nekmard and Zinawar, Hutan continued, "Now, on to the caravan; we must report to Balthasar!"

The three rode quickly and, as they approached the caravan, the Magi walked out from the depths of the trees to meet them. Hutan jumped from his horse before it came to a stop and ran alongside it for a moment until he reached his friends.

In an excited voice and, with only half of his breath, Hutan blurted, "Ten riders in armor... not Seres. I do not recognize their armor. They came toward us at full speed... raised swords... bows ready!"

"Where is Pulan? Are any of you injured?" asked Balthasar.

"No, we are fine. Pulan is watching the bandits. Two of their men were wearing our arrows, but none fell from their horses," responded a panting Hutan, although he was managing longer breaths.

"Some armor is quite strong. Unless you released your arrows at close range, I doubt they are seriously hurt," Gaspar responded.

"They were surprised by our arrows and are considering their next move, I suspect. If we strike them quickly, we can easily defeat them," suggested a confident Hutan.

"No, we are not on a military mission. Let us give them a few minutes. We are in a good position here. But if they attack again, they will lose their lives," answered Balthasar.

Several of Balthasar's men joined Pulan to keep watch over the bandits. The Magi positioned their men near the caravan to ensure protection on all sides. After an hour without movement, Pulan and his companions watched as the bandits mounted their horses and began a slow retreat in the direction of Merv. Pulan trailed the bandits at a distance to make sure they kept in that direction. He did not want the bandits to circle back to the caravan through the brush and trees. When Pulan was

73

certain the riders were no longer a threat, he returned to the waiting caravan to report what he had seen.

After listening to Pulan's observations, Balthasar instructed the men, "We appear to be out of danger for the moment. Let us pull our carts onto the road and continue. Hutan, post two men here and have them trail us by a quarter of an hour. That should give us enough time to prepare our defense if the bandits return once more."

Now standing on a cart, so he could be heard by all of his men, Balthasar shouted, "Be alert! Watch in all directions!"

When the sun reached the horizon, the caravan pulled off the road into a level clearing that provided good visibility. Pulan returned to the caravan with word that there had been no further sighting of the bandits. Although it was a quiet evening, the men remained restless from the day's excitement and worried about the possibility of the bandits returning in the night.

The next two days provided good weather and comfortable travel. The road was in good condition and the rest stops were brief. It was on their third day of travel from Merv when Nekmard, who was posted behind the caravan with Hutan and Pulan, galloped toward the caravan shouting for Balthasar.

"Magi! Magi!" shouted Nekmard as he rode to the front of the caravan.

Balthasar heard Nekmard's call and turned from the front of the caravan to meet him. As Balthasar neared, Nekmard spoke. "Seres are approaching. There are many, at least twenty in full armor."

"I see," replied Balthasar. "Do they ride swiftly?"

"No, they ride at a steady pace."

"Do they escort a caravan? Do they pull many carts?" asked Balthasar as he slowly stroked his beard and processed the information.

"No caravan, and they pull only one cart."

"Have they seen you?"

"Yes, I am sure they have seen us, but we are keeping a safe distance. I rode to you as soon as we saw them," Nekmard replied.

"Thank you, Nekmard. You have done well."

As Balthasar spoke to Gaspar, the caravan came to a stop. "I will ride to Hutan and Pulan. Will you take the caravan to a safe place?" he asked.

"I will find a safe place. What is your plan?" Gaspar asked in response.

"I will speak to the Seres. I am sure that they mean us no harm," replied Balthasar with a smile.

"Speak to them? How can you be sure? At least let me organize our men quickly so we may show them our strength," pleaded an excited Gaspar.

"No, I will go to them alone," answered Balthasar.

"Alone? Please reconsider! These may not be honorable men," Gaspar continued to plead.

"I do not believe that trained militia will strike down an old, unarmed man without first hearing him speak. Besides, they will have to pass us at some point. If they do not, we will be looking over our shoulder all the way to Rhagae!" Balthasar replied, still holding his smile.

Balthasar asked one of the men to bring him two sheep's skins filled with water.

As Balthasar waited for the skins, Gaspar asked, "Are you certain this is wise?"

"No, but Ahura Mazda is with us. He will lead us through this. Do you not feel his presence?"

"I sensed Ahura Mazda's presence on the day I departed Asdin for Shahnaz," Gaspar replied while nodding. He paused for a moment and then continued, "That feeling remains. I cannot explain it. When I returned home from Asdin, I told my wife that this feeling reminds me of riding a horse for the first time. I could enjoy the excitement because I knew that my father was holding the reins and his arms held me steady. I knew that I was safe, just as I know now that Ahura Mazda guides us. But I fear that the Seres down the road may not care if Ahura Mazda is with us. They may be desperate men!"

"If we were further north, closer to their land, perhaps we would have a problem. But we pose no threat to them here," Balthasar replied.

After pausing to gather his thoughts, Balthasar continued, "But if you see Nekmard riding fast up the hill shouting and I am not with him, then I was probably wrong in my thinking."

The Magi shared a laugh as Balthasar was handed the skins of water. He placed them over the front of his horse. "I will offer them a gift of water and let them know that we are friends, but capable of defending ourselves," Balthasar said softly.

"That might work, but they also may view your offer as a sign of weakness and fear," replied Gaspar.

"Perhaps," answered Balthasar with a shrug of his shoulders.

"Let me join you?" offered Gaspar.

"No, it is better that I go alone," Balthasar replied as he trotted his horse to the end of the caravan.

"May Ahura Mazda be with you!" shouted Gaspar. "But if you do not return, may I have your cart?"

Balthasar glanced back with a smile and responded, "I will see you in a moment!"

When Balthasar reached Hutan and Pulan, he told them, "Pulan, take your place with the caravan. Hutan, wait here and watch. Report back to Gaspar if anything happens to me."

"No, I must come with you. You do not carry a sword! If these men are evil, you will be slaughtered!" warned Hutan.

"I will be safe," assured Balthasar.

Balthasar rode slowly toward the Seres. He held his reins with his arms high. He wanted the Seres to clearly see that he was not armed. As he approached them, he began to search for the words that he would use. He knew some of the Han language, but wanted to make sure that he was not misunderstood. He mumbled to himself as he rode, practicing his words. Then finally, he bowed his head briefly and prayed silently for Ahura Mazda's help.

When he reached the Seres, a few of the men had their bows drawn, but they lowered them once they saw that Balthasar carried no weapons.

In the language of the Seres, Balthasar asked, "My friends, who is your leader?"

There was only silence. Balthasar held his smile, but beads of sweat formed on his brow and he began thinking about what to say next.

Just then, the man Balthasar suspected to be their leader spoke in Persian, "I am the leader. What is it you have to say?"

"My men told me that you were approaching. I come to greet you with some water," answered Balthasar as he held out the skins.

"I am Zheng. It is kind of you to offer us water. It is also brave of you to come to us alone."

"Friend, I am not brave. I come alone because I mean you no harm," Balthasar replied in a confident but soft tone.

Zheng jumped off his horse and accepted the skins from Balthasar. Zheng's men also dismounted and took turns drinking from the skins.

Zheng takes a drink and spat the water onto the ground to clean his mouth before speaking to Balthasar, "We have been traveling two days from Merv. This morning, we saw a group of men ahead of us. Just when we thought that we would be upon them, they disappeared. Did they pass your caravan?"

"No one passed us today. But three days ago, the day we left Merv, we were attacked by bandits, ten men perhaps. After the attack, they rode in the direction of Merv," Balthasar replied.

Zheng took another mouthful of water and, again, spat it to the ground. He said, "Those bandits did not return to Merv; they have been trailing you. No doubt they will ambush your caravan when you are further up the road."

Zheng took yet another drink, this time swallowing and wiping his mouth with the back of his hand and said, "A day from here is a good place for such an attack… large boulders on both sides of the road. Archers on those rocks can quickly overtake a caravan of your size."

Wary that the Seres may have been the same group of riders that attacked the caravan, Balthasar wanted to learn more without aggravating the situation. "Thank you for sharing the news of our bandit friends and for warning about the danger ahead. The bandits carried short bows like yours," Balthasar said as he looked over the bows held by Zheng and his men.

"Do you believe they are Seres because they carry short bows? Anyone can have bows such as these for a price!" Zheng replied as he spat on the ground again. Zheng paused for a moment and then asked, "Where does your journey take you?"

"Our next stop is Nishapur. Our final destination is Jerusalem," Balthasar answered as he kept his eyes focused on Zheng.

"I do not know Jerusalem, but we have been to Nishapur many times on our way to Rhagae. Rhagae is where we go now," Zheng replied.

"So, you have escorted caravans to Rhagae?" asked Balthasar curiously.

"Seres, Persian… many caravans. We have traveled west to Rhagae and traveled many months to the south. We go to Rhagae now to meet a Seres caravan, which we will escort to Merv," Zheng quickly answered.

Balthasar paused for a few moments as he assessed Zheng's men. He spoke to Zheng in a voice loud enough for all of Zheng's men to hear and said, "Our caravan could use the assistance of an escort that has made the journey to Rhagae. I will need to discuss it with my men, of course, but if they agree, will you be willing to accompany us?"

Zheng quickly looked to his men and then responded, "It is said in my land that the lone sheep is in danger of the wolf. You are wise to seek the protection of others. If we can agree on a price, we will deliver you safely to Nishapur."

Zheng's men nodded in approval.

"Very well, I will check with my men," Balthasar replied as he turned his horse and trotted toward Hutan.

When he reached Hutan, Balthasar greeted him with a smile and said, "Well, friend, my head remains attached."

When Balthasar reached the caravan, Gaspar and several others waited to greet him. Balthasar dismounted his horse and asked the men if he might speak with Gaspar alone. The men dispersed as the Magi walked to a nearby rock to sit.

"The Seres appear to be friendly. They have seen our bandits trailing us and believe that the bandits are waiting to ambush us in a day or two, in a place where the land will give them an advantage," Balthasar reported.

"How do they know this?" asked Gaspar.

"This militia escorts caravans, so they know the road well. I made them an offer, but told them I needed your approval," Balthasar explained as he studied Gaspar's face for his reaction.

"What kind of offer?" asked a surprised Gaspar.

"As I was speaking with their leader, I thought about whether this is just the beginning of our trouble with bandits. We just began our journey and we are already defending ourselves. Our men are capable, but we do not want to put them at risk if we can avoid it," Balthasar explained.

Gaspar's head was down as he nodded in agreement with Balthasar. He looked up to ask, "We did discuss bringing more men and weapons, but we decided against a larger party. What are you proposing?"

"I am proposing that we hire the Seres to escort us to Rhagae. I believe that we can trust them. They are disciplined and trained, and part of a militia," Balthasar answered.

Gaspar stood and glanced at the sky as he responded, "If they are willing to protect us, we could use their help. Their armor and weapons alongside our caravan should discourage any bandits. But I do worry if they can be trusted. Let me go with you so I may see for myself. Still, if we reach an agreement, we must be wary of these strangers, so we will keep close watch on them until we reach Rhagae. We should still continue posting our own guards and extra guards on our cargo!"

Hutan asked to join the Magi as they rode to Zheng and Balthasar agreed, realizing the importance of reasserting the caravan's strength in case the Seres had any ulterior motives. When they reached the Seres, Zheng's men are along the side of the road, sitting in the shade of nearby trees.

Zheng stepped forward and asked, "What have you decided?"

Balthasar, Gaspar, and Hutan dismounted and Balthasar asked Zheng to speak privately with the three of them for a moment.

Zheng said a few words to his men and motioned for the Magi to follow him to a fallen poplar tree lying next to the road.

"We are interested in your help, but we are curious as to how you and your men, members of a militia, can free yourselves of your responsibilities for such a length of time. Our carts cannot keep your pace. When do you need to be in Rhagae?" Gaspar asked as he studied Zheng's face, looking for any hint of deception.

"If we are late by a week or two, it will not be of consequence," replied Zheng.

Not satisfied with this explanation, Gaspar asked, "Should we worry that you will change your mind along the way and abandon us to keep to your original schedule?"

"My superiors allow me to be flexible with my schedule," Zheng confidently replied.

"What will you require from us?" Gaspar asked.

"We are reasonable men. You provide us with our food and once in Nishapur, perhaps one of your horses, some silk, or whatever we agree upon. I am sure that we will reach an agreement. In my land, we say that a man's conversation is the mirror of his thoughts. What I say to you is what I am thinking. I hide nothing from you," Zheng answered.

"We could use your help if your offer is reasonable. But what assurance do we have that we are not putting our men at risk?" asked Gaspar.

Zheng replied, "Dogs have many friends because they wag their tails, not their tongues. All I can offer is my word and my honor. If we cannot agree, my men and I will be on our way."

Gaspar paused for a moment and then nodded approvingly to Balthasar.

"We are pleased that you will join us," Balthasar said as he embraced Zheng.

"Come join us when you are ready and we will introduce you to our companions," Gaspar said before embracing Zheng and kissing him on his cheeks. The Magi mounted their horses and began trotting toward their caravan as Zheng called his men together to explain what was discussed.

As the caravan moved toward Nishapur, Balthasar's men were uneasy about their Seres escorts, and some had no trust for their new companions. Confident that they could defend the caravan themselves, Hutan and a few others even resented the Seres. Zheng kept his men at a distance from the caravan, but some of the Seres rode with Balthasar's men, although language differences limited conversation to the basics. There were no further signs of the bandits and the caravan met few travelers on the road. When necessary, Balthasar sent hunting parties into the hills to find game, but it was not an easy task to feed so many men. The Magi rode with Zheng for much of each day, although their conversations were few and limited to the choice of rest areas and routes of travel.

One morning, when the Magi rode alone, Balthasar asked, "Are you surprised by our men's distrust of the Seres? Perhaps we should speak to them."

"Some caution is healthy, but I thought that some signs of trust would surface after a few days," Gaspar replied with a shrug.

Later that same day, a Seres scout in advance of the caravan returned to inform of an approaching Persian militia. Zheng was concerned about this news and requested Balthasar to ride ahead.

"Tell their commander that we are your escort. I would not want them to be surprised by us," Zheng requested with a concerned tone.

Balthasar nodded, "I will go speak with him. Do not worry, there will be no trouble."

As Balthasar approached the Persian militia, he was surprised to see such a large number of armed men. He understood why Zheng and his men were apprehensive about encountering such a formidable Persian force. When Balthasar reached the Persians, he asked to speak with their leader. He was led along the caravan to where the officers were riding.

"Good day friends. How goes your travel?" Balthasar shouted.

Continuing to ride while shielding his eyes from the sun with his hand, the leader of the Persians spoke, "Our travel goes well. What is your destination?"

"We travel to Nishapur, then west to Rhagae. How is the road from here?"

The leader replied, "You wear the yellow cap of the Medes and only their leader would ride such a great white horse. You are Magi." Turning to look at the road behind him, the leader continued, "You are heading into dangerous territory. Are you able to defend yourself?"

"We are escorted by a modest-size Seres militia," Balthasar replied.

At this, the Persian officers looked at each other with puzzled faces and brought their horses to a stop.

The Persian leader responded, "Seres?"

"They have been riding with us for several weeks. We were attacked by bandits before the Seres joined us. They have kept us safe! They will be meeting a Seres caravan in Rhagae before returning to Merv," Balthasar boldly answered.

"Perhaps the Seres were your bandits. Could that be why you have not been attacked again?" asked the leader.

"I assure you, these men are not bandits," replied a frustrated Balthasar.

"We will see!" snapped the leader as he kicked his horse into a trot toward Balthasar's awaiting men.

Balthasar accompanied the Persian officers to the caravan where Gaspar and Zheng were waiting. Balthasar introduced them to the Persian, whose name was Marzban, which meant "Governor of the Frontier." Zheng began to answer Marzban's questions and the conversation went well until the remainder of the Persian militia arrived and surrounded Zheng and his men. If Zheng was nervous about their presence, it did not show. He continued to speak calmly with Marzban. Zheng's men, on the other hand, were quite anxious. They watched as the Persian militia moved around them. Their nervousness excited their horses, making it difficult to keep them in place.

"All of a sudden, this road has become a very crowded place," Gaspar whispered to Balthasar. Marzban drew the attention of his men by raising his right hand and then spoke to Zheng in a loud voice, "You must hand over your weapons and dismount from your horses!"
Marzban's men quickly closed in around Zheng's men.

"You arrest us? What crime have we committed?" demanded Zheng.

"No! No! I protest! These men are our friends. We will be at great risk without them," Gaspar pleaded as he positioned his horse between Marzban and Zheng.

Out of the corner of his eye, Zheng saw two Persians positioning themselves on the hillside next to the caravan. Zheng motioned his head toward the two and said to Marzban, "I trust that they are a hunting party looking for game and not Seres."

Hearing Zheng's comment, Marzban smiled and said, "If you have done nothing wrong, then you will have no problem with us. There has been much trouble in this region. We check everyone who is unknown to us."

Zheng looked at his men, shrugged his shoulders and slowly drew his sword and untied his bow. He handed them over to one of Marzban's men. Zheng's men also complied and surrendered their weapons.

"Let us talk this through, friend," Balthasar appealed to Marzban in a soft voice.

Marzban dismounted his horse and handed his reins to one of his men. He motioned with his hand for Balthasar to follow him.

Balthasar dismounted and told Zheng, "Come with me so we can set this matter straight."

Balthasar and Zheng followed Marzban to his caravan where Marzban took a seat on the back of a cart.

When Marzban looked up and saw the two approaching, he said, "Keep back, Seres, I speak only with the Magi."

Balthasar gave a nod to Zheng and Zheng turned and began walking back toward to caravan, with his horse trailing behind him.

When Balthasar reached the cart where Marzban sat, Marzban asked, "How long were you in Merv? Any trouble there?"

"We had no trouble during our three days," Balthasar quickly responded.

"Many Seres?" Marzban asked with his arms folded across his chest, his eyes glancing toward Balthasar's caravan to make sure Zheng and his men were not approaching.

"Yes, quite a few. We heard they were stranded until the weather improved."

"So that is where you met your friends?" asked Marzban with raised eyebrows, as if he was about to prove his assertion.

"No. We met them several days after we left Merv. They were coming from the south," Balthasar

quickly responded in a tone that hinted of his growing annoyance with the questioning.
"I see, and how many bandits attacked you?" asked Marzban.
"I believe that ten were their number, maybe a few more," Balthasar answered.
"Were they Seres?"
"We do not know who they were," replied Balthasar, shrugging his shoulders.
"And what is your destination?" Marzban asks as he unfolded his arms, once again surveying the scene around him.
"Our journey takes us to Jerusalem. We will leave our Seres friends in Rhagae."
"Jerusalem? For what reason do you journey such a distance? Is it a matter of great importance?" asked a puzzled Marzban.
"We travel to see the Hebrew messiah. We have been studying his star."
Balthasar's comments took Marzban by surprise, as he asked, "Messiah? Studying what star?"
As Marzban mumbled to himself about studying stars, before Balthasar could respond, Balthasar noticed someone lying in the cart next to them.
"Is one of your men injured?" asked Balthasar as he walked to the cart. When he was beside the cart, he saw someone covered with blankets, a moist cloth covering his forehead.
"Why, he is but a boy! What happened to him?" asked Balthasar. Marzban did not respond.
Gaspar, hearing the commotion, walked over to join Balthasar and also asked what happened.

"He will not say," answered Balthasar. "But he looks to be with fever." He felt the boy's forehead.

Gaspar called out to Marzban in a stern voice, "How long has this boy been sick?"

Marzban's face grew angry. He hopped off the cart and looked as if he was about to shout. But when his eyes met the boy in the cart, he dropped his head and softly spoke.

"Four days, he has been sick four days. We tried everything, but he only gets weaker. He is hot one moment and cold the next. He cannot eat and today – today, he cannot even hold his water. We can only keep him awake for a few minutes at a time. He is very weak," Marzban said, his voice cracking with emotion.

"Why does he travel with militia?" Gaspar asked.

Marzban lifted his head to reveal tears streaming from his eyes. "He is my son, my only family. Until now, he has not been sick one day in his life."

"I am sorry," replied Gaspar softly, so as to not cause the boy further distress.

Having made his way toward the Magi, Zheng overheard the conversation with Marzban and offered, "Perhaps Shen, one of my men, can help. He helps us back to good health when we are sick, and is very knowledgeable."

"We need no help!" Marzban snapped.

"Of course you need help! Your son is dying! His time may be short," Gaspar snapped back, in a hushed shout.

Marzban was silent for a moment, thinking about Gaspar's harsh-but true-words. His head was down as he said softly, "Yes, I do need help. Do what you can."

Zheng hurried to his men, calling for Shen, which means "deep thinker" in Seres. He found him and the other Seres huddled next to their horses, surrounded by Persian militia.

Zheng spoke briefly to Shen in the Han language and then motioned with his hands for the Persian militia to make room as he shouted, "Make way for us so that we may help the boy."

Shen untied a leather sack from his horse and walked quickly with Zheng to the sick boy.

"Shen does not understand Persian, so I will explain the boy's illness to him," Zheng explained. When Zheng had finished speaking, Shen nodded a few times and then spoke to Zheng, seeming to ask a question.

Zheng asked Marzban, "When did the boy become sick and what were his symptoms? What did he eat and drink before he became sick? And has anyone else fallen ill?"

"I am afraid that I do not have much information for you. He became ill four nights ago, shortly after supper. We all eat the same food and drink the same water, but no one else has been sick," Marzban replied, shaking his head in sadness.

Zheng relayed this information to Shen. Shen scrunched his face as he studied the sick boy, pressing on the boy's stomach and feeling his throat. Shen asked Zheng another question, which Zheng again relayed to Marzban.

"Did he complain of any pain?" Zheng asked.

"He said something about a pain in his stomach," Marzban answered, trying to think of any more details.

Zheng told Shen these things and Shen replied that he would go fetch some hot water and then return.

Zheng then called to his men as Shen departed, "Help Shen with whatever he needs, and quickly!"

Zheng, Gaspar and Marzban sat next to the boy as they waited for Shen. When Shen returned, he carried a pot of hot water, a cup and his leather sack. He carefully selected some items, which were too dark and dry to identify, from his sack. Although the other men could not be sure, the mixture appeared to be dried flower tops and a piece of twisted root. He threw these items into the pot of hot water and closed the lid, removing another pouch from his waist and pulling out a small ceramic box. Placing the box in the palm of his hand, he opened it slowly and took out a pinch of brown powder, which he dropped into the pot and again closed the lid.

Shen spoke to Zheng once more and Zheng relayed to the others. "We need to sit the boy upright and make him drink. He must drink three cups of Shen's potion," Zheng says.

"This will not be easy. The boy is barely breathing and that awful smelling syrup will be difficult for him to swallow," cautioned Gaspar.

For the next several minutes, they took turns steadying the boy and holding his head back so he could swallow the liquid. Prying the boy's mouth open, they slowly poured. Although they managed to spill most of the pot, they were successful in getting three cups into the boy's mouth. When they were finished, they put dry clothes on him and laid him back down. Before they covered him with blankets, Shen climbed into the cart and placed his ear on the boy's chest. After a few moments, Shen climbed out of the cart and spoke briefly with Zheng before joining the other Seres.

"What does your man say?" asked Marzban.

"He said that the boy probably ate poison berries. It may be too late to save him, but his heart appears to be responding to the medicine. He says this is a good sign," Zheng said with a tone of encouragement.

Zheng handed the pot to Marzban, "You are to add more water tonight and have him drink, and again tomorrow morning. If he survives this night, there is a good chance that he will recover. Remember: no drink but water, and no food but bread for at least a week."

"Understood, friend. I am grateful for your help. You may have your weapons. You are free to go," replied Marzban.

As the Magi and Zheng walked toward their caravan, Zheng grinned and said, "This is good news, I cannot leave this place quickly enough."

"We cannot leave! We must spend the night in case the boy needs Shen's help," Balthasar replied with Gaspar nodding in approval.

"Spend the night? What if the boy dies?" But the Magi did not respond; they only stare at Zheng. "Oh, I suppose you are right. I will share the news with my men; we will spend the night with our new friends."

The caravans of Balthasar and Marzban soon made camp together. They traded supplies and shared food, and the Magi gathered their men for an Afrinigan, where they prayed for their safety and for the healing of the boy. As the men began to assemble, Gaspar assisted Balthasar with the Padan, the ritual in which Balthasar washed to purify himself. Balthasar covered himself with the Sudre-Kusti. Gaspar prepared the Atash Dadgah fire and offered some frankincense to consecrate it. Many Persians joined in the Afrinigan, but they did not understand much of it. Zheng and his men stood and hummed along as the hymns were sung; it was a pleasant evening. Every hour or so, Shen checked on the boy's condition and the group was updated on the boy's progress through Zheng's translations. Zheng and his men no longer felt threatened and the Persians were beginning to relax.

When dawn arrived, the Magi accompanied Zheng and Shen to check on the boy. As they neared Marzban's tent, they saw Marzban with the boy in his lap, covered with blankets, sitting next to a fire.

"He is awake!" greeted Balthasar.

"His fever has broken. He wakes briefly, but remains very weak, although he is much better," Marzban answered as he wiped tears from his eyes with the sleeve of his coat.

"Our hearts are joyful with this news!" Gaspar replied.

"Joyful indeed!" added Balthasar.

Shen picked up the water pot and removed the top to peer inside. He took the box of powder from his waistband, added another pinch to the pot and placed the pot on a rock next to the fire, speaking briefly to Zheng.

Nodding his head, Zheng relayed the instructions to Marzban, "Shen said that the boy should drink another pot of his mixture, for it takes a considerable amount to remove the poison from the body."

Marzban picked up the cup next to him and handed it to Zheng, asking, "Would you fill it with more of the potion?"

Both men smiled as Zheng said, "It is my pleasure to serve my Persian friends."

Marzban kissed his son on the head and spoke softly into his ear to wake him. He held the cup to the boy's lips. As he drank, Marzban spoke to the Magi.

"We sat by the fire all night. When his fever broke and he opened his eyes, the first thing he did was lift his weak arm and point to the star. I suppose that it is your star. Strange that I never noticed it. It was as if the star spoke to us. It was a wonderful night!"

"Not everyone sees the star, but Ahura Mazda revealed it to you last night." Balthasar replied. Before they left, the Magi reached out to touch the boy before returning to their tents to wake their men and pack their carts. Within the hour, Balthasar's men were packed and ready to move.

As they mounted their horses, Marzban came to say goodbye. He embraced Zheng and handed him a rolled parchment.

Smiling, Marzban said, "In case you are stopped again by Persian militia, present this parchment. It is my personal statement commending you for saving the life of a Persian and for assisting this militia."

Zheng looked at the scroll, but he could not read a word of Persian. "I am greatly honored, dear friend. Perhaps we will meet again," he said.

Balthasar shouted for his caravan to move.

Marzban saluted him and said, "May the god of the star be with you. Carry our good wishes to the messiah whom you seek."

Balthasar returned the salute and led the caravan down the road. Spirits were high as Balthasar turned to Zheng.

"We experienced something extraordinary in this desolate place!"

"Yes, we Seres are greatly relieved to be among the living. It did not look good for us yesterday," Zheng quickly replied, completely missing Balthasar's reference to the boy's miraculous recovery and of God's presence among them.

The encounter with the Persian militia put Balthasar's men at ease with the Seres. Hutan, who had been most distrustful of the Seres, was even beginning to tolerate them. As they rode, Hutan turned to Pulan and the others near him to say, "If the Persians do not consider the Seres a threat, perhaps we need not worry."

Pulan shrugged his shoulders, "We are on a long journey and they will only be with us a short time. It is often said, 'Do not cut down the tree that gives you shade.' We should make the best of the protection our friends provide!"

For much of the journey, Nekdel had been riding with his cousin Rushad in the center of the caravan. This day, Balthasar had the young men ride with him. It was heartbreaking to see Marzban's boy so close to death, so Balthasar felt compelled to keep close watch on the boys for the remainder of the journey. He contemplated if the two should have stayed in Asdin, but for this moment, he was overjoyed to have them close.

When the caravan stopped to rest for the night, there was some conversation between the two groups of men, and some of Balthasar's men joined the Seres as they ate their supper. They did not understand much of what was being said, but there was laughter, which had more meaning than words.

For the evening's Afrinagan, Balthasar's men unpacked their musical instruments, something they had seldom done so far on the journey. One of the men used a short bow to play a "kamancheh," a long, narrow fiddle. Another stringed instrument called a "tar" was being strummed, as well as a flute-type instrument that produced sound by blowing into a reed. Many drums were tapped, including one in the shape of a goblet, a tombak and another, a daf, which looked like a large plate. Accompanied by several lutes and a small harp, the instruments were played skillfully as the well-honed harmony of men's voices completed the magic of this evening's performance.

After the music, when the men retired to their tents, the Magi shared a seat by their fire with Zheng. Every few minutes, the Magi took turns moving away from the fire to gaze at the star, which shone brightly in the western sky.

After watching his friends stare at the sky and then return to the fire, Zheng leaned back and asked, "Friends, why do you search the sky? Each night I watch you search the sky. Do the stars speak to you? Do you wait for them to do something?"

Gaspar looked up from the fire at Balthasar and nodded his head for Balthasar to respond.

Balthasar leaned back on a boulder to get more comfortable, stretched his legs and said, "Yes, the stars are important to us. We believe that they reveal things to men. Tell me, Zheng, you have traveled with us many days now and you have not asked about the purpose of our journey. Are you curious as to why we would travel such a great distance?"

"I suppose that I am a little curious about your journey, but it is not my concern. I take orders and give orders. It is not my place to ask many questions. Getting you safely to Rhagae is my only concern," Zheng replied.

The men were quiet for a few moments as Zheng poked a stick into the coals and asked, "Why do you go to Jerusalem? Traders do not usually travel for more than a few weeks. I know that kings will travel great distances to visit other kings. As kings of your people, you must be on such a mission. Of course, kings will also send their warriors to invade another's kingdom, but you have no legion of warriors. Whatever your purpose, it must be important for you to take such a risk!"

"Have you seen the bright star shining behind me?" Balthasar asked.

"I suppose I have seen it, but I do not spend my time looking at the sky, unless I am watching for storms or vultures," laughed Zheng.

"But you do see it? Is it brighter than the other stars?" asked Balthasar as he tried to engage Zheng.

"I suppose it is," Zheng responded with a shrug.

"Zheng, this star is like no other. So much about it cannot be explained. Not everyone sees the star. Can you imagine? A star that shines so brightly, yet cannot be seen by everyone," Balthasar instructed with a smile.

"That is quite strange. I do not understand. Maybe their eyes lose their strength," replied Zheng, trying to make sense of what Balthasar told him.

Gaspar stood and pointed toward the star. "We have been studying the stars since we were children. Our fathers studied the stars, as did their fathers. There has never been such a star. It burns with a great flame, yet it is hidden from many."

"Impossible! How can that be?" asserted Zheng, now fully engaged in the discussion.

"See for yourself. Ask your men if they see the star. You may find that not all see it," offered Gaspar.

"If what you say is true, then this must not be a star," replied Zheng as he tried further to reason an explanation.

"If it is not a star, what is it?" asked Gaspar.

"I do not know. Perhaps it is one of the gods. Whatever it is, it is best to leave such things to themselves!" Zheng replied as he shook his head.

"We cannot ignore this wonder. We believe it holds something important for men. We are following this star to the place that lies beneath it," added Gaspar.

"You may wish that it holds special meaning, but it may not. We all wish for something, but as it is often said, 'If wishes were horses, beggars would ride,'" Zheng replied with a laugh.

Gaspar did not respond and his expression was a most serious one. Zheng realized that he may have offended his friend, so he chuckled as if his comment was not meant to be taken seriously.

After no change in Gaspar's demeanor, Zheng slowly rose, brushed the dirt from the seat of his pants and said, "So, the purpose of your journey is to go to the place of the star. Friends, you must be having fun with me. Surely there is more to your story."

Balthasar stood and put his hand on Zheng's shoulder. "There is much more to our story, but we shall save that for another night. We need to rest our weary bones."

As the three men walked to their tents, they sensed that the evening had brought them closer. The Magi were reminded that the star that fascinated them remained a mystery to all who saw it.

The next morning, groups of men were making their way through the bushes, picking from the abundance of berries. The plants were lush and bore much fruit. In another month, the summer's destructive sun would burn the plants away.

    Balthasar did not mind that the caravan would have a late start this morning; it was good to see his men and the Seres enjoying themselves. Besides, fresh berries served with dinner was something that all savored. Balthasar and Zheng rode together on this lively morning. On most mornings, the caravan was quiet while the men fought the morning chill. This morning, however, most of the men were warm from berry-picking and some carried warm tu in their cups as they mounted their horses.

    Zheng was very much awake and attempted to engage Balthasar in conversation. "It seems that there are never enough coats or blankets to warm the body on mornings such as this. Your wool is thick and heavy, does it keep you warm?" asked Zheng.

    "Yes, it holds the warmth well. But it is hard to keep my feet warm while riding. Sometimes I must walk to get the blood flowing," answered Balthasar.

    "Yes, I agree. Sometimes we jump up and down and shout as if we are wild men. The jumping gets us warm quickly," replied Zheng.

    "What about the shouting? Does that warm you?"

    "No, we shout to keep the bandits away. Even bandits avoid wild men!" laughed Zheng.

    As they rode, Zheng continued, "My coat is not of good quality, but it was cheap. As we say in my land, 'Cheap things are never good and good things are never cheap.' Someday I will have a coat as fine as yours!"

    A silent Balthasar prompted Zheng to continue after a few moments, saying, "I kept awake most of the night thinking about your star. What is its meaning? A star so mysterious must have a special meaning. You did not tell me its meaning!"

Balthasar looked toward the distant horizon and pointed to the star, which was visible in the morning sky, "Our eyes and our hearts tell us that the star is a sign of the Hebrew messiah. That is why we believe that it hangs over Jerusalem."

"Is the Hebrew messiah a god, a god with special powers? Surely only a god would have such a star? In my land, we have many gods, so many gods that I do not know all of their names. What about you Magi? You have your god or do you now follow this Hebrew god?"

"I do not have answers for all of your questions. Tonight, if we are not too tired, let me ask Ethan if he will speak with us. Ethan is a Jew and knows the Hebrew writings. He will answer your questions."

"Thank you, my good friend. May the sun keep you warm," Zheng responded as the two rode out into the new day.

Chapter VI: Ambush Among the Rocks

The caravan rested briefly in Nishapur; it took only a day to make repairs and resupply the caravan before the men were once again ready to move. With full confidence in their Seres companions, Balthasar's men wanted to take advantage of their added protection and quickly cover as much distance as possible.

As the Magi rode with Zheng the morning after leaving Nishapur, Gaspar asked their Seres friend, "How will our ride be this day?"

"We should have a good ride until mid-day. Then the hills will become a bit longer and steeper. We will see fewer trees and more rocks. By evening, we will be surrounded by large boulders and we will be in the midst of the place where bandits surprise their prey," replied Zheng.

After a few minutes of silence, Gaspar asked, "Will there be a safe place to stop this evening? Should we make camp before the boulders so we do not place ourselves in danger? I worry that the bandits have an advantage; they know the road far better than our scouts."

"We will be among the boulders for several days. As we ride, we should take our time and keep our caravan close together. This evening, we will post men on top of the rocks so we are not ambushed," answered Zheng. Never shifting his gaze away from the land that sprawls before them, Zheng added, "Remember, a thief is a king until he is caught. If we are surprised by the bandits, they will pay a steep price."

Balthasar pondered this wisdom and asked, "Have you had trouble in this area?"

"No trouble in my last trip to Rhagae; that was an easy ride. But a year ago, I lost two men. Several more were injured," replied Zheng, shaking his head.

"What happened? Was it a surprise attack? Were you escorting a caravan?" asked Balthasar, both excited and nervous to hear Zheng's answers.

"We were escorting a large caravan to Merv when the sky opened and the rain turned the road to mud. Some of our carts became stuck, so we were easy targets for the bandits. The caravan was too long for our men to protect," answered Zheng.

"How did you escape?" asked Gaspar.

"Their numbers were too great. We could not find them among the rocks, so we left one of the carts on the road, which satisfied them. I buried two of my men among those rocks and we killed several bandits… very unpleasant business!" Zheng replied quietly while dropping his head as he was saddened by the thought of his slain friends.

Balthasar directed his attention to Gaspar and said, "When we enter the rocks, we will alert the men to follow Zheng's instructions."

Trying to put his friends at ease, Zheng replied, "It is always good to be on alert, but no reason to worry. Your Persian militia went through that area recently, so bandits will worry they may still be near. We are most vulnerable when there are few people on the road."

By early afternoon, the flat road narrowed and began to give way to rolling hills. Even the smallest of hills were hard on the horses pulling carts. Gaspar rode along the caravan every hour to check on the condition of the men and their horses. After one of his hourly checks, he spoke to Balthasar and Zheng.

"We need to rest the horses. We should probably rest each hour until we reach level land," he advised.

As the caravan slowed to a stop, Balthasar noticed a table made of stones along the road. He and Gaspar dismounted and walk toward the unusual sight in this desolate area.

"A traveler must have built this altar to thank his god for guiding him through the rocks safely, or perhaps to ask his god for help in navigating through them," suggested Zheng.

Balthasar removed his boots, shaking them to empty the pebbles and dirt and exclaimed, "This is a good place for us to ask for Ahura Mazda's help. Let us prepare for an Afrinagan."

The altar reminded the Magi of the many different people who traveled this road, bringing their religions and gods with them.

"What religion do you suppose was practiced by those who built this altar?" Gaspar asked his two companions.

"People of many religions use this altar. No one wants to travel without their god as company, it is too lonely and too dangerous a road," answered Balthasar.

Zheng, the most experienced traveler of the three, told the Magi, "This is a good place to look for water to fill our skins. We may not see water again for several days."

"Very well, but first we will pray with our men. You are welcome to join us," replied Balthasar as he turned toward the caravan.

Zheng did not respond. He walked towards the caravan, shaking his head and mumbling to himself. He shouted something in Han to his companions and raised his water skin above his head. Zheng's men retrieved their skins and followed Zheng to a grove of trees in the distance.

When the Afrinagan was complete, Balthasar's men filled their skins and jars with water and returned to their carts and animals. The caravan was readied and began moving past the altar toward the top of the next hill. Zheng rode to the front of the caravan to speak with the Magi.

"I have seen many different religious customs, but I have not seen people worship fire. Why is it that you praise and sing to the fire?" asked Zheng with a grin.

Gaspar's face grew red and he clenched his teeth. As he was about to speak, Balthasar burst into one of his boisterous laughs. "It is not the fire we worship, Zheng! Fire reminds us to purify our minds when we call upon our god, Ahura Mazda. Our god is most wise and the source of all justice and goodness in this world. We seek his protection from all who wish to harm us."

"Oh, I think I understand your fire now. The fire is like a messenger. It is used to get the attention of your god?" asked Zheng.

"Almost. You are not the first to think of us as fire worshippers. I suppose that our fire is more of a reminder than a messenger, but I can see how it must seem strange to you," replied Balthasar.

"Once along this road I saw a group of Persians sacrifice a bull as part of their ritual. They said that killing the bull had something to do with a struggle between good and evil," Zheng responded. After a moment of silence, he continued, "I am not sure who won that struggle, but we ate bull for many days; it was quite tasty!"

"There are many ideas about god that I do not understand," replied Balthasar.

"That reminds me, did you see the stone house standing along the road near Merv, the house with many altars?" asked Zheng.

"Yes, I remember seeing that house," nodded Balthasar.

"That house is a temple built by people who worship Buddha. Many merchants who travel this road know Buddha," said Zheng. "Are you familiar with this god?"

"I have heard of Buddha. His followers believe that men are reborn many times, living many lives. If they are good and do many good things, they might eventually enter paradise," replied Balthasar.

"Yes, that is right! Is that not marvelous?" replied Zheng with obvious excitement in his voice.

"I know that many hear this message with favor. Ahura Mazda does not put men through such pain and frustration. One good life of obedience is all that our god requires of us," replied Balthasar.

"We worship many gods in my land. It is most confusing. Some of our leaders worship their own fathers. Can you imagine? And they worship them in great temples that were built in their honor," replied Zheng

"I understand the power held in a man's ancestors. I have heard it said that to forget one's ancestors is to be a brook without a source, a tree without a root," Balthasar responded in an understanding voice.

"Ah, but it doesn't stop with the worship of our ancestors. As I have said, we have many gods. We worship the god of the Soil, the god of the Four Directions, the god of the Mountains and Rivers… so many gods. I cannot remember all of them. For a simple man such as myself, God is too complicated. I will likely have to be reborn many times before I solve this puzzle. How do we know which god to follow?" Zheng asked Balthasar with eyes that begged for answers to his questions.

"I do not possess all the answers my friend. No man has such knowledge. The god who created this world and placed his stars in the heavens must want us to seek and be able to find him. If this is not true, why would he go to all of this trouble?" replied Balthasar.

Zheng let Balthasar's words linger through the day's warming air. After accepting his words, he asked, "Do Persians build temples to honor their great kings?"

"Persians do not honor their kings in this way. We remember our kings for what they accomplished, not for their lives, luxuries or grand palaces," explained Balthasar.

"And what have your great kings done?" Zheng asked inquisitively.

"Our greatest king, Darius, united Persians by building many great roads, roads that we still use today. Darius also created a delivery system for Persians to send things to each other and he paid for everything by collecting money from all Persians. Through these acts, Darius brought Persians together as a nation," Balthasar replied, reflecting on his great king.

"So, Darius became a great king by building roads and making deliveries?" asked a grinning Zheng.

"Darius was a great king because he was fair to all people, including the foreigners who were living in Persia. He allowed the foreigners to worship their own gods and to keep their own customs. But it has not been easy for Persians to accept some of these customs. For example, have you seen those places along the road where unfortunate travelers died and are buried?" asked Balthasar.

"Yes, I have seen them. Why do you ask? Are you warning me to stop talking?" Zheng asked, uncertain as to where Balthasar's answer will lead.

"No, this is one of these unpleasant customs. Persians would never foul the earth with an unclean, rotting body. Persians bury their dead above the ground and cover them with rocks. We Medes also bury above ground, but we make sure that the body's bones are free of skin before we cover them with rocks," Balthasar stated matter-of-factly.

Zheng cocked his head and smiled. *Surely he must be having fun with me,* Zheng thought. Without responding to Balthasar's comments about skin off the bones, Zheng offered another thought. "We Seres also have strange customs. One of them is that we bury our dead with their valuable jewelry and fine clothes," he said.

"Why is this done?" asked Balthasar.

"Seres believe that they will be reborn and they do not want to come back into this world poor and naked. We toil so hard for everything. I will never understand why anyone would put something of value into the dirt. Can you believe such a thing? Seres kings are buried with much more than clothes and jewelry. It is said that men are also buried with our kings… men who are not yet dead!" Zheng exclaimed, letting his emotions show on his normally expressionless face.

"Buried alive with their dead king? I agree with you, Zheng; that is most strange and frightening. It must be hard for your kings to make friends!" replied Balthasar with a laugh, trying to lighten the conversation.

"No, it is the opposite. It is a great honor to be buried with the king... but I have never been terribly excited about such an opportunity," Zheng replied as they both shared a laugh at the odd subjects being discussed.

After a few moments, Zheng asked Balthasar, "Were your kings great warriors?"

"Darius was our most famous warrior. He won many battles and expanded the empire far to the west, until he began claiming Greek cities. King Cyrus also had many great conquests. That is, of course, until Alexander and his great army took control of Persia. It seems that every ambitious warrior eventually falls to a more ambitious warrior," Balthasar offered with reflection.

As they rode, Balthasar was reminded about Rhagae and its rich history. "Zheng, our last great Persian king, Darius the Third, fled on this very road trying to escape from Alexander. Darius did not make it far. In fact, I believe that he was killed close to where we ride at this moment."

"That is most unfortunate for your king," Zheng replied solemnly.

"A nation's people suffer when their king dies in battle and the pain is far greater when a king is killed on his own soil. It was a sad day for Persia," Balthasar said.

After a brief moment, he continued, "Soon after Alexander's victory, a terrible earthquake took place here that destroyed many villages. My people believe that Ahura Mazda sent the earthquake to show his displeasure with Alexander."

As Zheng looked to each side of the road, he saw large rocks covering the hillside and said, "It would not be good to be in this place when the earth begins to shake!"

Reflecting on their conversation and keeping a watch for bandits, the two men rode in silence among the boulders on each side of the road. Balthasar was unable to find a suitable place for the caravan to rest this evening, so he brought the caravan to a halt at the base of one of the hills and directed the men to set up their tents on the road, while some of the men made their beds near the animals among the rocks. After a restless night, the men were anxious to get moving and underway at dawn. Everyone hoped to travel beyond the difficult terrain today. It was mid-morning when Pulan and one of Zheng's men, Yon, rode quickly over the hill from their position ahead of the caravan. As they approached the Magi, Pulan raised his arm for the caravan to stop.

"What is the trouble?" asked Balthasar.

"We have company among the rocks!" answered Pulan. Nodding in Yon's direction, Pulan continued, "I did not see anything until Yon pointed to something shiny among the boulders. When I got a better look, it appeared to be a man hiding behind one of them. The sun was reflecting off his shield. Unfortunately for us, Yon says there are more. How many Yon?" Pulan asked.

Yon held up both hands, displaying all of his fingers, and said in Persian, "Six."

"I am not sure what that means," Balthasar replied, confused by Yon's reply. Balthasar quickly took charge. "Zheng... Zheng to the front!" he called out.

Zheng quickly rode up the line to Balthasar, who sat at the front. "Yes, I am here!" he exclaimed.

"Zheng, ask Yon how many men he saw among the rocks" Balthasar said.

"Of course," answered Zheng as he turned to Yon to ask him in the Seres language. "Yon says that he saw ten men on the right side of the road, but he saw many large rocks on both sides of the road where men can hide," Zheng responded, translating Yon's answer into words Balthasar could understand.

"I see. This is not good," Balthasar said to himself, but loud enough for the men around him to hear.

"Pulan, do the men in the rocks know that you saw them?" Balthasar asked.

"Perhaps. Yon pointed briefly in their direction, but the sun may have been shining in their eyes, so I cannot be sure," Pulan answered.

"Did you race back to us as soon as you saw them?"

"No, we were over the top of the hill before we began our gallop," answered Pulan.

Contemplating the matter at hand, Balthasar asked, "What are your thoughts Zheng?"

"It is good that we saw them before they attacked. Let us protect the high ground around us. If they move into positions above us, they will shoot our horses and we will be at their mercy. If they are among the rocks, their horses must be nearby, probably on the other side of the hill. I suggest that we send two men to the top of both hillsides. Pulan and Yon, take positions ahead of us on the road, on top of the hill. From that position, it will look as if you are waiting for the caravan. Hopefully that will hold the bandits in their positions," Zheng responded.

It was clear that his years of training brought him unparalleled experience and wisdom. The Magi also had much knowledge in warfare, but they realized their caravan would be at a disadvantage without Zheng.

"Why do we want them to hold their positions among the rocks?" asked Gaspar.

"So we can steal their horses, of course," Zheng snapped back. "This will take a few minutes at most. If we surprise them, we may escape with little damage. But we take a risk. Since we are unsure about their numbers, it may be we who are surprised."

"We have few options," Balthasar said as he looked at Gaspar, waiting for him to agree.

"I suppose you are right," Gaspar answered. "Let us go over the plan quickly with our men so we understand what is required of us."

Zheng jumped on top of a cart and motioned for all the men to gather around. As he spoke, he pointed to the men, directing them to move to different areas near the cart.

"Pulan and Yon, ride ahead to the top of the hill. You must act as if you are waiting for the caravan. You must be convincing. Do not let the bandits know that you have seen them!" Zheng pointed to Xun and the other Seres, directing them into position. "Walk quietly and move up the hill among the rocks. Their horses may be under guard on the other side."

"I will take four of my men and we will come in behind the bandits on this side," Zheng said, alerting each man to his role in the attack.

"How can my men help?" asked Balthasar.

"Take your men and wait just below the top of the hill from Yon and Pulan. Once the fighting starts, you will need to decide how to best deploy your men. Until we find the bandits, we will not know where to take the fight," Zheng answered defiantly.

"You want us to wait while you and your men engage the bandits? They will have the advantage!" Balthasar answered, unwilling to miss part of the action and risk surrender or death at the hands of the bandits.

"You must be patient. A hasty man drinks his tea with a fork! Your delay will take the bandits by surprise."

"We will be ready," replied Balthasar, understanding that Zheng's experience had to be trusted.

The men readied their bows and checked to see if their quivers were full of arrows. Their swords hung on their sides and some of the men carried a shield in one hand.

As the men checked their equipment, Zheng whispered to Balthasar, "If we find that we are outnumbered and it is not going well, turn the caravan around and make haste, friend."

"I will not be able to keep our men from the fight!" Balthasar answered without looking at Zheng. Balthasar and his men were ready for the battle; they knew this journey would bring conflict and reaching the star was far more important than the obstacles placed in front of them.

The men tied their horses to the carts and begin scaling the hillside, quietly maneuvering around the rocks.

Gaspar dismounted, checked his horse and readied his bow. He spoke to Balthasar, who was watching Zheng's men move through the rocks. "You should stay with Nekdel and Rushad and I will ride to Pulan," he said.

Balthasar replied, "No, they will be safe. I will speak with them. Wait for me; I will only be a moment."

Balthasar then hurried to the boys who were standing next to a cart with their bows at their sides.

Balthasar placed a hand on the shoulder of each boy and asked, "Do you understand what is happening"?

"Yes, we have been listening," replied Nekdel.

"We are ready!" blurted Rushad, young in years, but fearless and ready to fight.

"Listen to me carefully because I must ride up the road. Untie these two carts, empty them and turn them onto their sides. Stay between the carts for protection. You will be easy targets for the bandits if you do not take cover. Do you understand?" Balthasar directed in a firm tone.

"Yes, Father, do not worry about us. Watch out for yourself," replied Nekdel.

Nekdel reached into his cart and pulled out a round, plate size, flat object and handed it to his father.

"What am I to do with this?" asked Balthasar.

"It is a shield, Father. It is as hard as a rock. I made it from reeds and deer skin and it has dried tight and strong. Place your hand in the strap."

"Perhaps you should keep this," replied Balthasar as he began to hand it back to Nekdel.

"No, keep it, please. We have more shields," Nekdel pleaded.

"Very well… hurry with the carts! I will return when this is over." With the shield in his hand, Balthasar hurried back to Gaspar.

"Are the boys excited?" asked Gaspar.

"Yes, their eyes are as big as cart wheels," answered Balthasar.

Looking at the shield in Balthasar's hand, Gaspar asked, "What are you going to do with that, protect your knee?" asked Gaspar with a smile.

"Nekdel made this. I suppose I will carry it." Balthasar replied.

The Magi shared a laugh for a moment as they rode toward Pulan and Yon with ten of their men following on horseback.

As they got closer to Pulan and Yon, Balthasar said to Gaspar, "Let us stop just short of the hill. Once Zheng and his men appear, we will join Yon and Pulan and then decide where we are needed."

But, before Gaspar could respond, shouting began on the other side of the hill.

"Quickly… to the top!" shouted Balthasar as they rode to join Yon and Pulan.

"Zheng has surprised the bandits!" announced Pulan.

With their hands shielding their eyes from the sun's glare, Balthasar and Gaspar scanned the hillside.

"Look, the bandits on the north side are surrendering!" Balthasar shouted with obvious surprise and excitement.

"The sun is shining directly into their eyes on the north side; I doubt they can see much of anything above them. But they are not surrendering on this side. I will take five men with me on foot and close in on them. There must be ten or more bandits on this south side," Gaspar responded.

"We will position ourselves on the road. Pulan, keep an eye on the boys and call to me if they are in trouble!" Balthasar shouted.

As the Magi moved their men into position, they saw that Zheng's men had the situation well in hand on the north side. Crossbows were targeting the bandits who were walking down the hill with their hands held high.

The fighting was intensifying on the south side. Balthasar could see fallen men and one man lied near the top of the hill; Balthasar feared it is one of Zheng's men, as this was where his men were positioned, shooting arrows into the rocks below.

"The bandits are taking cover behind the rocks. I see only two of them!" Balthasar shouted to Gaspar. "Let us space ourselves along the road!"

"Good! We will come in behind you," Gaspar added in agreement.

Balthasar said to Kanuka, who was riding behind him, "Kunuka, watch to the north and on the road ahead of us. Shout if you see trouble."

Balthasar gave his horse a kick and led his men down the road. Balthasar began to raise his arm to signal a stop when a bandit stepped out from behind a rock. With bow drawn and his arrow pointed toward Balthasar, the bandit released. Immediately, the bandit was hit by Kanuka's arrow. Still holding Nekdel's shield in his right hand, Balthasar instinctively moved his hand in front of him to stop the bandit's arrow. But the arrow pierced Balthasar's small shield, cutting his finger, while the tip of the arrow moved through Balthasar's coat, barely breaking the skin on his chest. The bandit fell to the ground with Kanuka's arrow deep in his shoulder. Balthasar dropped his shield, raised his bow and looked for a target while his men sent arrows into the rocks.

"Take cover behind the rocks and wait for my command!" shouted Balthasar.

Zheng's men continued to make their way down the hillside, shouting and whistling as they went, trying to frighten the bandits. Balthasar could see the bandits, groups of two and three, making their way to the base of the hill. Balthasar pointed to an opening in the rocks.

"Men, get ready. Two are heading for this place and several more are to the left!"

Balthasar drew his bow. Two bandits appeared in the opening between the rocks, one with a sword in his hand, the other with a bow. As the bandits moved through the opening, Balthasar targeted his arrow just ahead of the bandits to send them a warning. Balthasar drew back on his second arrow, but the bandits dropped their weapons and fell to the ground.

Balthasar called out to Kanuka to take control of the bandits. And so, without waiting for help, Kanuka quickly grabbed each bandit by the arm, brought them to their feet and shoved them against a boulder. Kanuka then placed the blade of his sword under the chin of one of the bandits and said, "Call on your friends to surrender or you will lose your head!"

With Kanuka's cold blade against his throat, the bandit called out in Persian, "Surrender! It is no use. There are too many. We will all be killed!"

One after another, the bandits emerged from behind the rocks. Dropping their weapons, they walked down the hillside with their arms stretched above their heads. In a few moments, six bandits took their positions on the road with the others who had surrendered. Zheng's men made their way down the hill, picking up weapons dropped by the bandits and making certain that no others remained hidden.

"Is that all of them?" shouted Balthasar as he surveyed both hillsides.

He heard a loud whistle behind him and turned quickly to see Zheng with his sword in the air, following several bandits with their arms raised.

"We have them!" Zheng shouted.

Balthasar turned his horse and slowly moved in Zheng's direction. "What are the injuries?" he asked.

"Three bandits and one of my men," Zheng answered. "One of the bandits has a stomach wound. His injury is the most serious. Shen is tending to him and believes that he may survive if he can stop the bleeding. Another has a shoulder injury, which also appears quite serious."

"How are the others?" Balthasar asked while he considered the effects of the injuries.

"One of my men had his arm cut by a sword. It is a clean cut and not too deep. In time, he will heal, but the bandit who cut him is suffering from a head injury he received when he was thrown against a rock. Another had an arrow through his hand and one of them injured his foot jumping from a rock," Zheng answered.

"We are fortunate; it could have been much worse," Balthasar said to Gaspar as he approached the two men.

"Praise Ahura Mazda for sending us Zheng and his men!" shouted Gaspar.

Gaspar noticed that Balthasar's finger was bleeding and asked, "Were you hit by an arrow?"

"Had I not been holding the shield, the arrow would be deep into my chest!" Balthasar answered, looking to the sky.

"Imagine that!" Gaspar laughed as he shook his head in disbelief.

Zheng joined the Magi and announced, "We can all be thankful that the gods made these bandits quite dim. Half-starved, poorly equipped… had we stayed on the road, they would have likely put arrows into each other!" laughed Zheng.

"We are grateful for your help!" Gaspar said as he embraced Zheng. The Magi and Zheng watched as their men searched the bandits for weapons and then ordered them to sit with their backs against each other on the road.

"What shall we do with them?" asked Balthasar

"Feed them to the buzzards!" Zheng said with a pause, and then said, "Unless of course, you Magi object," answering himself with a laugh.

"No, that will not do," replied Gaspar as he gave his head a shake.

"We should not be so hasty. Those poor birds need to eat!" replied Balthasar with one of his belly laughs. Gaspar rolled his eyes and shook his head.

"Do not worry about the fate of these misguided men. They are fortunate that we rescued them," Zheng replied.

"Rescued?" asked Balthasar.

"That is what it is - a rescue! This starving bunch has no food and few horses. They will surely slow us down. They can take turns riding, but we must lead their horses. It will be necessary to tie the others to carts so they can walk alongside their injured friends. I suppose that we will need to feed them, so we should include their food and water requirements in our plans," Zheng answered.

"Have they any valuables from their victims?" asked Balthasar

"A few trinkets, but not much more. Their swords are of good steel, but nothing else of value. They may have buried some things among the rocks. I do not yet know their story, but we will learn more when we get them to Rhagae. The Persian militia will be happy to take them off our hands. Maybe we will pass a militia on our way and be rid of them sooner," Zheng responded. Over the next few hours, the men tended to the injured and prepared beds in the carts. Balthasar was anxious to get the caravan moving and asked Zheng to inquire why Shen needed a fire.

"He is tending to an injured man. He needs a few minutes to make a paste and apply it to the man's wound."

"Is the man able to travel?"

"The wound is on his side, just above the stomach. There is much bleeding, but Shen says that the paste should numb the pain and thicken the blood enough to stop the flow. He will wrap him so he cannot move, but it will take no longer than an hour more." Zheng answered.

"Very well. Remind the men to be careful with the water. Our numbers have doubled and it may be some time before we find another water source," Balthasar shouted for all to hear.

"I will share the message and will come to you as soon as we are ready," replied Zheng.

Once the caravan was ready, Zheng's men guarded the prisoners while Balthasar's men took their positions in advance and behind the caravan. Nekdel and Rushad were called to duty, riding a short distance behind the last cart. There was no talking among the men as they continued through the area of the rocks. They knew it would be much more difficult if there was trouble again;

they would need to keep an eye on their prisoners as they defended themselves, and no one was comfortable with the possibility of having to fend off another attack while keeping their prisoners restrained.

After two days of travel, the caravan traveled beyond the hills and boulders. The prisoners took turns riding in the carts and made no attempt to break free. On the third morning after the attack, the Magi spoke with Zheng about the day's travel.

"Zheng, will we make Rhagae today?" asked Balthasar

"The land is level and the road is in good condition. If we keep our stops short, we should be there this evening," he responded. "I suggest that we also keep a close watch on our prisoners."

"They are not a problem. They appear to be content with just being fed every day," answered Gaspar.

"Ah, I remind you that the bandits know this territory well. They know our location and they know what will happen to them when we reach Rhagae. If I were them, I would make my break for freedom while I had the chance. We have been watching the bandits closely. Last night, we found a small knife with one of them and another had a large sharpened stone in his pocket," Zheng replied while running his clenched fist across his throat.

Balthasar glanced at Gaspar with raised eyebrows. Gaspar returned the glance with a shrug of his shoulders.

"Thank you for the warning. We will instruct our men to take the necessary precautions," Balthasar responded.

While Zheng checked on his men, Balthasar said to Gaspar, "Zheng is always thinking about his next move. He has much experience in these matters."

"The trip from Merv would have been much more difficult without Zheng and his men. We will reward him properly when we reach Rhagae," Gaspar responded.

With each passing hour, there were more travelers on the road. By early afternoon, there was a steady stream of people on horseback passing the caravan in both directions. Zheng studied the caravan, making sure there were no problems. He stopped to speak with the Magi and said with concern, "The prisoners are getting anxious and it is making my men nervous."

"We will be in Rhagae soon. Are the ropes secure on the bandits?" asked Balthasar.

"I am not worried about their bindings, but I do worry about all of the people we are passing. For all we know, some of these travelers may be friends of the bandits. Have you noticed the two riders who have passed us in both directions within the past hour?" Zheng asked.

"I did not notice," replied Balthasar as Gaspar shook his head. "What do you suggest?" Balthasar asked.

"We should blindfold our prisoners. If there is an attempt to rescue them, they will be of little use to their rescuers if they are tied to the carts and cannot see," Zheng responded.

"What are your thoughts?" Balthasar asked Gaspar, liking Zheng's suggestion, but wanting to include Gaspar in the final decision.

"The residents of Rhagae will no doubt consider us ruthless captors when we pass through their gates, but I suppose that would be better than getting ourselves killed in a rescue attempt," Gaspar reasoned.

"I agree. Once we reach Rhagae, they will no longer be our problem. Zheng, shall we stop the caravan?" Balthasar asked.

"No, we can cover their eyes while we are moving. It will only take a moment," Zheng quickly answered.

Just as their conversation ended, Pulan arrived, having ridden swiftly to Balthasar from his position ahead of the caravan. "Several armed riders are coming our way, just beyond the next turn," he said.

"Are they militia?" asked Gaspar.

"No, they do not appear to be militia, nor do they pull carts."

"Return to your position and wait for us while I speak with Zheng," ordered Gaspar.

As Pulan rode to rejoin the caravan, Zheng called six of his men to follow him to the front.

"Is there trouble?" Zheng shouted as he neared Balthasar.

"Not certain… armed riders, no carts, coming our way!" Balthasar shouted to Zheng.

"We will escort them past our caravan. Pull the caravan to the side of the road and place our bandits on the other side of the carts," ordered Zheng as he and his men kicked their horses with a shout, causing the dust to kick up behind them when they broke into a gallop.

"I will get the boys and take charge of the carts to the rear," Balthasar told Gaspar.

"Be careful, we could also be attacked from that position," Gaspar responded.

A quarter of an hour passed as the caravan waited for Zheng and the armed riders to appear. Balthasar's men were quite anxious; some had their swords in hand and several archers had taken positions on higher ground. Tied to the carts with their eyes covered, the bandits began to shout, demanding their release. An impatient Balthasar regretted leaving his position in the front of the caravan, but saw Zheng and his men returning just as he was about to lead his men back to Gaspar.

"What is happening?" asked Nekdel.

"I do not know, son. This is quite puzzling. I do not see the armed riders, only Zheng and his men. Let us speak with Zheng before we make any more decisions." Balthasar answered.

But before Balthasar and the boys reached the front, Gaspar raised his arm and waved his hand in a circular motion as a signal to get the caravan moving. The men brought the bandits to their feet and positioned the carts onto the road.

"What news do you bring, Zheng?" asked Balthasar.

"When the riders saw us coming, they turned and rode toward Rhagae. We followed them for a few minutes, but we did not want to become separated from you. We will watch, but I doubt we will see them again," Zheng answered.

"You frightened them away," laughed Balthasar.

"Obviously. You forgot that I am well known in Rhagae!" Zheng replied with a smile.

As the caravan once again started moving and made its way around the next bend, a large building sitting high atop a hill came into view.

"What is that?" Nekdel and Rushad shouted in unison.

"That is Ustunawand!" answered Balthasar, who was also captivated by what stood before him.

Immediately, the entire caravan stopped for a moment to take in the sight.

"It is magnificent, Father," said Nekdel.

"Ustunawand was built more than a thousand years ago to honor Zoroaster. At one time, it was the fortress of the greatest of Magi leaders, our Masmoghan," Balthasar answered, wanting to teach the boys of his traditions and the awe that they brought.

"Are we going to stop?" Nekdel asked curiously.

"We will plan our next steps once we get to Rhagae. Magi live in Ustunawand. It is where the Varharam is kept, the most important fire of the Magi," Balthasar answered.

Within the hour, the caravan approached the gates of Rhagae.

"We have made good time!" Balthasar shouted enthusiastically to Gaspar.

"Our trip has not been without difficulty, but we can thank Ahura Mazda for getting us this far without sickness or injury," replied Gaspar.

Balthasar nodded approvingly as he responded, "Let us ride to Zheng and see where he wants the caravan to rest." As they trotted ahead to Zheng, Balthasar pressed his thighs against his horse so he could raise up to get a better view.

"I see Zheng's men, but I do not see Zheng."

"He must have gone ahead to find a place for us," replied Gaspar.

When they reached Zheng's men, Balthasar asked Yon, "Has Zheng gone ahead?"

Yon nodded and replied, "He will meet us at the gates."

Balthasar motioned for Pulan to join them. When he arrived, Balthasar told him, "Keep the men together and move quickly once Zheng directs us. Place our prisoners in the carts so we can control them. If a prisoner escapes, it will be hard to find him in the city."

As they neared the gates, they saw Zheng with several Persian militia members. Zheng waved for the Magi to join him. "My friends, I have found some men of authority who are interested in our prisoners. This man's name is Advi, he is their leader."

The Magi dismounted and brushed the dust off their clothes. Zheng called for his men to assemble the prisoners and motioned for the caravan to follow him to a place just south of the gates. Zheng's men removed the coverings from the prisoner's eyes and helped them out of the carts as Balthasar began to describe to Advi how the bandits attacked.

"We were a week's ride from Merv. They were hiding among the rocks, but one of Zheng's men saw them just before we were within their range, so we were able to come in from behind and surprise them. The fighting was brief with only two serious injuries. If it was not for Zheng, we would have lost many men," Balthasar recounted.

Advi, who had listened intently to Balthasar's story, looked over the bandits and instructed his men to take them to the militia station. After embracing the Magi, Advi said, "We had many reports of bandits in that area several months ago. Many travelers were killed and robbed, but we could never find the bandits. We thought they had moved on. Friends, we are grateful for your assistance. Tell me, why did you go to the trouble of caring for them? Others would have lopped off their heads and left them for the birds!"

"Our god would not be pleased if we took a life when we were no longer threatened," replied Balthasar without hesitation.

"Ah, of course, the yellow caps. You are Medes and you are their leader, a Magi. I am sorry that you came under attack, but it could have been much worse. You have reached your destination with few injuries," replied Advi, very impressed by the condition of the caravan and the men after such an attack.

"We are fortunate indeed! But our journey does not end here. We are just beginning and have many more months to go," replied Balthasar.

"Many more months!" Advi answered, surprised by this duration. "What is you final destination?" has asked the Magi.

"We are on our way to Jerusalem," answered Balthasar.

"Jerusalem? What does Jerusalem hold for you? Such a journey is quite dangerous. You need a militia and many riches for such a journey!" Advi warned.

"We seek the King of the Jews. A messiah has come to the Jews!" replied an excited Gaspar, unable to contain his enthusiasm and unconcerned that Advi may not approve of the journey.

"The Jews have a messiah? There are many Jews in Rhagae, yet I have not heard talk of this messiah. The Jews are under Roman rule, are they not? Where have you learned this news?" Advi asked, confused by the words of the Magi.

But before Gaspar could respond, Advi asked, "If the Jews have a messiah, why is he so important that you risk your lives to reach him?"

"This messiah is unlike any man who has walked the Earth. You see, Ahura Mazda has placed a great star over Jerusalem as a sign of the messiah's arrival. We follow that star," Gaspar stated.

Advi had no response. With his eyebrows raised and his mouth open, he looked at his men for their reactions, but they too had puzzled faces.

"It is strange that a star would ignite such a fire within you! I do not have time for such things, but what you say must be true. Wise and knowing Magi would not risk such danger without good reason. When will you leave Rhagae?" Advi asked.

"In a day or two, as soon as we make repairs and trade for horses and supplies," Balthasar answered.

"If you can wait four days, a militia group is leaving there to escort a caravan to Ecbatana and you can travel with them as well," Advi suggested.

"We can most certainly wait until then for the protection of your militia. That is very good news!" Balthasar responded with a smile as he looked to Gaspar.

"Then I will have one of my men find you tomorrow to tell you where to take your caravan," Advi answered with a nod and then hurried off to the militia station.

Balthasar's men were relieved to have turned over their captives and to be free from the dangers of the road, if only for a few nights. Rhagae, although a welcome sight, would bring no music or feasting this evening for the caravan's men. The travelers were exhausted and, once the animals were fed and the tents in place, they found their beds, some not even taking time to eat before they slept.

The Magi sat by a small fire when Zheng and Pulan approached. Zheng spoke first, saying, "Everything is secure. We will only have two men on watch this evening and we should split the shifts between our men." Nodding his approval to the precautions taken by Zheng, Balthasar motioned for Zheng and Pulan to sit with him and Gaspar by the fire. Zheng asked, "Is the tu hot?" "

"No, not hot, warm," answered Gaspar as he reached for the pot.

"Zheng, have you found the caravan that you will accompany to Merv?" asked Balthasar.

"Yes, I spoke to the driver and we are to leave in two mornings," Zheng replied.

"So soon? Can you not rest with us for four days?"

"There is nothing we would enjoy more, but our Seres friends are anxious to travel and I do not want to discourage their enthusiasm," Zheng answered as a smile spread across his face.

"Very well, but Zheng, we need to discuss our agreement. You will need to prepare for your trip tomorrow and you will need supplies. What would you like from us?" asked Balthasar.

"We could use a horse and a cart, and some of my men need clothes and boots. I suppose enough silk, jade or whatever you have that we can trade for these things would be enough," answered Zheng.

"In the morning, you can choose from the items we have. If you like, I will help you with the merchants," Balthasar offered.

"Yes, please, your assistance is most appreciated." Now standing, Zheng continued, "As much as I enjoy the company of such good friends, I have an appointment with my bed that I must keep. I hope your sleep is most restful. Let us meet in the morning for a filling breakfast!"

Even before dawn, many people were scurrying around Rhagae. By sunrise, the city was bustling with activity. Zheng had been awake for some time and was waiting outside Balthasar's tent. As Zheng waited, he thought about the items he would like from the merchants. A heavy wool coat for himself would have been nice, but there were many things the men needed, like several pairs of boots, but his mind kept returning to the prospect of a warm coat.

When the Magi emerged from their tent, Balthasar greeted Zheng and said, "Gather your men and we will provide you with a great breakfast!"

Over the next few hours, the group moved from merchant to merchant, sampling, buying and eating. Some items, such as fresh eggs, were prepared for the men immediately on the merchant's cook fires. Other items such, as sweet treats, partially ripened fruits and root vegetables, were packed so Zheng's men could carry them on their trip to Merv.

When the morning's leisure time had passed, the afternoon was spent locating a cart and other necessary items for Zheng. Then finally, the last stop of the day was to the stable area where a fine horse was acquired for Zheng.

"This beauty is not as fine as the animal you ride, but he will serve me well," a grateful Zheng said to Balthasar, as he led the horse to the caravan.

"Do you have all that you need?" asked a pleased Balthasar

"We have more than we need and unfortunately for you, we have more than for what we bargained," Zheng replied with a smile.

Zheng's men worked into the evening packing their carts, inspecting their weapons and caring for their horses as Balthasar's men assisted in repairing one of their carts. Pulan, wanting to ensure that his new friends were protected, made sure that Zheng's men had a good supply of arrows.

The most relaxed night of the trip for Balthasar's men, they prepared a supper of hens and fruit soaked in syrup for Zheng and his men. They did not have to worry about the dangers of the trail while camped within the confines of the city, and with plenty of good food and wine, played their instruments and sang as they took comfort in knowing that they could rest for two more days. At dawn, Balthasar's men gathered outside the tents as Zheng's men prepared their horses.

Zheng shouted to the Magi who were standing together, sipping Tu, "Why are you not sleeping? Did you think we could not manage by ourselves?"

"We want to make sure that you are pointed in the right direction," replied a laughing Balthasar.

Zheng's men mounted their horses as Zheng gave his Magi friends a warm embrace and a kiss to each cheek, both surprising and complimenting the Magi, as the gesture was not Han tradition.

Gaspar, placing his hand on Zheng's shoulder, said earnestly, "We cannot thank you enough, good friend."

"As we say in my land, if there is a strong general, there will be no weak soldiers. You have trained your men well, Magi. It was my pleasure to ride with you. If I did not have an obligation to my superiors, it would have been nice to ride with you to the place of the star. But now I can only wish you well on your journey," replied Zheng.

Zheng walked to his horse and took the reins from one of his men.

Just as he was about to mount, Balthasar shouted, "Hold on friend! You forgot something."

Zheng turned to see Balthasar walking toward him as he removed his fine wool coat. "A present for you," said Balthasar as he handed the coat to Zheng.

"I cannot accept this. You have already paid me in full, and even more than we bargained."

"Take it, please. You need it more than I do. We may have seen the last of cool weather for our journey, but it will be cold many more weeks for you."

"This is the coat of a king and should not be worn by a beast like me," replied Zheng as Balthasar hung the coat over Zheng's shoulders.

Balthasar laughed as he said, "I hope it keeps you warm. At night, when you cover yourself with it, look to the star and think of us."

"I will never forget my friends and our time together. May your god protect you!" Zheng shouted as he and his men rode to the gate to meet the caravan they would escort to Merv. When the dust from Zheng and his men had all settled and they were no longer in sight, the Magi shared a relaxing breakfast of cakes, fruit and syrup with Nekdel and Rushad, thinking of Zheng and contemplating the journey that would further distance the Magi from their Seres friends.

Chapter VII: Melchoir; a Friend from the Past

    The following morning after Balthasar's men had finished their breakfast, Nekdel asked, "What will we do today, Father?"
    "I thought that our time would be best spent going to Ustunawand. Gaspar, will you join us?" Balthasar asked.
    "Most certainly!" replied Gaspar, eager to accept the invitation.
    "We can ask the others to join us, but we will need to leave a few men to guard the caravan," responded Balthasar.
    "I am sure we will have volunteers; some would like to rest. How soon shall we leave?" Gaspar said as he poured water onto the fire.
    "Half an hour should give us enough time to get ready. Let the men know that we will return by early evening."
    Soon the Magi, the two boys and six of the men passed through the gates of Rhagae. Within an hour, Ustunawand could be seen in the distance, where its mighty walls were impressive even from afar.
    "Father, have you visited this place before?" asked Nekdel
    "I have, but it has been many years since my last visit; I was younger than you when my father first brought me here," Balthasar responded.
    "Why was it built so high on the hill?" asked Nekdel.
    "My father told me that it was built on high ground so it would be closer to Ahura Mazda. It is a

mighty fortress on top of a mountain, a safe place that is difficult for enemies to attack."

"Father, we are getting smaller as we get closer."

Gaspar laughed as Balthasar nodded with a smile, both men enjoying Nekdel's innocence. The eyes of the boys were wide with wonder. "Enemies could not get through walls built with such great stones. I have never seen such a place!" shouted Nekdel, never letting his gaze fall from this spectacular sight.

Balthasar motioned for the men to stop and they dismounted their horses. An outer gate and wall surrounded the entrance to Ustunawand; behind these gates, two men appeared and greeted Balthasar and his men with an embrace and kiss to the cheeks. Balthasar and his companions handed the reins of their horses to their hosts, who would provide the animals with water and food, and the group was led to large wooden doors where they were greeted by several others.

"We are on a great journey and have stopped here so that we might worship," explained Balthasar.

"You are most welcome. I am Izadyar. Come with me, I will take you to Husvak, the High Priest of Ustunawand."

Izadyar gave a shout and immediately, one of the great doors slowly began to open. Made from large timbers, the doors were too heavy for one man to manage, so two men could be seen pulling a rope used to operate the entrance. The group was led to the center of the fortress where they entered the Chamber of the High Priest, a magnificent room covering the length of the fortress. Large stone columns on each side of the room supported the roof and narrow openings on the walls allowed sunlight to trickle in. Balthasar's men stood in the center of the chamber with their heads tilted back, admiring the night sky, which was painted on the ceiling.

"Father, we could fit all of Asdin into this room!" exclaimed Nekdel.

"I suppose we could," Balthasar replied as he considers the incredible size of the chamber.

"How was it possible to build such a structure?" asked Kanuka.

Izadyar walked to the far end of the Chamber to speak with Husvak, an elderly man with a long white beard, wearing a Sudre-Kusti, the sacred shirt and girdle, beneath a dark blue silk robe featuring elaborately designed, gold-colored embroidery. Husvak left Izadyar and walked to the center of the Chamber with his robe dragging on the floor behind him.

"Is it not magnificent?" asked Husvak.

A startled Balthasar flinched, and then responds, "We are sorry to delay you. We could not resist pausing to study this great chamber."

"Please, take your time. I am here every day and yet I continue to be overwhelmed by this sight," Husvak answered the travelers as he greeted Balthasar and his men with and an embrace. "Welcome to Ustunawandm brothers. Does your kingdom lie near or far?" asked Husvak.

"Our people live north of the mountains, a month's ride from Merv," replied Balthasar.

Considering this, Husvak answered, "You have traveled far. Do you travel to Rhagae or Ecbatana?"

"We have many months before our journey is complete," Gaspar replied.

"Where do you travel?"

"We follow the star that shines in the western sky," responded Balthasar.

"We know the star! Why do you follow it?" asked Husvak with a puzzled look.

"We believe that the star is a sign of the Hebrew messiah. We go to pay homage to him," Balthasar answered.

"We know of the Hebrew prophesies, but we have not determined that the star is the sign of the messiah. How are you certain of this?" Husvak asked.

"The Hebrew Scriptures are clear: the star is one of a kind and in our hearts, we feel its draw upon us!" responded Gaspar.

Husvak paused for a moment, studying the faces of his visitors and then replied, "Perhaps you are right. But travel to… Jerusalem? That is a long and dangerous journey. Yet, I have discussed this same subject with another Magi who is also determined to make such a journey."

"There is another Magi going to Jerusalem?" Balthasar quickly responded.

"Is it the star that he follows? Is he here, in Rhagae?" asked Gaspar, too excited to withhold his questions.

"No. I spoke to him here, at Ustunawand, perhaps two weeks ago. He was on his way to Ecbatana to prepare for his journey."

"What is his name?" asked Balthasar.

"Oh, I do not remember names. I forget many things," Husvak said with a laugh. "But this Magi is not one who is easily forgotten. He was loud and very generous, as I recall. A dark-skinned man… he gave us many things, but tried to sell us some items that were not of much use to us. He is a Magi, of that I am certain. He stayed two days with us. A man of good humor and much laughter, but I am afraid that I cannot recall his name. Perhaps Izadyar can remember what I have forgotten."

Balthasar and Gaspar were excited by this news and Balthasar asked, "Did you notice if he wore such a ring?" The two raised their hands, clinched in fists, near Husvak's face, exposing large, shiny gold rings that held a magnificent, five pointed ruby.

"Yes! He wore the exact ruby ring! You know this man?" Husvak asked.

Gaspar and Balthasar laughed loudly and then Balthasar explained, "His name is Melchoir, an Ethiopian. His father made us these rings soon after our village survived an attack by Han tribesman. We were terrified boys, but we managed to hold back more than a dozen attackers."

"We have not seen him in many years. He returned to Ethiopia with his father, but he manages to get word to us occasionally. He chose a life of travel; we know him as a man with a pure and generous heart who can out bargain any merchant!" Gaspar added.

Turning to Gaspar, Balthasar explained, "If we can reach Melchoir, we can travel together. He knows the road well!"

"He may already be too far ahead of us, but it is worth trying to reach him," replied Gaspar.

"If it is Ahura Mazda's will, you will find him," interjected Husvak. "But at this moment, you are with us in Ustunawand. Take time to worship with us before you hurry back down the road. The next prayer watch, the Rapithwin, will be upon us within the hour. We will prepare the Adar Burzin, the most sacred fire, in your honor. Izadyar, instruct the priests that we will gather here in a few minutes," directed Husvak.

Husvak walked to the far wall where the fire would be prepared. Balthasar and Gaspar were overjoyed, their faces beaming with wide smiles.

"So Melchoir is alive and well! I did not expect to see him again," Balthasar said to Gaspar with a smile.

"Do not get your heart set on finding Melchoir. He may have already changed his mind. For all we know, he could be moving south or even north to the Caspian," replied Gaspar.

"I do not believe there is any question where he travels. He spoke to Husvak about the star! He must have come to our same conclusion. If he has heard Ahura Mazda's call, he will not ignore it," said Balthasar.

Studying the great ceiling as they stood in the center of the chamber, Gaspar contemplated Balthasar's words. "Are those stars carved into the ceiling? Why yes, it is the summer sky. Amazing! How could they reach the ceiling to chisel such a heavenly map?" asked Gaspar.

Balthasar did not glance at the ceiling, but instead fixed his eyes on Gaspar, waiting for his thoughts about Melchoir. Gaspar dropped his head and moved it from side to side to ease the strain on his neck until he saw that Balthasar was staring at him.

"Why do you stare?" asked Gaspar.

Balthasar did not respond, only waited for Gaspar to respond.

"Melchoir? Of course he is on his way to Jerusalem. Do not worry. It will not be hard to find him. He will try to bargain with everyone he meets. If he is already beyond Ecbatana, we need only speak with those we pass on the road, for surely they will remember if they passed him," assured Gaspar.

"You remember him well," Balthasar replied.

"Leopards do not change their spots. We will find him, do not worry."

Meanwhile, Nekdel and Rushad had been exploring the chamber on their own, darting from one side to the other.

When they rejoined their group, Nekdel tapped Balthasar on the shoulder, "Father, Izadyar wants us now."

The sacred fire began to burn and the residents of Ustunawand gathered for the daily watch. But today, instead of prayer, Husvak had arranged for an Afrinagan and a full ceremony in honor of Balthasar and his men. Prayers would be offered and animals sacrificed for their safe travel. After the ceremony, Husvak took a burning torch from a wall holder and asked Balthasar and his men to follow him. He led them to very narrow stairs rising along the fortress wall, where it took the group several minutes to climb to the top, as Balthasar and Gaspar followed closely behind Husvak for his torch light. The other men had to rely solely on occasional glimpses of light from slits in the walls to light their paths. In a short time, Balthasar and Gaspar climbed far ahead of the group.

Every minute or two, Balthasar shouted jokingly to the men behind him, "Can you not keep pace with old men?"

The climb eventually ended at a small door and Husvak placed the torch in a holder on the wall to open it. For a few seconds, the men were blinded by the bright sunlight; Husvak had led them to the roof of Ustunawand.

A moment later, the others stumbled onto the roof, breathing heavily and covering their eyes as they bumped into each other while their eyes adjusted to the sun.

Seeing this amusing sight, Gaspar said for all to hear, "It is a miracle that our caravan has made it this far!"

Nekdel and Rushad were already running across the roof to see what lied below.

"Careful, boys, many of the stones are loose. We do not want you toppling over the side," warned Husvak.

Out of breath, Nekdel came to a stop next to Balthasar. "Look, Father, there is Rhagae! All of it!"

"We can see everything from here. I see why the fortress was built on this location," Balthasar replied.

Husvak pointed to the road below, "The only path to Ustunawand is the road up the hill. From where we stand, we can see the trade road and anyone who leaves it. Over the centuries, this place has provided safety from our enemies."

Balthasar and Gaspar turned from the view of Rhagae to fix their eyes on the western sky.

"We have studied the star closely from this roof. Is it not amazing that we can still see it in the midst of sun?" asked Husvak.

"We see it in the sun light because it is God's star," Gaspar responded.

"Whose god?" Husvak asked with a smile.

"We cannot be certain whose god placed the star in the sky, but it speaks to us and we are drawn to it," responded Gaspar. He paused for a moment and then asked, "Do you not see it as a sign of the Hebrew messiah?"

"When you return from your journey, you can tell me what you find. Then I will know," Husvak responded as he moved away from the wall. He added, "Please take your time here. I must return to my duties, but you are welcome to stay on the roof."

"No, it is time for us to leave. You have been more than generous to us," Balthasar answered.

Once the men returned to the Chamber, Husvak wished them well before making his way to another part of the fortress. Balthasar and Gaspar took their time walking to the main doors and spoke to each other in a whisper, because even the smallest sound carried well in this great room.

"One would think that a man such as Husvak would be most understanding of the star. How can he not see what is so clear to us?" asked Gaspar.

"He raises the same question that troubles us. Do we seek the star of another god? Some reason a relationship to Hebrew Scriptures, but some do not. Some are drawn to the star, while others are not. Some see it, some do not. Some Jews do not see the star or believe it involves their scriptures, yet we feel as we do because a fire burns within us. I am coming to believe that unless Ahura Mazda ignites the fire within someone, the star will not be understood," Balthasar answered.

"I have no doubt that what we believe is true, but I must confess, at times, I wish that I had doubts. This is such a long trip and I have no excuse for staying home in Shahnaz," Gaspar replied.

Balthasar and his men waited briefly as the great door was opened for them. They retrieved their horses and made their way down the hill, stopping one last time to take a good look at Ustunawand before turning onto the trade road and returning to Rhagae.

During the next two days, Balthasar's men made repairs and traded for the supplies they would need for the trip to Ecbatana. They estimated that the trip would take three months and they could not be certain about what items they would be able to acquire along the way.

On their third morning in Rhagae, Balthasar called his men together and said, "Men, we will leave for Ecbatana at day break. Pack the carts before supper so we are organized before dark. Gaspar and I will inspect the carts as soon as they are packed."

As the men went about their tasks, Gaspar spoke to Balthasar.

"I expected to hear some groans, but the men appear to be excited about resuming the trip," he said.

Balthasar surveyed the sky and responded, "I have been anxious to move on since we learned of Melchoir. It looks as if we will have wet weather, so I hope it does not slow us down."

While the carts were being packed, some men filled their jars and skins with fresh water, while others took a cart to the market area to fill with fresh fruit, flour and other items.

Early the next morning, a voice called for Balthasar. Standing outside their tent in the dark and in heavy rain was Advi.

Throwing open the flap to the tent and Gaspar called, "Here! In here! Advi, is that you?"

Advi entered the tent where lamps burned and men were packing their belongings into sacks.

"My men will not be leaving this morning. Not in this rain," said Advi.

"We understand. We are not anxious to spend the day freeing our carts from the mud," Balthasar replied.

"Tomorrow… it will be better tomorrow," said Advi as he turns to go.

"Advi, join us for some tu," Gaspar offered while holding a cup in his outstretched hand.

"Is it hot?"

"No, not hot, warm," Gaspar answered.

Advi nodded his head in approval while Gaspar walked to the corner of the tent where a small fire smoldered and puffs of smoke floated from the glowing embers and escaped through a small opening in the tent roof. Gaspar lifted the pot of tu from the embers and poured a cup for Advi before pouring one for himself.

Nekdel alerted the others to the change in plans while the Magi and Advi sat together, sipping tu. Not many words were spoken. The rain beating down on the tent said all that needs to be said this morning.

As the men sat, drops of water fell from the tent roof. When a drop landed on Balthasar, he inspected the material above them.

"It looks as if the goat hair has had all the rain it can handle this morning," Balthasar said as he took another sip from his cup.

The rain began to slow by late morning and came to an end in the afternoon. The men emerged from their tents to check on the carts and their animals, which had been covered with sections of tent material. The remainder of the day was spent cleaning up after the rain. Clothes and sections of tent were hung to dry on ropes stretched between poles while fires were started to assist in drying clothes and cook the evening meal.

Chapter VIII – Trouble on the Road to Ecbatana

As the caravan prepared for travel in the morning, one of Advi's men came to Balthasar with instructions to follow him to the east gate where they would meet their Persian militia escorts. But when they reached the east gate, the militia was already on the move and nearly out of sight, while two militia members were waiting for the Magi.

As Balthasar greeted them, he asked, "Good morning, friends. Have you made this trip before?"

"We have made this trip many times and it is a difficult ride," gruffly replied one of the militia as he kicked his horse and began riding toward his fellow militia members, who were now out of view.

"Can we make it to Ecbatana in three months?" Gaspar asked the soldier who remained.

"Perhaps three months, but it could be much longer. We will have a month's ride through the mountains before we enter the hill country. Many steep hills on a narrow road. Use great caution!" responded the soldier as he, too, gave his horse a kick and trotted ahead, eventually disappearing over the hill.

"Not ones for conversation," Gaspar grumbled to Balthasar.

"He has much responsibility. We will learn more when we speak with his leader," Balthasar replied.

"It appears that there will be no militia riding with us today," Gaspar said.

"The militia will not be far, but our men must keep alert," replied Balthasar as he turned to make sure the caravan behind him was keeping pace.

It was early evening when Balthasar's caravan reached the camp of their Persian escort at the base of a mountain. Fires were burning and the men were watering the horses when Balthasar's men arrived and occupied a clearing next to the militia.

As the Magi directed their men, Balthasar turned to Gaspar and said, "One of the advantages of travel with a militia is that we do not have to worry about the best place to camp or where to find water."

"Yes, and they know the villages, they know where to find game and they know the places to avoid," replied Gaspar as he nodded in agreement.

Balthasar's men were busy tending to their animals and preparing their supper when the leader of the militia walked into their camp. The Magi introduced themselves, but the militia leader did not respond. He walked back and forth briefly, inspecting Balthasar's men, their animals and their carts.

"Hmmmm," was the only noise the militia leader made as he walked around the carts. When he completed his inspection, he announced, "I am Jangi," which meant "brave warrior." "It is good that you caught up to us, Magi," he said with a stern look.

"You must have had an early start this morning because we moved at a good pace and took few breaks," Gaspar replied.

"We get an early start every morning!" Jangi replied sharply.

"Do not worry about us, we will keep pace," Balthasar said in an assuring tone.

"That is why I speak to you. My only responsibility is to see that my caravan arrives safely and on schedule in Ecbatana; the safe delivery of my cargo is my only concern. You are welcome to join us. We will try to help you when we can, but we cannot delay if you run into trouble. Understood, Magi?" replied Jangi as he stood at attention.

Gaspar's face became red and his mouth tightened, something he tended to do when irritated. Gaspar turned away from Jangi and looked in another direction without responding.

"We understand. We are grateful for the opportunity to follow you and we will not be a problem," replied Balthasar with a nod of his head. He looked to Gaspar for a nod, but Gaspar was not making eye contact.

Focusing his attention again on Jangi, Balthasar continued, "Let us know if we can be of any service to you." He asked quickly as a cue, "Gaspar?"

Gaspar turned his face toward his two companions and replied, "Yes, of course, we are your humble servants."

"We will leave at first light," Jangi said as he turned to rejoin his men.

Once Jangi was out of hearing distance, Balthasar asked with a smile, "Gaspar, is that as pleasant as you can be to our new friend?"

Gaspar's face became red again as he replied, "Did you hear him? He thinks of us as helpless chickens! We fought mightier foes than he will ever see and we have traveled more dangerous territory, all before he was born! It was all I could do to…"

Balthasar interrupted with a laugh and said, "He is young and a bit rough, but he does not have much time for conversation. Did you see his eyes? Well, of course not, because you would not look at him. If you had been looking at his eyes, you would have noticed that he was watching closely for our reaction to his words. Did we take offense? Did we cower? He was measuring us. He needs to know if he can trust us, if he can count on us if there is trouble."

"You came to all of that by watching his eyes? I have another theory. I believe that we should keep our distance because he does not know what he is doing. Two caravans are one too many for him!" replied Gaspar with his arms folded across his chest.

Balthasar laughed, placed his hand on Gaspar's shoulder and said, "Good friend, I have not seen you this irritated in quite some time. Do you feel better now?"

"Yes, much better," responded Gaspar with a laugh. Gaspar paused for a moment, reflecting briefly on their conversation with Jangi and then continued, "I guess that I am just tired, tired from hurrying all day. Hurrying to catch up with this man only to have him say that he will not bother with us! I hope that he does not slow us down. If he does, we will pass him!" he said with another laugh.

Balthasar removed his hand from Gaspar's shoulder and now placed his arm around his friend, turning him slightly toward the west where the star brightly shone. As they fixed their eyes on the star, both men became silent, their contentment reflected in warm smiles.

Travel was tedious over the next few weeks and the slow pace tired the men and their horses as they navigated the road through the mountains. The road was very narrow in places and it was necessary for the caravan to stop several times each day as boulders and other debris were cleared from their path. Balthasar's caravan managed to keep pace with the militia, but Jangi's men keep to themselves. Occasionally, when the caravan stopped, Jangi or one of his men would tell the Magi when the group would rest next; the many heavily packed horses were easily fatigued on the steep hills, so it was helpful to know the approximate time between stops. Every few days, a caravan or a small group of riders approached from the other direction. Some of these travelers were on their way to Rhagae while others were moving between mountain villages.

On their third week of travel from Rhagae, the caravan began the slow descent from the mountains. The hills became less steep, allowing the animals to travel a bit further between stops. For the first time since Rhagae, level land could be seen in the distance. It would only be another day or two before the hills would be behind them.

Jangi doesn't visit the Magi's tent often, only when delivering a news report, and tonight he had come to speak with the men. As he walked into Balthasar's camp, the men gathered around in hopes of hearing what was said. When Balthasar emerged from his tent and saw his men, he motioned for them to join him and Jangi.

Jangi stepped on top of a crate and said, "I have good news to report and also a warning. The good news is that if we make good time tomorrow, we should be out of the hills and onto level land."

The men did not react to Jangi's statement; they waited for the warning. "The warning: do not leave your guard down as we leave the hills. We will be entering the most dangerous area between Rhagae and Ecbatana."

"Who presents a threat?" asked Balthasar.

"Bandits, well trained murderers. They frequent these hills leading into Ecbatana and take refuge north, toward the Caspian. They also attack on the road northwest near Tabriz and in the mountains to the south near Isfahan. They could be anywhere, so be alert!" shouted Jangi with his hands on his hips.

"Have any of the caravans that passed us had any trouble?" asked Gaspar.

"No one reported any problems. But, for all we know, some of those travelers may be bandits. Be cautious, stay alert. You are responsible for keeping us safe from attacks coming from the east," Jangi instructed. Without waiting any longer to see if any of the men had questions, Jangi stepped off the crate and made his way up the road to his caravan.

"Did you hear that? We are responsible for his safety!" complained an angry Gaspar.

Ignoring Gaspar's comments, Balthasar instructed his men, "You heard the warning! Keep a sharp eye out tomorrow, in all directions."

Knowing that Gaspar was angry with Jangi's manner, Balthasar said to him in a reassuring voice, "See, he trusts us now. We have earned his respect. Otherwise, he would not ask for our help."

"Let us pray that he knows what he is doing. If we are in danger, he should have told us to post additional guards this evening. Would it not be wise for us to pull our carts closer together for protection?" asked Gaspar as he pointed his index finger in Balthasar's face.

Balthasar was enjoying the sight of his red-faced companion mumbling about their Persian friend. In a reassuring voice, Balthasar said, "Beyond any doubt, you are correct on both points. Extra guards and a defensive position for our caravans are good advice that you should share with Jangi," Balthasar jokingly responded with a big smile.

147

"I am pleased that you agree. I will go to him immediately," Gaspar replied as he began walking briskly up the road.

Balthasar's eyebrows raised and his jaw dropped in disbelief as he watched Gaspar disappear behind the carts and tents on his way to speak with Jangi.

Balthasar shook his head and grumbled to Pulan, "He will be back here in a few seconds madder than a hornet shaken from its hive."

Several minutes passed and Gaspar had not returned. Balthasar stood on a crate to get a better look, but Gaspar was not in sight. Balthasar joined his men for supper, expecting Gaspar to return at any moment.

As they finished their supper, Balthasar spoke to Pulan, "It has been nearly two hours since he went charging up the road. I cannot imagine what is keeping him. I worry that they have him bound in chains. I suppose that I should go rescue him."

Balthasar began walking toward Jangi's caravan when he saw Gaspar returning with his arm around Jangi. When they reached Balthasar, Gaspar spoke, "We agreed on a plan for protecting the caravans. I volunteered Pulan and Hutan for scout duty, but I want your approval."

"Of course, they are our best scouts. What is the rest of the plan?" asked a surprised Balthasar.

"We discussed how we will bring the caravans tightly together, putting our carts into two circles in case of attack. We also agreed that some of our men should scale the hills as we travel through problem areas to protect against an ambush in the narrow passages," explained Gaspar.

"It sounds like a good plan. Let us give the men their assignments now so we are ready to move in the morning," replied Balthasar.

When morning arrived, the men took their positions and the caravan resumed its descent through the hills. The many carts in the two caravans now formed one continuous line, making it easier to take cover when necessary.

The first two hours passed quickly as the caravan kept a good pace. Just as one of Jangi's men signaled for a rest stop, shouts could be heard in front of the caravan. All eyes turned to see their scouts, Hutan and Pulan, riding quickly toward the caravan.

Gaspar asked Balthasar, "What can be the problem? They do not signal an attack."

They watched as Hutan stopped to speak briefly with Jangi, while Pulan made his way to the Magi.

"What happened?" shouted Gaspar.

"A small caravan was attacked ahead of us. Yesterday, perhaps two days ago. Six men dead! Four with arrows, two hacked by swords. Animals gone, carts empty!" Pulan responded in a nervous voice.

"Can you tell how many bandits?" asked Balthasar.

"I cannot say for sure. We will know better once we can check the road ahead. There are many horse tracks, at least a dozen, but we do not know how many horses belonged to the dead men," answered Pulan.

"What is Jangi's plan?" asked Gaspar.

"He said that he would organize a party to ride ahead in search of the bandits."

The Magi shook their heads and Balthasar replied, "That could be a deadly mistake. Let us speak with him before he is gone."

The Magi joined Pulan in riding swiftly to Jangi.

When they reached Jangi, Balthasar pleaded, "Do not go looking for them. That is what they would have you do. If we are separated, we all become easy targets. You do not know the number of bandits or where they hide!"

"Then what do you suggest should be our response?" asked Jangi.

"Let us keep together and take our time. Send four scouts ahead to draw out the bandits. If the bandits attack, we are capable of defending ourselves. There may be no need for fighting if we stay together," answered Balthasar.

"If we keep moving today, we will be in more open space by this evening. If they are going to attack us, they will need to do it soon. The caravan that was attacked was probably small in number. They were easy prey," added Gaspar.

"I understand, but if we do not find and kill them now, there will be others to serve as their prey," Jangi quickly responded.

"What you say is true, but are you willing to risk your men and sacrifice your cargo?" asked Balthasar.

Jangi was frustrated and becoming angry. He held his reins tightly as if he were ready to race away, his horse raising its head in response.

"Let us consider our options; at least three come to mind," said Balthasar in a calming tone.

Upon hearing Balthasar mention options, Jangi nodded his head in interest and dismounted from his horse. Handing the reins of his horse to one of his men, Jangi joined the Magi to hear what Balthasar had to say.

Having Jangi's full attention, Balthasar said, "One option is to take our caravan down the hill with our archers in front of the carts so they can respond quickly to an attack."

Gaspar interrupted, "If the bandits are waiting for us on the hillside, they will have the advantage!"

"Yes, that is the risk with that option," Balthasar answered. Pausing for a moment, Balthasar continued, "Another option is to send a group of our men in search of the bandits. If they find them and attack, that may give us enough time to move our caravan ahead, out of danger."

Again, Gaspar interrupted, "But we do not know how many bandits may be waiting for us and we have no idea where they hide. If we search for them, we may put everyone at risk."

"I agree; there is a risk with any response," Balthasar replied.

There was no immediate response from Jangi to these suggestions. He stared at Balthasar for a moment and then asked, "And the third option? You said that there were three!"

"Yes there is a third option, but it may be too risky," Balthasar answers.

"Let us hear it and then we will discuss the risk," snapped Jangi.

Balthasar grimaced and continued, "We could set a trap for the bandits."

"A trap? What kind of trap? Tell me more," replied a curious Jangi.

"I have not completely thought this through, but consider this question: Why would the bandits leave their victims to rot along the trail? Their scouts must have known that we were the only travelers nearby. If they wanted to surprise us, they would have cleaned the area," Balthasar said as he studied Jangi's face for his reaction.

"Perhaps they are lazy bandits," quipped Gaspar.

"So, you believe the bandits are nearby?" asked Jangi.

"That is my guess. By leaving their victims on the road, they may want us to panic and split up the caravan. Their scouts must have seen us. I suspect that they hope your militia will move out ahead of us to protect your cargo," answered Balthasar

"I see, sacrifice the remainder of the caravan, leaving you to fend for yourselves makes you much easier prey for the bandits. So you will serve as the bait in this snare?" Jangi asked with a smile.

"We are the bait?" gasped Gaspar.

"Yes, we are the bait. You cannot catch a cub without going into the tiger's den!" replied Balthasar.

"Please continue!" Jangi replied with enthusiasm.

"If the bandits are near, they need to believe that the militia is deserting us. Jangi, if you send several of your men ahead of us, we will appear vulnerable. Your horses will pull empty carts covered with blankets. With any luck, the bandits did not get an accurate count of your men. Your men will pull only two carts, so the bandits will leave you pass."

"Empty carts? Where is our cargo?" asked Jangi

"You and the remainder of your men will hide in our carts under blankets with your weapons. When the bandits attack, we will let them draw close before we pull the blankets and hit them with more arrows than they can count. Our scouts will signal your men ahead of us so they can leave their empty carts and race back to join the fight," Balthasar answered with enthusiasm.

"That is your plan?" asked Gaspar, rolling his eyes.

"Well. I know that it is a bit rough… that is all that I have at the moment," Balthasar replied with a shrug of his shoulders.

"I like it. It is a good plan. How long will this take? I do not like riding in carts," asked Jangi.

Balthasar placed his hand on Jangi's shoulder and replied, "For the plan to work, your men will have to follow it. There can be no movement under the blankets. As for the duration, I cannot be certain." Balthasar pointed to the road ahead. "The next two hills provide the most cover for the bandits… many large rocks and groves of trees. They will probably hit us from the right side, so the sun will be in our eyes. What are your thoughts, Gaspar?"

"I suppose you are right; if the bandits are in the area, to our right would be the best place to mount an attack."

Over the next few minutes, the plan unfolded. When they reached the base of the next hill, Jangi's cargo was unloaded into Balthasar's carts and everyone was instructed as to their roles. Jangi's men took their positions in the carts and Balthasar's men stretched blankets over them. When the lead caravan reached the slain victims, the drama began. Balthasar and one of Jangi's men staged a shouting match, accompanied with some spirited shoving. The shouts echoed through the hills. For effect, a few of Jangi and Balthasar's men drew their swords and waived them in the air.

Every few seconds, Gaspar cupped his hands over his mouth and warned in a loud whisper, "No laughter, no smiles, this has to be convincing!"

With a nod from Balthasar, Jangi's men mounted their horses and began pulling their carts forward at a quick pace, made easier by the empty crates. Within minutes, they were over the next hill. Once out of sight, they slowed their pace and listened for the sounds of an attack behind them.

As Balthasar's carts moved along, Gaspar suggested to Balthasar, "If we are going to be attacked, it should come before we reach the second hill. After that, the hillside widens. They lose their ability to surprise and attack quickly. The open area gives us more space to defend ourselves."

"You can see beyond the second hill?" asked Balthasar.

"No, but I do not see a third hill. There must be a wide sloping hillside stretching to level land."

"Ah!" replied Balthasar.

Every few minutes, Jangi was heard calling from beneath the blankets, "Anything? What is happening?"

"Nothing yet. But if we are going to be attacked, it will be soon," spoke Balthasar in the direction of Jangi's cart.

"Is that one of Jangi's men ahead?" asked Gaspar.

"Where? I do not see anyone," a squinting Balthasar answered.

"Ahead, just to the right of the road," replied Gaspar as he pointed to show Balthasar.

"Oh! Now I see him. His horse has large white patches. I do not recall seeing such a horse. Jangi! Any of your men ride a brown horse with large white patches?" Balthasar asked.

"More brown than white?" asked Jangi from under the blankets.

"No, more white!" responded Balthasar.

"No, our horses are mostly brown," Jangi quickly replied.

"Men, get ready, pass the word quickly," Balthasar called out.

"What is happening?" shouted an impatient Jangi.

"Jangi, get ready, it could be any moment," answered Balthasar as his eyes studied the hillside.

Within seconds, men on horseback appeared on top of the hill to the right of the caravan and several men on foot emerged from behind rocks halfway up the hill. One of Balthasar's men gave three shrill whistles to serve as an alert to Jangi's men, who rode ahead.

"Hopefully the bandits believe those whistles are meant for us. Let us hope Jangi's men are not too far away to hear it," Balthasar shared with Gaspar.

"Look at them slithering as snakes out from under their rocks," Gaspar said as he checked on his men and motioned for them to keep in place. "There must be twenty."

Gaspar maneuvered his horse to the left side of the carts. This was the signal for his men to take their positions on that same side.

"Are we being attacked?" shouted Jangi.

"There are twenty bandits to our right. About half of them on horseback," replied Balthasar.

"What are their exact positions?" asked Jangi.

"Those on foot are walking slowly toward us, not yet within range for their arrows. The men on horseback are carefully making their way down the hillside. The hill is steep; their horses move slowly," Balthasar replied with his eyes fixed on the hillside.

"Good! The men on horseback will have trouble with their bows on the slope," answered Jangi.

"But those on foot will be within range before the riders. They must think it strange that we do not take cover," Balthasar said in a loud voice as he rode next to the cart carrying Jangi.

Balthasar turned around to send a command to his men, shouting, "Keep moving forward until those on foot raise their bows."

"Tell me what is happening!" shouted an anxious Jangi.

"The men on foot have not drawn their bows. They walk slowly now; looks as if they wait for the riders to join them," Balthasar replied.

"Good! How soon will they be within range?" shouted Jangi.

"Another moment," Balthasar shouted.

"Are we on level ground?" Jangi shouted as he placed an arrow in his bow string while lying on his back under the blankets.

"Yes, level ground. Just a few more moments and I will give the command," answered Balthasar.

"Do not let them get to level ground, we want to keep them off balance," a restless Jangi replied.

"Their ground is steep with many lose rocks, they watch their feet as they walk," Balthasar said as he raised his hand to signal the caravan to stop.

As the caravan came to a stop, Balthasar shouted, "Jangi! They are bringing up their bows. I am going to give the order to dismount and once off our horses, I will give the order to pull the blankets."

"We are ready! My men will find a target for their arrows as soon as the blankets are pulled!" shouted Jangi.

"Dismount!" Balthasar shouted.

Balthasar's men quickly jumped from their horses and took their places on the left side of the carts. Balthasar stayed on his horse and looked for Gaspar, who had moved to the end of the procession. Gaspar turned his horse toward Balthasar, the signal to pull the blankets.

"Pull the blankets!" Balthasar commanded and immediately his men removed the coverings from the carts carrying Jangi's men.

Within seconds, arrows were flying in the direction of the bandits. Before Balthasar's men were even able to release an arrow, four bandits were down. Jangi's men were standing in the carts, shouting at the bandits as they released their arrows while one bandit on horseback fell. The other riders tried to turn their horses around and climb the hill, but it was too steep. Two horses stumbled, throwing their riders. The bandits on foot sought rocks for cover, but the larger rocks were further up the hill. Three bandits on horseback dropped their bows, signaling their surrender. The horses of four remaining bandits made a run for it, down the hill, ahead of the caravan. Once they reached the road, their horses quickly reached a gallop.

"Leave them! With any luck they will run into our men," Jangi ordered. Then Jangi directed his men to spread out to form a half circle. He then led his men as they closed in on the remaining bandits. The bandits were partially exposed behind the small rocks and brush on the hillside.

"The hill is too steep for them to run. They know they will be easy targets for our arrows. Give them time to think this through!" Jangi shouted to his men.

Several wounded bandits were calling for help, in great pain from their wounds, while two other bandits lied motionless on the ground.

"Surrender and you will live!" shouted Jangi

"What if they do not understand Persian?" asked one of Balthasar's men.

"Do not worry, they understand!" Jangi responded. One by one, the remaining bandits stood and dropped their bows, knives and swords.

"Well done, Jangi! Well done!" shouted the Magi as they joined their men in banging their bows against the carts in approval.

Balthasar's men assisted in taking control of the bandits and tending to the wounded.

"I saw not even one arrow fly in our direction," Balthasar said to Gaspar.

"They never had time to get off a shot. It all happened so quickly. They put themselves in a poor position and were taken by surprise with our hidden cargo!" added Gaspar.

In a few minutes, Jangi returned and said, "They carried many weapons, but did not get a chance to use them. They do not seem to know what has happened. Two of their men are dead, so we will bury them along with their victims down the road."

"Will our prisoners be with us until Ecbatana?" asked Balthasar.

"No, but we will have them for a week or so. We will pass two of our stations before we reach Ecbatana.

Someone will take them off our hands so they can receive their justice."

Returning from his position ahead of the caravan, one of Jangi's men gave a loud whistle and waved his cap to alert the caravan of his return.

"I am guessing the other bandits rode into my men," said Jangi with a smile.

Within a few minutes, Jangi's men appeared over the top of the hill, surrounding four bandits on horseback.

Jangi put one arm around each of the Magi and said, "I underestimated you. Your plan worked very well. You think as warriors and your men are well trained. I have never seen a fight won so easily!"

"We have plenty of help that you do not see," Balthasar replied.

"Help that I do not see? You are men of good fortune?"

"Our god is with us. He was with us before we left our homes. He calls us to this journey. Each time we get into trouble, our problems are solved in most unexpected ways. Our god is making sure that we get to Jerusalem safely," explained Gaspar.

"God is traveling with you to Jerusalem? Well it is often said that some roads are not meant to be traveled alone!" Jangi replied in an understanding voice.

The caravan proceeded cautiously over the next several days without any additional problems. The prisoners were cooperative, but the attention they required slowed the caravan and one of the wounded died from an infection that Balthasar's men could not remedy.

The following morning, several prisoners requested to Gaspar that their friend be buried according to their customs. Relaying this to Balthasar and Jangi,

Gaspar said, "The prisoners request that their friend be buried by a covering of rocks above the ground, not by our custom."

"It is of no concern to me. They may bury their friend as the wish. What is your way?" answered Jangi.

Balthasar responded, "We believe that bones are sacred. We bury our bones above the ground after covering them with wax, so that we may also keep the earth pure."

A very puzzled look appears on Jangi's face. Realizing that Jangi may have found this custom odd, Balthasar continued as he took delight in Jangi's discomfort, "Left in the open, the birds make use of the flesh within two hours. Then we bury the bones. There is a purpose in us leaving the flesh for the birds. The bandits, however, had no reason to leave their victims rotting on the road for the birds."

Now appearing a bit distraught, Jangi shouted, "Burial with rocks it shall be! Quickly, before the birds arrive!" Jangi motioned with his hand for his men to assemble the prisoners. Jangi paused to look briefly at the two dead bandits and then looked to the sky, as if searching for birds. Jangi, thinking about birds eating flesh, shivered briefly before mounting his horse.

"He must believe us to be horrible animals," said Gaspar.

"I am sure that he knows our tradition. He is having fun with us," replied Balthasar.

The caravan moved on with the men in a somber mood. No one was comfortable with any man losing his life, even if he was an enemy. They traveled without any problems and ten days after taking the prisoners, the caravan reached a Persian militia station where Jangi delivered their captives. Jangi and his men were eagerly received by fellow militia for the capture of the bandits. Jangi outlined with great detail how he carefully planned and directed the operation with precision. Several militia men surrounded Jangi and hung on his every word.

At one point during the tale, the leader of the militia station walked to the Magi and asked, "You were among the travelers who were saved from the bandits?"

Jangi, following close behind the militia station leader, looked quite concerned as he tried to encourage a favorable response from the Magi by nodding his head vigorously. The Magi did not respond immediately, choosing to let Jangi worry a bit longer, until Balthasar ended the silence and said, "Only a masterful militia leader could conduct a dangerous operation with such precision!"

Gaspar added for his and Balthasar's amusement, "Hiding beneath our carts, we watched in amazement. The operation was carried out just as Jangi tells… except for one thing."

The militia station leader and a nervous Jangi waited for Gaspar to continue.

"Jangi is much too modest of his accomplishment and the danger he faced!" Gaspar finished with a smile, turning to make eye contact with Jangi.

With a quick wink to the Magi, a relieved Jangi put his arm on his leader's shoulder and directed him back to his men, while the Magi returned, laughing, to their carts.

"Did you see the look on Jangi's face?" an amused Balthasar asked.

"Terrified! Did you see the sweat dripping from his forehead? I thought he gave himself away," Gaspar said between laughs.

"Jangi is a good man. He has a difficult job that provides few rewards, so who could blame him for taking all of the credit?" Balthasar replied.

"His arrows stopped the bandits and he was wise enough to listen to your plan. Hopefully some reward will come his way." Gaspar said with a nod.

Chapter IX – A Close Call on the Road

As the caravan finally departed the militia station after a day's rest, the men saw the mountains in the distance that would lead them to Ecbatana. Spirits were high among Jangi's men as they neared their destination, and Balthasar's men were also excited about reaching the city that held special meaning, as many of the men had family roots there.

Much of the evening's discussion was about Ecbatana. Many of Jangi's men had been to Ecbatana, but among Balthasar's men, only the Magi had visited Media's capital.

Gaspar stood to speak to his men and said, "Ecbatana is a jewel that god chiseled from the great mountains that surround her. She sits in the shadow of the greatest of these mountains, named Elvend. While we will not reach Ecbatana for some time, it will not be long before you see Elvend, standing tall for all to see."

When Gaspar finished, Balthasar added, "Several hundred years ago, a great warrior named Deioces united the seven Median tribes. Deioces became the first king of the Medes and the peace he brought to this region allowed his people to prosper. He built a magnificent palace in Ecbatana, but it is mostly rubble today. The palace was surrounded by seven great walls, each a different color, much of which remain, but they, too, are crumbling."

"Why would he build so many walls?" asked Nekdel

"Deioces wanted a palace that would show strength and dignity to all who cast eyes upon it. The great walls surrounding the palace were strong, standing in circles, one within the other, a wise decision to protect his palace from attack."

The men were silent, imagining such a great structure and the man who built it, when Balthasar continued, "Each wall is built higher than the next. Within the last circle stood the royal palace and the houses that once held great treasure. The outer wall is white, the next black, then crimson, blue and red. Am I correct, Gaspar?"

"Yes, that is how I remember them. And the two walls closest to the Palace are colored with silver and gold," added Gaspar.

Nodding, Balthasar continued, "I believe that Gaspar even witnessed the building of the walls. But, as you can imagine, after one thousand years, it has lost most of its former glory, unlike Gaspar, who continues to sparkle and retains much of his color!"

Gaspar opened his coat and slowly turned around in place to exhibit his physique. Balthasar, laughing with the rest of the men in the group, offered a bow to Gaspar for his perfectly timed performance.

Resuming the Ecbatana story, Gaspar explained, "During Deoices' rule, Ecbatana was the most prosperous and most beautiful city in the world, but much has changed since then. The city has lost much of its splendor, although it remains a jewel among the mountains. When King Cyrus attacked Median King Astyages about 500 years ago, Cyrus took control of Ecbatana."

Balthasar interrupted, "King Astyages might have prevailed had his warriors been trustworthy. When Astyages ordered his troops to march against Cyrus, Astyages' men revolted, instead delivering him to Cyrus, who seized the palace, the gold, the silver and everything else of value."

"Ecbatana has fallen through the hands of many kings, but the city continues to prosper because of its location and the abundant land which surrounds it," added Gaspar.

"Can we visit the palace?' asked Nekdel

"I am afraid that not much remains of the palace, but you will see what stands. When the palace was new, it rivaled any structure ever built. The builders used the finest cedar and cypress wood, covering the columns and ceiling with silver and gold. Can you imagine? Even the roof tiles were covered in gold!" explained Gaspar as the men attempted to imagine such a sight.

A few days later, the caravan reached a ridge near the top of the Elvend.

As the caravan rested, Jangi announced, "We have reached the summit and the most difficult part of our ride to Ecbatana is now behind us!"

In hearing the announcement, the men gave a shout, tossed their caps into the air and clanged their supper pots on the rocks where they sat.

"But danger remains and there are some things that you need to remember as we ride the ridge," continued Jangi as he climbed onto the back of a cart to make sure that all could see and hear him.

"We will ride the ridge for a week and then make our descent into Ecbatana. We have climbed high where the air is thin, so although you may not feel its strain on your body now, you will. Although the road is fairly level, we must ride slowly and take many breaks for the animals, who will also struggle from the thin air. Water will be available along the way, but not every day. Where we rest this evening, the road is wide and there is much room for us, but within a day or two, the road will narrow and we will pass through areas where we will have only a small patch of land on either side. If you or your horse stumbles on these narrow ridges, you will be lost forever, as the bottom of the mountain is so far below it cannot be seen," warned Jangi.

The men grumbled to each other and then grew quiet as Jangi continued, "We will not have trouble if we are cautious. We will not ride in rain, strong wind, or even when the clouds settle on us and hide the road. We will find places to rest for the evening early, while there is still plenty of light, and we will safely gather wood during our breaks in the daylight, as we cannot look for wood at night. We must make sure our animals are tied securely at rest and at night. If they wander off, they will be gone, and if you leave your tent at night, do not go far, or you too will be lost. I have just one question: do any of you walk in your sleep?"

Balthasar saw that the men were troubled by Jangi's comments and, wanting to calm and reassure them, he offered a prayer. In closing, he said, "We thank you Ahura Mazda for keeping us safe from our enemies and for guarding us against illness. We ask that you deliver us safely to Ecbatana. Protect us and guide us to Jerusalem."

When Balthasar was finished, the men remained gathered with their heads down, contemplating Jangi's cautions and Balthasar's prayer.

But before the men could make their way to their tents, Balthasar reminded them, "Why such worry on your faces? Considering what we have been through, staying on the road should be easy!"

The following two days were cool, the nights cold and the sky clear. The animals adjusted to the thin air, but

Jangi made sure that the caravan kept a slow pace and rested frequently, and that the men and their animals drank plenty of water to prevent dehydration. On the third evening, it rained steadily through the night.

At dawn, Jangi entered Balthasar's tent and said, "There is no use readying ourselves this morning, as the clouds have settled on us. My tent sits only twenty paces from yours, yet it cannot be seen. As the sun rises, perhaps it will clear the air."

As the fog began to rise near the noon hour, Jangi and Balthasar gave the order to break down the tents and pack the carts. Within the hour, the caravan was moving with caution on the muddy road. Although the clouds were gone from the ridge, they continued to provide a thick covering over the valley below.

Nekdel, riding with his father, said, "We are riding above the clouds! We must be getting close to Ahura Mazda."

Balthasar looked below to see the sun shining brightly on the clouds and answered, "It is quite a beautiful sight, one that not many are able to see. You have made quite an observation Nekdel. We seem to be getting closer to Ahura Mazda with each step."

Jangi and his men inspected the road carefully, alerting everyone to spots with deep mud or slippery areas of exposed wet rock.

In the afternoon, Jangi told the Magi, "Within the hour, the most dangerous stretch of the road will be upon us. The road narrows and the slopes become steep."

"How should we proceed?" asked Gaspar.

Jangi paused for a moment, looked to make sure the sky had no rain clouds and replied, "We should take the carts through this area one at a time. It will take much of the afternoon, but it will be safer than moving all the carts and horses through at once. Let us take the small carts first so there will be no delay if a heavy cart becomes stuck. We do not want the animals getting restless in this narrow passage."

"We will alert the men and begin arranging the carts so we will be ready when we reach the danger area," replied Balthasar.

Gaspar stopped his horse and directed his men pulling the heavier carts to leave the line and wait with him on the side of the road, and Balthasar led the caravan, glancing back occasionally to make sure there were no problems.

When Jangi and two of his men reached the danger area, they began clearing rocks that had fallen onto the road from the hillside. Several of the rocks were too large for the three of them to move, so Jangi waited for the remainder of his men to arrive to clear it. When a turn in the road revealed danger ahead, the Magi stopped their horses.

Balthasar sighed and said, "I can see why Jangi is so concerned. The slope is steep and the road is narrow. We may need to get on our hands and knees to pass through here."

"You have to look hard to see the road. It must have been much wider and was narrowed by snow and rain," added Gaspar while shaking his head in frustration at what awaited them.

But before Gaspar and Balthasar had any more time to worry, a man sent by Jangi arrived for rope to remove the remaining rocks. Jangi and his men tied rope around each rock and looped the other end around a horse's neck. Once the rock was moving, the horse was led to the side, dragging the rock behind it. In a few minutes, the rocks were removed from the road.

Jangi said to the Magi, "The road is clear, but here is where the most treacherous area begins, continuing beyond the turn in the road. We will tie a rope around each horse pulling a cart so we can guide it because even the best trained horse will become nervous if they look over the side!"

One of Jangi's men led the riders without carts. Moving slowly, they eventually disappeared from view around the turn. Jangi then secured a rope around the neck of the horse pulling the first small cart and its rider. As this cart was led around the bend, out of danger, the next horse and small cart was put into position. Once the last of the small carts were through, Jangi motioned Balthasar to hold the heavy carts as Jangi and his men inspected the road.

He rode to Balthasar and reported, "The surface is very slippery. The small carts have knocked the dirt and mud from the road, exposing the rocks. The rocks do not lie flat, so the cart wheels may slide off of them. This could be a problem for the heavier carts."

"We will take our time and find our way through this," Balthasar confidently replied, aware that he had relatively no other options.

The Magi directed the heavy carts into position and Balthasar instructed his men, "If your cart begins to slide and you hear us yelling for you to jump, do not hesitate! Jump to your left and forget about the horse and the cart. We do not want to tell your family that you disappeared over the side of a mountain."

With that, Jangi led the first of the heavy carts down the road. One after another, he led the carts through the dangerous area. When a cart began sliding over the rocks, Jangi gave his horse a kick and quickly pulled the cart back on to the road.

When Jangi returned with his rope, he shouted to Balthasar, "Two more carts to go!"

When Hutan's cart was positioned and the rope was placed around the neck of his horse, Jangi sent them on their way. Jangi led the cart halfway through the danger area when Gaspar shouted, "Look out! Falling rocks!"

Hutan and Jangi looked to the top of the mountain to see many large rocks tumbling in their direction. Jangi quickly kicked his horse and gave a shout, while Hutan also kicked his horse hard and shouted to Jangi, "Can we outrun it?"

"We have no choice!" Jangi shouted in reply. The rocks were halfway down the hill, gaining speed and heading directly for them. The Magi watched in horror as the scene unfolded.

"It is going to be close!" Balthasar said, holding his breath.

"Should we tell them to take cover under the carts?" Gaspar shouted back.

"No! Those rocks will knock everything into the valley. Their best chance is to get ahead of it," Balthasar quickly replied.

Hutan's cart was moving too fast over the slippery rocks and began sliding toward the valley side of the road. Jangi continued kicking his horse, trying to pick up speed, but he felt his horse being dragged by Hutan's cart toward the edge.

"We are not going to make it!" yelled Jangi.

Hutan quickly drew his sword from his side. In one motion, he leaned back and swung the sword, severing the rope that tied the cart to his horse. In an instant, he and Jangi were free. Frantically, they kicked their horses, galloping for their lives as they heard the rocks crashing the cart behind them. Just ahead of Jangi, a boulder hit the middle of the road before bouncing over the hillside. They continued kicking their horses as a boulder passed between them and another barely missed Hutan's head. Then, just as quickly as the chaos began, all was silent. Jangi looked to his left, checking for more rocks, then raised his right arm and slowed his horse. He and Hutan came to a stop and turned to look behind them.

"Whoa!" shouted Hutan as he tossed his cap into the air.

Balthasar and the others cheered loudly for their friends.

"What just happened?" asked a stunned Jangi. He and Hutan turned to see that the road behind them was completely clear of debris.

"It has all gone over the side!" replied an astonished Hutan.

"We were being dragged over the side and then suddenly we were running free! I thought we were dead men! What did you do? How did you get free so quickly?" panted a puzzled Jangi, out of breath from the excitement.

His sword now back in its sheath, Hutan tapped it lightly with his hand and said, "A lucky swing cut us loose!"

"We are most fortunate men," Jangi replied as he slapped his hand on Hutan's shoulder.

"You are more fortunate than I. I am the one who must tell the Magi that their tent went over the side with their cart!"

"I will say a prayer for you. Join the others while I go back for the last cart and break the news to your leaders. I am sure they are most happy you are alive. If I learn otherwise, I will let you know," replied Jangi with a hearty laugh, grateful to be alive.

When Jangi returned to Balthasar to retrieve the last cart, the Magi greeted him with clapping hands and shouts of praise.

"It is not all good news, friends. The lost cart was carrying your tent!" replied Jangi with a big smile.

Balthasar laughed loudly and answered, "That old tent needed to go. Gaspar, was it not your grandfather who gave you that tent?"

"Old? Yes. But made of the finest material by a great craftsman. It was improving with age!"

"Improving with age? That explains the smell!" answered Balthasar, still laughing.

All of the men enjoyed a good laugh before the last cart was moved down the road. Soon, the caravan was moving along smoothly and Jangi announced that two hours of daylight remained. "Let us keep a good pace so we can find a suitable clearing before we lose the sun."

Once a clearing was found, Jangi directed the men to a location to erect their tents. As the Magi arrived, Hutan greeted them nervously. Before Hutan could speak, the Magi give him a strong embrace.

"Praise Ahura Mazda that you were not hurt," greeted Balthasar.

"It was quite a site, Hutan. We could not believe our eyes! It is a miracle that you are still with us. A rock missed your head by this much," added Gaspar, holding his finger and thumb a couple of inches apart.

"Your tent is gone!" replied Hutan with his head down.

"Yes, we know. I cannot thank you enough!" answered Balthasar.

"But where will you sleep?" asked a confused Hutan.

"Why, with you of course!" answered Gaspar with a wink to Balthasar.

As they walked, Gaspar asked Balthasar, "But really, where will we eat and sleep? Our cookware was also in that cart."

"Let us wait until the tents are set and then split up our group. We will be in Ecbatana in two days and will replace what was lost," answered Balthasar.

After supper, as the men prepared for bed, the Magi brought together the men who were sharing their tent. With their supplies in hand, they followed Balthasar to one of the tents, outside of which Balthasar called, "Hutan!"

A surprised Hutan emerged from within, unsure of what to think of his visitors.

"Since we have no tent, we have come to join you," greeted Balthasar.

"All of you?" Hutan asked with a troubled look.

Balthasar could not hold back his laughter and was quickly joined by his companions.

"Will you make room for four of us? The rest will squeeze into other tents," asked Balthasar with a smile.

"Well, in that case, of course, we have plenty of room," replied a much relieved Hutan.

As the caravan was organized the next morning, Jangi stood on a cart and instructed, "Before we stop this evening, we should be able to see Ecbatana in the valley. With good weather, we should arrive in the city tomorrow afternoon."

Jangi was interrupted by cheers, but after a few seconds, he motioned for quiet and then continued. "Yesterday, we had a difficult time on a stretch of road. Hutan and I barely escaped with our lives. We survived because we were cautious and we stayed alert. I am told that your god may have been a help to us. I urge you to likewise be cautious because travelers often become careless when they near their destination. Even the gods have trouble helping those who are not careful. Until we descend the mountains, we will be at risk. Be careful and look out for each other. If you see someone being reckless, say something, or else, or tell me. Understood?"

"Understood!" responded the men.

A few minutes later, when the carts had been checked to make sure everything was secure, Jangi gave the signal to begin moving. By midday, the road led the caravan to lower elevation, away from the ridge and, as the sun set, Jangi found a clearing for the caravan overlooking Ecbatana and the valley below. The men marveled at the sight of Ecbatana, sparkling in the rays of the setting sun. Balthasar motioned for Gaspar to join him as he stood on the mountain side to take in the view.

"Is it not marvelous?" asked Balthasar, focusing his gaze on the western horizon.

Gaspar took his position alongside his friend and asked, "The star is brighter than I have seen it. Is it not clear this evening?"

"Yes, everything is becoming clear to our eyes; how far we have come, our destination, our purpose, it is all quite clear," replied a contented Balthasar.

The Magi watched as rays of sun faded and Ecbatana slipped into darkness. The star's light intensified in the darkening sky and was reflected in the eyes of both men as night fell around them. They prepared for bed in anticipation of tomorrow's final push to Ecbatana.

Packing began before dawn as everyone was anxious to reach the magnificent city. Jangi made his way along the caravan as the carts were packed.

"Be ready to move with the sun!" he shouted as he walked along the row of carts.

Balthasar, standing outside his tent as it was taken down, asked the approaching Jangi, "Join us for tu?"

"Is it hot?" Jangi replied.

"No, not hot, warm," Balthasar answered with a smile.

"That will do," Jangi replied, returning the smile.

Jangi joined the Magi as Gaspar poured him a cup of tu. Jangi held it under his nose for a moment, enjoying the scent of the spices.

After taking a long sip, Jangi said, "We need to get moving soon to be certain we arrive in Ecbatana before evening."

"Is there a chance that we will enter her gates this afternoon?" asked Balthasar.

"The city is close, but the road moves back and forth as we descend, making it twice the distance to Ecbatana. There is another road, a much shorter route, but it is steep and not in good condition, although a rider without a cart could make it to Ecbatana on that road in a few hours. We should have no trouble with bandits if you want to send some of your men on that route," suggested Jangi.

"No, we will keep together. If we fall behind schedule, alert us," Balthasar replied.

Within a few hours of traveling, the road straightened, allowing the carts to move at a faster pace. Travelers soon appeared and a farmer's goats even crowded the road, briefly slowing the caravan. Once the caravan emerged from the mountains, the men were surprised to see many farmers and merchants living outside the city's gates.

As they rode, Balthasar said to the men who rode near him, "In the early days of Ecbatana, its residents took advantage of the shelter provided by the city's walls. After a few generations without an attack, the people have grown comfortable living outside the city. The city's walls are still close enough for many people to seek safety in times of danger."

As they rode, a goat and some fruit were purchased from a farmer, which would provide them with the evening's celebration feast. The Magi joined Hutan and Pulan in front of the caravan, riding side-by-side, as they discussed their arrival in Ecbatana.

Balthasar began loudly, saying, "Pulan, let us go over your assignment one more time. You and Hutan will locate the temple and find the Chief Priest. You are looking for an Ethiopian, a Magi named Melchoir. He is a trader with a loud voice and a generous heart. Return to us after you have finished at the temple. Jangi said that he will lead us to a place east of the gates."

Hutan and Pulan left the caravan and rode toward Ecbatana in search of Melchoir. Nekdel and Rushad rode up the line to take their places next to the Magi.

Nekdel pointed ahead and said to his father, "I see why Deioces built his palace here. It sits up high for all to see! Can you see the walls? I can see them, all seven of them."

"Yes, I see them. They would have been an imposing site for Deioces' enemies," answered Balthasar as he delighted in the wonder reflected in the faces of the two boys.

As they approached the city, they realized how difficult it would have been to take control of all of the walls and capture the palace. Ecbatana was large, covering much of the great valley.

It was late afternoon when the caravan approached the east gates and Jangi alerted the Magi that he was sending two of his men ahead to find a suitable area for the carts.

"Follow them, for we must leave you now. We go to the militia station to deliver our cargo, but I will find you tonight," he said.

Balthasar's men had finished their supper when Hutan and Pulan returned to the caravan.

"Any sign of Melchoir?" asked an anxious Balthasar.

"We have not seen him, but we spoke with people who saw him two days ago," replied Hutan.

"We asked the Chief Priest and the militia commander to send Melchoir to us if they see him. The Priest said that Melchoir was planning a long trip, but he does not know if he has left Ecbatana. He travels with a group of traders, but no one is certain of their location," Pulan added.

"We will find him tomorrow. Come, have some supper while it is warm," Gaspar said to the two tired men.

He turned to Balthasar, who sat near him by the fire and tried to comfort his friend by saying, "Do not be troubled that Melchoir was not waiting for us by the gates. It may be weeks or months, but I am sure that our paths will cross on the way to Jerusalem."

Gaspar pauses for a moment, took a drink of his tu and asked, "Has there been a problem on this trip that Ahura Mazda has not resolved for us?"

Without responding, Balthasar raised his head to reveal a smile, then lifted the pot of tu from the fire to fill Gaspar's cup.

Jangi returned to the caravan alone to say goodbye to the Magi. As he embraced the Magi, he said, "Friends, I have been given another assignment and must leave you now. I have enjoyed our time together. It is often said that long roads test the horse, long dealings, the friend. The two of you will always be my friends. I know that your journey is of great importance and I will remember you in my prayers while I keep an eye on your star."

Jangi turned and departed quickly, returning to his men and to his next assignment. After supper, the Magi joined their men in singing hymns, while Balthasar offered a prayer, thanking Ahura Mazda for their safe delivery to Ecbatana. Before retiring to their tents, the Magi stood next to the carts to discuss their plans for the next day.

"Would you feel better if we search the city for Melchoir tomorrow?" asked Gaspar.

"We need not search for him. We have much to do. Let us make our repairs and purchase supplies. If he is near, we will find each other," Balthasar responded, as Gaspar nodded in agreement.

While walking to his tent, Balthasar stopped to speak with Zinawar, one of the men assigned to guard duty. "I know that we all feel free from danger, but make sure that you stay alert."

Zinawar nodded and then continued on his walk, inspecting the carts and the horses. When Gaspar saw Ushtra, who was also assigned to guard duty, sitting in a cart with a blanket over him, he spoke in a voice loud enough for Ushtra to hear and said, "And remember, it is difficult to draw one's sword while sitting in a cart, covered with a blanket!"

Ushtra immediately removed the blanket and jumped out of the cart while Gaspar, shaking his head, told Balthasar, "I know that the men are tired, but they must be vigilant in carrying out their duties."

Nodding in approval, Balthasar said in agreement, "Sloppiness will be seen as encouragement to those who may want to separate us from our cargo. We carry many things of value, much more than our men realize. Our journey will end abruptly if we are robbed."
"Discipline and order are the keys to our safe arrival in Jerusalem. Let us keep in mind that we have done quite well keeping our routines. Reaching Ecbatana is a major accomplishment for us, something we should celebrate. We have been keeping a good pace, the problems we encountered were all resolved and, for the most part, our men are in good condition," added Gaspar.

The Magi rested comfortably, knowing that it would not be necessary to assemble the men before dawn to take down the tents and pack the carts. But a few short hours after they drifted off to sleep, they were awakened by a voice calling, "Magi! Magi! Wake up, please!"

Standing in the doorway of their tent was Zinawar holding a lamp.

"Please forgive me, but your friend insists that I wake you. He has built a fire and has prepared your breakfast. He instructed me, 'Tell the Magi to rise and eat, time is wasting!'" Zinawar relayed.

"Friend?" an annoyed and sleepy Balthasar snapped.

"Who said these things?" added Gaspar before Zinawar could reply.

"He would not tell me his name. He is alone, with no weapons. He says he knows you. He is tall with a clean-shaven head, a dark-skinned man."

"Melchoir!" shouted the Magi.

At once they were on their feet, throwing their robes around them as they hurried barefoot from the tent. Stumbling toward the fire, they felt the ground with their toes to avoid stepping on a jagged rock. When they looked up, they saw the outline of a man standing next to the fire. The man bent over the fire briefly, revealing the star behind him in the sky, its light blazing as it held its place over the horizon.

Balthasar and Gaspar stopped for a moment as their friend opened his arms and shouted, "Good morning, old friends!"

Gaspar was first to embrace and kiss their friend, saying, "Melchoir! How good it is to see you!"

Balthasar followed with an embrace and a kiss and asked, "How did you find us?"

"The Chief Priest said that you were looking for me," Melchoir replied as he tended to a pot resting on a rock next to the fire.

"The Priest? He told us that he did not know where you were," responded Balthasar.

Melchoir laughed. "He probably thought that I owed you money! Come! Join me in a breakfast feast of Ecbatana's finest: fresh quail eggs, sweet bread, sweet fruit and cakes with plenty of syrup!"

Before they sat, Balthasar gently grabbed Melchoir's arm, turning him in the direction of the star, and said, "Husvak, the Priest of Ustunawand, told us that you were on your way to Jerusalem. We left Rhagae in search of you."

Placing a hand on each of his friends' shoulders, Melchoir replied, "I know that many Magi are studying this strange and marvelous star. I have spoken to some who are fascinated by it, but none have enough interest to seek its source. None, that is, except for the three of us. I knew that if either of you were alive, you would seek this star."

"When did you first see it?" asked Balthasar.

"I had just left Ecbatana on my way to Rhagae. I considered returning to Ecbatana, but decided to continue with the trip. That was many months ago, just as winter was beginning. At first, I thought the star would shine for only a few days. A sign from Ahura Mazda, surely, but I never dreamed that it would be with us for so long," answered Melchoir as he began serving breakfast to his friends.

Stepping away from the fire, Melchoir again placed an arm around each of his friends, drawing them closer, and asked in a loud whisper, "Do you know the strangest thing about this star?"

But before he could answer his own question, Balthasar and Gaspar said in unison, "Not everyone sees it!"

"That is it! And the Hebrew Scriptures – you are familiar with what they have to say?" asked Melchoir.

"The sign of the Hebrew messiah!" replied Gaspar.

"Yes! Most Magi are in agreement about these things, but there are still many who do not reason as we do. Even here in Ecbatana, many priests do not consider the star special or do not believe that there is a connection with Jerusalem," Melchoir responded.

"Do you believe the star to be the sign prophesized in the Hebrew Scriptures, a sign of the messiah?" asked Gaspar.

"Perhaps, but we should consider all of the possibilities. The star appears to point to Jerusalem. But there are respected people who have different opinions," cautioned Melchoir.

The Magi talked as they ate their breakfast. As dawn flowed into morning, Balthasar's men had fed and watered the horses and had now moved on to other chores. Yet the Magi continued their discussion, oblivious to all of the activity around them.

"Tell us Melchoir, is Ecbatana your home?' asked Gaspar.

"I call many places home. Ethiopia is home, but Egypt will always have a special place in my heart. I have not been to either place in twelve years," answered Melchoir

"Twelve years? What have you been doing all this time?" asked Balthasar.

Melchoir shrugged his shoulders and responded, "The weeks drift into months and the months to years. Tomorrow becomes yesterday so quickly that we do not take notice until the past is difficult to remember. What have I been doing? For much of this time, I was an emissary to Prince Sohrab from Persia's western province. Then, about two years ago, I began trading again. There is much profit to be made on this great road and always much to learn, but I never intended to travel this far to the east and I never dreamed that I would be sharing breakfast with my two oldest and closest friends here in Ecbatana!"

Melchoir paused for a moment and held up his hand to display his ring. With his eyes welling up with water, he said in a soft voice, "I see that both of you still wear it." He gave his friends an embrace and said, "It is good to be with you again. I cannot believe this is happening." Then he turned to Balthasar and asked, "How is your sweet flower, Dinbanu?"

"She is more beautiful than she was on the day we met. She is home with my youngest son," answered Balthasar.

"Gaspar, your wife is well?" asked Melchoir as he picked up a piece of cake drenched in syrup.

"She is quite well and most happy that I am not creating problems for her at home," Gaspar replied.

"It must be hard for you both to leave everything behind for such a long journey. We are not young men; we cannot be certain that we will return from such a journey," Melchoir said as he studied the faces of his friends.

"I cannot be certain that I will return to my house after retrieving water from the well each morning, but it is a risk that I am willing to take," replied Gaspar with a laugh.

"All of us had to consider these things. It has not been easy, but it has been worth the sacrifice. We are having an exciting and wondrous time!" Balthasar replied.

"Melchoir, did you ever marry?" asked Gaspar.

"Marry? What woman would have me? Oh, I thought about it a few times, came close to marriage once. But a woman needs to have a place to call home. She cannot spend her life being dragged over mountains and through deserts!" he responded. Then after pausing for a moment, he asked, "Why do you ask? Do you have someone in mind for me?"

Gaspar laughed and replied, "If Ahura Mazda has someone in mind, he will make sure that you find each other."

Balthasar added, "Ahura Mazda will be kept busy finding a woman strong enough to tame you!"

With that, Melchoir jumped to his feet and said, "Enough about a woman for me. We have more important things to discuss. My place is not far from here, just west of the city. Bring your caravan there, as there is much shade for your horses and a cool stream filled with fish. It is there that I can show you my charts and we can arrange to trade some of your horses for a few good camels."

"Trade our horses? Is it necessary to abandon our horses now? So much of our journey remains," asked Balthasar.

"Horses are no match for the mountains on the way to Cresiphon and your horses are not rested. Once past Cresiphon, horses have trouble in the heat and the loose sand of the desert road. Camels are what you need!" Melchoir answered confidently.

"Camels! Ahura Mazda does not intend for men to ride those beasts!" grumbled Gaspar.

Melchoir laughed and replied, "Granted, they are not comfortable at first, but you will get used to them. I have passed by enough rotting horse carcasses in the desert to be content bouncing on top of my camel. Over time, you will appreciate them. It takes some time adjusting to the ride, but you will be glad you have a reliable animal when you are boiling under the desert sun."

One of Balthasar's men interrupted the conversation to ask Balthasar about purchasing food and supplies. Balthasar, realizing he had no idea where was best to find such items, asked Melchoir, "Could you tell us where we can find a wheel for a cart?"

"Of course! We will find the items you require on the way to my place," Melchoir assured his friends.

Balthasar's men were not anxious to break down the tents and pack the carts, but within the hour, they were once again on the move. By late afternoon, they had acquired food and supplies and had set up their tents near Melchoir's hut, a humble house consisting of one large room with a bed, a table, two chairs and several crates.

As Melchoir invited his two friends in, he said, "This is not much, but it serves me well."

Melchoir motioned for Balthasar and Gaspar to sit at the table as he dragged a crate containing his charts over to them. As Balthasar and Gaspar opened their own leather pouches containing their charts and scrolls, Gaspar asked Melchoir in a serious tone, "I sense that you are not convinced that the Hebrew Scriptures carry the message of the star: the coming of the Messiah?"

"I have read Balaam's prophesies. I understand what he says about the star that will come out of Jacob and the scepter that will rise out of Israel. I also know of Daniel's prophecy of when the Messiah will arrive. But I have traveled to many lands and I have heard compelling prophesy for other messiahs. Confucius and Zoroaster tell of a great prophet who will come and possess extraordinary powers. But the star is not in the sky over Han China or Persia. It appears to be over Jerusalem. With that, I have reasoned that it must be the sign of the Hebrew messiah, but my mind is open to other explanations," answered Melchoir.

Melchoir selected a scroll from his crate and unrolled it, revealing a map. Laying the map on the table, Melchoir said, "I drew this while on my travels. It is quite crude, but it is accurate as to general location and distance measured by days of travel." Melchoir pointed to a place on the map and said, "See this land to the west, between the two great rivers? We will pass through here on our way to Jerusalem. The people in this land have many gods. It seems that every village and city has its own god, and they worship, sacrifice and make offerings to him. Their gods do not make sense to me, but I mention this because there are many who expect a messiah. I tell you, from Han China to the Great Sea, every nation holds out hope for a messiah, someone who will deliver them from their misery. Perhaps the star we see points to the Hebrew messiah, but who can be certain?"

Balthasar placed his hand on Melchoir's shoulder and said, "We know the prophecies of which you speak; we heard many of them as children. I hold hope that

Zoroaster's prophecy will come true and that the arrival of the powerful Persian will restore our country to greatness. Maybe there will be messiahs for people of other lands, but for now, the evidence is strong that a messiah has come to the Hebrews and his star hangs over Jerusalem. The Hebrew Scriptures are convincing and their prophecy is clear. If the great star has been placed in the heavens for the Hebrew messiah, then he must be unlike any man who has come before him!"

"What you say may be true, but there is just one thing troubling me. If the star is a sign of the Hebrew messiah, why do not all Jews see the star? We see it shining bright, but how do not all of the Jews see it? Tell me how this can be true!" exclaimed Melchoir.

Balthasar laughed and then offered, "Friend, we will need to speak with the Hebrew god himself to learn the answer to that great mystery!"

Gaspar added, "Do not let this puzzling question stop you from seeing the truth! A Jew from Asdin travels with us. He sees the star as we do and is making the trip to see the messiah with his own eyes, yet we encounter Jews, Persians and Seres who do not see the star or simply cannot tell it apart from the other stars in the sky."

"We traveled many months from Merv to Rhagae, escorted by a Seres militia, people very different from us and very different from the Jews. Yet the Seres leader could see the star as we see it. He is drawn to it, but resists it, even though he understands it to be a wonder that only a god can create. If we had all the answers, there would be no need for us to make this journey. But we have been given enough to stir our souls and we will learn much more once we arrive in Jerusalem. Can you imagine the excitement in that great city? Surely everyone in

Jerusalem is celebrating under the great star shining above them. If we can see the star in Asdin, Shahnaz and Ecbatana, Jerusalem must be bursting with people from many lands who come to discover the source of the light!" added an excited Balthasar, who grew more animated with each passing remark.

Nodding in agreement, Gaspar said, "To witness the star and to experience the Hebrew god revealing himself in this way must be the cause of great rejoicing in Jerusalem!"

After hearing all of this, Melchoir sat quietly, stunned by what had happened so quickly in the last few hours. For several minutes, he was silent with his elbow on the table, his hand propping up his head.

Suddenly Melchoir stood and blurted, "Of course! It is just as you say. I have had the same experience. Some see it, some do not, and some Jews see it, while other Jews do not. But all who do see it share something, the one thing that brings us together in this marvelous experience: That fire burning within us, a voice speaking to our hearts. If the star is revealed to us, we can resist it, as your Seres friend has done, or we can seek the star and its meaning."

Gaspar placed a hand on Melchoir's shoulder and said, "Balthasar and I have talked many times of how the star pulls on us. To stir such feelings, the power of its light can seem terrifying, yet it calms our spirit with…" Gaspar trailed off, as if trying to put the star's great meaning in to words was impossible. But then, raising his right index finger, he exclaimed with excitement, "Love! An overwhelming sense of love!"

When Gaspar was finished and the three men agreed that they felt an unexplainable calling toward the star, Balthasar playfully slapped Melchoir on his back and said, "I am glad that we have settled this matter. Now, when can we continue our journey?"

Melchoir laughed at his friend's restlessness and explained, "We need two days, friend. It will take us that long to find camels, but first thing in the morning, we shall find you ones that suit."

Chapter X – Life with Camels; a Bumpy Ride

When morning arrived, Melchoir took his companions an hour or so from his camp to a place where many camels were kept.

After inspecting the camel pens for several minutes, Balthasar asked, "There are dozens of them. How can the merchant afford to keep so many?"

"Do not worry about the cost of keeping camels. They are a source of much profit. Beyond Ecbatana lies the desert, land too dry to herd sheep and cattle. Even the goats have a difficult time. But camels do well with little. This merchant gets a good price for his camels and for their milk. Have you tasted it?" asked Melchoir.

"Yes, it is thick and quite sweet," replied Balthasar.

"Not my favorite, but I know that it is good for the body," responded Gaspar.

"Quite right! And in many places, camels are raised for their meat. The best meat comes from the young males. A bit tough to chew, but its flavor is quite good," added Melchoir.

"I hope that you are not planning to eat our camels!" Balthasar said with a smile.

"It is good to have that option if we run into trouble," answered Melchoir, returning the smile.

As the men continued to look over the animals, Melchoir continued to share his knowledge of the camel. "When water is in short supply, there is no better animal. He does not drink much more than a horse, but once he is full, he can go for several days without needing another drink, perhaps a week without food or water," Melchoir shared.

"How do you suppose he can survive so long without water?" asked Gaspar.

"Ahura Mazda has given this animal the ability to resist the heat. We would shrivel up quickly without water in the midst of the desert sun, yet this animal can lose a great deal of water, almost half of its weight, and survive. It uses its water sparingly. Its urine is as thick as syrup and full of salt, while its dung contains little water. It comes out so dry that it can be burned as fuel as soon as it hits the ground," Melchoir replied as he studied the herd of camels.

"Will they carry our loads a long distance? Our horses have trouble in the heat, but they are strong and do well in most conditions," asked Balthasar.

"Except for a few, your horses are at the end of their journey. They are tired, worn out. They need much rest and should be replaced," Melchoir replied, shaking his head.

Melchoir climbed over the fence into the pen, pet a large camel and said, "This one molted in the spring and is growing a new coat. We have coats, rugs and tents made from the hair of this beast, so we know its value. This one probably produced five pounds of hair. Add that to the hair from the rest of these animals and you can see the value they bring their owner."

Melchoir placed his hand on the side of a camel and said, "Look closely at this camel's legs. From a distance, their legs appear quite thin. But when you get close, you can see the great muscles supporting the legs. He can carry twice as much as your best horse."

Now patting the camel softly on its side, Melchoir continued, "But they will not run forever. At best, we will get six, maybe eight months, out of them. But by then, we should be in Jerusalem and they will have done their job. We can rest them well in Jerusalem or trade them for fresh ones."

"Or we could can eat them!" snapped Balthasar, throwing his hands up in the air to signal his continued disbelief.

"Ah, you laugh, but we may be eating them before Jerusalem. Any questions before we barter with the merchant?" asked Melchoir.

"Just one question," replied Gaspar. "Our horses are trained to our command – ah, well, for the most part, they are trained. How will we get these animals to respond? It does not appear that they have ears to hear us!"

"These are smart animals and we will have no trouble controlling them. Do not worry about their hearing. Their ears are small, but their hearing is quite good," replied Melchoir.

Standing next to a camel, Melchoir gently lowered the animal's head by pulling down on its neck and said, "Look at this ear. See how the ear is lined with fur? The small size of the ear and all of that fur inside keeps the dust and sand from clogging the canal. Now, look at his eyes. Quite large, but ample protection is provided by these long lashes, two rows of them. These large, bushy eyebrows protect his eyes from the desert sun."

Melchoir reached outside the pen to pull a patch of grass from the ground and held it in front of the camel's mouth. As the camel began to eat, Melchoir continued, "Such a large mouth. He has two more teeth than we do and they are much sharper. With this mouth, he can eat almost anything, even thorny bushes, without damaging the inside of his mouth. Have you noticed that camels are always chewing? It does not matter if they have nothing to eat, they still chew. You cannot put the bit of the rein into his mouth."

"You cannot put a rein in his mouth?" asked Balthasar.

"No… never in the mouth! The peg is placed into the nose. You cannot pull on the reins as you do with a horse. If you do, you might break the reins or even hurt the animal," warned Melchoir.

Melchoir motioned for Balthasar and Gaspar to join him in the pen. Melchoir bent over to lift up a rear leg of the camel. The animal immediately made a loud, deep, bleating sound, which caused Balthasar and Gaspar to jump backwards, briefly losing their balance.

"Do not mind the noise, he is just saying hello," laughed Melchoir.

Holding the leg of the camel, Melchoir continued with his instruction. "Now, let us look at his feet. See how he has this wide, flat, pad that appears to be made of leather? And these two toes? When his foot hits the ground, this pad flattens, making it even wider. This prevents his foot from sinking into the sand."

Melchoir led the camel around in a small circle and said, "See how he moves both feet on one side of his body, then both feet on the other side? This helps him keep his footing on uneven ground and sand."

When the camel had completed the circle, Melchoir left him and returned to the fence to join his friends, exclaiming, "Ahura Mazda perfectly designed this animal for the desert!"

Balthasar asked Melchoir, "How many camels will we be purchasing?"

"Let us speak with the owner. Perhaps we can trade four or five horses for as many camels, although such an even trade is unlikely. We can complete our deal tomorrow when we return with your horses, preferably those in most need of rest. Once we reach Cresiphon and leave the mountains for the desert, we will only travel by camel," replied Melchoir.

"Once we have our camels, will we begin our trip to Cresiphon?" asked Gaspar.

"Yes, but we should first check to see if any caravans or militia will also be making the trip," suggested Melchoir.

"Surely with all of our men, we are a force of respectable size. We should have more men than we need for protection," replied Balthasar.

"Perhaps, but it is always safer to travel with as many as possible," Melchoir replied with a smile.

"Do you expect trouble on the road to Cresiphon? I thought it was of little risk," asked Balthasar.

"As Zoroaster teaches, whenever you seek Ahura Mazda and his truth, Angra Mainyu will try to obstruct your path. If the star is intended to draw us closer to our god, you can be sure that there will be trouble. You have already experienced much trouble; I doubt that those dangers were a coincidence," replied Melchoir in a serious tone.

"I agree that we should be cautious, but we know that Ahura Mazda is with us," replied Balthasar.

"Yes, he is with us, but you can be sure that Angra Mainyu is not far behind," warned Melchoir.

When the Magi finished negotiating with the camel owner and had acquired their camels, Melchoir sent some of his men to inquire with the merchants and authorities in Ecbatana about caravans or militia traveling to Ctesiphon. The Magi continued planning, checking supplies, reviewing charts and consulting previous notes Melchoir had made on locations suitable for evening stops and areas that provided sources of water and game, valuable information for planning a trip of several months or longer. The men also discussed areas that were particularly dangerous because of difficult terrain or exposure to attacks, and decided that if they were unable to join a militia or another caravan, they would need to plan for areas that provided little protection from bandits.

Before evening, Melchoir's men returned to share what information they had gathered in the city.

Melchoir's most loyal companion, Khursand, which meant "a contented man," entered Melchoir's hut and said, "After checking with merchants and militia, we did not learn of anyone planning to travel to Cresiphon. It may be a month or longer before anyone begins such a trip."

"That is most unfortunate news!" Melchoir responded, his mind already racing to produce alternate plans, as Balthasar and Gaspar sat in silence, disappointed by what Khursand had just told them.

"But there is a militia group leaving Ecbatana in two days, except they will travel west for only three weeks before turning north," added Khursand.

"That will do! They will give us protection for part of the way, which is better than no protection at all. Unfortunately, they will be leaving us just as the road becomes a problem," Melchoir replied with a nod, still weighing his options.

"Tomorrow morning, notify the militia that we would like to join them," Melchoir instructed Khursand.

Turning to his Magi friends, Melchoir said, "This great road provides many things, but certainty is not among them. You cannot be certain who might be traveling with you and you cannot be certain of what you may encounter. You cannot be certain of your safety and you cannot be certain if you will even reach your destination."

Just as Melchoir finished, Balthasar jumped to his feet, exclaiming, "That is what makes this journey so interesting! Why, if there were no surprises, the boredom would cause Gaspar to drift off to sleep and fall from his horse!"

Gaspar laughed and shook his head. "This old man has had enough surprises. I could do with a good dose of boredom. In fact, six or eight months of boredom would just about put us in Jerusalem."

The Magi enjoyed the remainder of the evening, sharing stories of past adventures and praying for Ahura Mazda's help as they continued on to Jerusalem. The following morning, the men traded most of their horses for camels and in the afternoon, a Persian militia leader stopped by their camp.

Melchoir greeted him, saying, "Commander, may I be of assistance?"

Melchoir could tell from his uniform that he was a Marzpawn, the rank of Commander for the frontier areas of Persia. The commander introduced himself as Sahi, which meant "straight."

"I understand that you would like to join us tomorrow, is this true?" he asks Melchoir. "Yes, that is correct. I hope that this is not a problem. We will be of no trouble to you," replied Melchoir.

"You are welcome to join us, but I want to make sure you know that we have different destinations. We are going to Nisbis and then on to Dara. We will only be with you for a few weeks. If Ctesiphon is your destination, you will not have us for most of your journey. You could be another two months through the mountains on your own," Sahi replied sharply.

"We understand, Commander. I have made this trip many times and I know the dangers through the mountains. We are well prepared with supplies and warriors," Melchoir assured Sahi.

"Very well. We will pass through the west gates tomorrow, just after day break. Be ready to go if you want to leave the city with us," advised Sahi.

When Sahi departed, Balthasar asked Melchoir, "His uniform is of significant rank, perhaps a hazarapatish. Why would he be leading a small group of men through the wilderness?"

"That is a good question. He may be training some of his men, or perhaps important business awaits him in Nisbis. We may learn more tomorrow," Melchoir answered.

For the next few minutes, the Magi discussed the hierarchy of the Persian militia, which consisted of many levels of command. There were dathabams, small groups of men led by a dathapatish, and larger groups of one thousand men were known as a hazarabam. Their leaders were commanded by a hazarapatish. Melchoir explained that it appeared Sahi was a hazarapatish. His escort of a small group for several weeks was somewhat unusual, as there was only one command unit above Sahi's rank and that was the baivarabam.

The following morning, Balthasar's men were readying for their trip well before dawn. Everything proceeded smoothly until the men began packing the camels. Almost suddenly, men began to shout and camels squeal, halting the packing process completely.

When Balthasar heard the commotion, he hurried to the scene of the chaos and, upon finding Hutan, shouted, "What is happening? Do you need help?"

"It is the camels. The stubborn beasts will not let us pack them!" shouted a frustrated Hutan.

"We do not have much time. Keep working!" replied Balthasar.

Balthasar made his way to Melchoir's hut where he found him packing and said, "Good friend! It appears that our newly acquired camels are rebelling and will not let us pack them. I am afraid that we will miss our militia. Will you help?"

"They can be stubborn beasts. It will take some time to settle them, so let the Commander know that we will find him later," Melchoir replied.

Balthasar retrieved his horse and rode to the west gate where Sahi and his fifty men were waiting.

As Balthasar approached, Sahi greeted him. "Magi… have you decided to travel alone?"

"No, I am sorry to report that we are having a problem with our camels," replied Balthasar with a troubled look.

Sahi and his men shared a good laugh before Sahi asked, "How much time do you need?"

"It may be well into the morning before we have the situation under control. One man has been bitten and another kicked in the head. No one wants to get close to the animals now," Balthasar answered with a shake of his head.

"Your camels have spirit! That is good. You will appreciate it when travel gets difficult. You and your camels will get used to each other soon enough. I need to get my men moving, so join us when you can; we will look for you," Sahi replied as he motioned with his hand for his men to begin moving.

Sahi and his men rode toward the mountains with smiles on their faces. Balthasar returned to his caravan and found Melchoir standing next to the kneeling camels. Melchoir held a long stick high into the air as he instructed the men on training the camels.

"If you have owned a camel, you know that they are gentle giants. And much like a woman, they require your love. You need to be gentle and speak softly. A kiss to the forehead and a sweet treat will win them over," Melchoir instructed.

Before he could continue, the men groaned and a few tossed their caps in his direction.

Balthasar walked into the group and announced, "I am sorry to break up this tender moment, but we need to get moving. The militia has departed and we do not want to fall too far behind. How soon can we move?"

"We will be ready soon," responded Melchoir as he pet a camel and made a kissing sound with his lips, which was immediately greeted with a loud bleat from one of the camels. Everyone had a good laugh as they finished packing, finally able to calm the camels enough to pack them.

Once packed and assembled, the caravan had a few starts and stops before the men had their camels under full control. But within a few hours, the caravan was moving smoothly. They made their way through Ecbatana's valley and soon began the climb into the mountains, but they were unable to reach Sahi and his men until the sun had set.

In the days that followed, the road through the mountains was treacherous in places, so care was taken when moving through these areas. Sahi kept with his men most of the time, but Balthasar was still able to discuss the road to Ctesiphon with him. With the aid of Melchoir's map, Sahi showed the Magi places that might have posed a threat from bandits, as well as the best places to find water and game.

On one afternoon while the caravans rested, Melchoir asked Sahi, "Why would someone of your rank, a Commander, be leading such a modest number of men to such a remote place as Nisbis?"

"Friend, I have important business in Nisbis!" Sahi said proudly.

"I have never been to Nisbis. I am interested as to what awaits you there," responded a curious Melchoir.

"Surely you know how important Nisbis is to Persia's security. From the mighty Tigris, its road leads west to the Great Sea and north to the mountains. A strong fortress with large, thick walls protects our King and his riches in Nisbis. Such a place would be of much value to our enemies. I will be commanding many men in the protection of Nisbis. This is an important mission for any commander!" Sahi curtly responded.

"Yes, of course! The protection of Nisbis is important to all of Persia!" replied Melchoir.

"What awaits you in Ctesiphon?" asked Sahi.

"Ctesiphon is another stop for us. We are on our way to Jerusalem," Melchoir replied as he looked for Sahi's reaction to his words about Jerusalem.

"That is quite a journey. What is your purpose? Do you travel for a king or prince?" asked Sahi.

"No, we seek the messiah of the Jews. Perhaps you have seen his star in the sky over Jerusalem?" asked Melchoir.

"The Jews have a messiah? Is he a warrior? What do you know of this messiah?" Sahi asked with a concerned look, confused by what Melchoir has said so suddenly to them.

"We know of the messiah from the Hebrew Scriptures and from his star," Melchoir replied, still studying Sahi's face.

"I have not heard of this messiah and I have not seen his star. Let us hope that this messiah has no interest in Persia. If you learn that he does, you must inform our militia!" warned an alarmed Sahi.

Melchoir decided not to elaborate further on their quest, as it held little meaning for Sahi. Instead, Melchoir gave Sahi a nod, then turned the conversation to the more immediate concerns of travel.

"How much further until you leave us for Nisbis?" asked Melchoir.

"Two, perhaps three days. Several roads wind north through the mountains. Some roads are quite steep, while others require traversing many streams. If the weather remains good, we may take our chances on one of the steep routes, which would even shorten our trip by a few days, weather permitting. That is the trouble with these mountains. The clouds riding the west winds shed their rain when they reach them. Strong wind, heavy rain and hail can come upon you quickly," Sahi replied.

"I know this to be true. I have traveled through these mountains and have learned to not take risks," replied Melchoir.

"You are wise to be cautious. Many travelers perish because of their foolishness," responded Sahi.

In the three days that followed, Sahi and his men traveled with the Magi, sharing information with them about the routes available to them and the danger they entailed. Then, unexpectedly, and ignoring his own word of caution to the Magi, Sahi and his men left Balthasar's caravan and turned north. They chose a difficult road to Nisbis that would take them through steep mountain passes. They, too, were anxious to reach their destination.

Chapter XI – The Wrath of Angra Mainyu, God of Darkness

Balthasar's caravan traveled at a steady pace as they moved through the mountains toward Ctesiphon. Melchoir's map and the information supplied by Sahi were helpful in planning their rest stops, locating sources of water and finding game. Sahi was also kind enough to mark Melchoir's map to show the streams where he had trapped fish.

No longer under the protection of the militia, Balthasar's men were now responsible for their own safety. Having traveled under the protection of both Seres and Persian militias, the men learned a great deal about guarding the caravan and avoiding the dangers of the road. Although much grumbling continued, Balthasar's men were growing used to their camels. They were not as comfortable as their horses, but they had proven their hardiness and had yet to present any problems during the trip.

On the morning the caravan began its descent from the mountains, Melchoir discussed an area of his map with his friends. "As you can see, we will not pass another village until we are down from the mountain. Perhaps tomorrow afternoon we will be on level ground and in Ctesiphon by week's end," he said.

"We should have an easy time of it these next few days," Balthasar responded as he studied the map.

"Travel is never easy, but the road will soon widen and there will be fewer steep hills," replied Melchoir.

Within a few hours into this day's journey, the gentle breeze that greeted them in the morning had grown in strength and as the wind grew, the sky began to darken.

Balthasar asked Melchoir, "Are we about to get wet, or will these clouds pass us by?"

"We cannot see enough sky from here to know. Perhaps it is just a shower that will soon pass. A little further down the road, we will be in an open area, where we will have a better view of the sky," Melchoir replied as he scanned the sky for more information.

But as the caravan entered the clearing, a few drops of rain began to fall.

"Let us wait here for a moment," suggested Melchoir.

The Magi watched the sky for a moment as the clouds grew darker and the wind became stronger.

"We are in for a storm. Hopefully it will be brief," Balthasar said as he counted men and carts to make sure all were in view. As they watched the sky, the rain drops became larger, making a faint "pop" sound as they hit the carts.

"Oh, that is not good," blurted Melchoir, looking in to the distance.

"What?" asked Balthasar.

"See how the sky is beginning to change color? It is taking on a shade of green," a worried Melchoir said as he pointed to a section of sky above them.

"How strange," Balthasar replied as he turned, looking at his men behind him to see if they had also noticed this development.

"And turning dark green quickly!" Gaspar shouted.

"We are in for trouble and we have no protection here!" shouted Melchoir, urgency in his voice that was not present mere seconds before.

"The trees behind us are closer, but it will take too long to turn around the carts," shouted Balthasar as it began to rain harder.

"Forward... Quickly... To the trees ahead... No time to waste... Seek shelter quickly... Follow Balthasar as fast as you can ride," shouted Melchoir, with pauses in his breath to increase the volume of his voice in competition with the sound of the heavily falling rain.

Hutan took an arrow from his quiver and used it to slap each camel and horse on its rear as he rode toward the end of the caravan, shouting for everyone to move. At that instant, the clouds broke apart and the rain poured on them, with the wind still strengthening, blowing the rain sideways.

It took several minutes for most of the caravan to take cover under the trees. As Melchoir assisted three men on horseback whose carts remained in the open, they shouted and kicked their horses as they struggled to stay on the road in the blinding rain. Then, just as quickly as it started, the rain stopped. The wind slowed and all became silent, an eerie quiet that consumed all of the men and everything around them.

"Keep moving! Do not stop. The storm is not over!" Melchoir shouted.

In a few seconds, small drops of hail began to fall. Like the rain, they dropped slowly at first, then picked up speed, hitting the ground with force. Then claps of thunder brought lightening flashes, frightening the men and their animals.

"Hurry, Hurry!" shouted Melchoir as he pulled on the reins of his camel, positioning himself behind the last of the carts.

The hail stones quickly became larger and fell in greater number, while the thunder and lightning remained constant. Melchoir pulled a blanket over himself as he rode, but it did little good to shield from the hail.

"Move! Move! Move!" Melchoir shouted to the men as they were pummeled by hail.

The men yelled as the hail pierced their skin and the horses pulling the carts slowed and whinnied from the pain of the hail.

Realizing that they had run out of time, Melchoir directed the men, "Untie the horses and leave the carts! Run to safety! Now!"

Leaving the carts behind, the four men kicked their animals and followed Melchoir toward the trees. The hail now covered the road, making it difficult for the animals to stand. Melchoir looked at the ground in amazement, as some of the hail stones were beyond his imagination. The horse carrying Zinawar lost its footing on the hail, stumbled and fell to the ground in great pain. As a result of the fall, one of its front legs dangled oddly, and the injured horse desperately tried to rise, but could not stand. The hail continued to add to the animal's pain, but Zinawar alone could not do anything to help his fallen animal.

"Help! My horse is down!" shouted Zinawar.

But Melchoir, ahead of Zinawar, did not hear his cry. Only Hutan, the last rider, saw what happened. As he rode toward his fallen friend, he drew his bow and shot an arrow through the heart of the fallen horse, ending its misery. Hutan reached for Zinawar and in one motion, lifted and swung Zinawar onto his horse. Zinawar clung to Hutan with both arms as they rode to the trees. But Hutan's horse was also overcome with pain from the hail and stopped abruptly, rearing up on his hind legs, causing Hutan and Zinawar to tumble backwards onto the ground. Before they could get to their feet, Hutan's horse was gone, racing toward the trees.

Both men covered their heads with their arms, while Hutan shouted to Zinawar, "Run to the carts, it is our only chance!"

Both men ran for cover by the carts. Although only a short distance, it seemed to take forever to reach them through the pounding hail. Hutan passed the first cart, leaving it for Zinawar, then dove head first under the second cart. When he hit the ground, he turned to see Zinawar slide under the first cart. Both men covered their heads with their arms and brought their knees up to their chests to protect their bodies as the hail stones smashed into the carts with great force, producing a loud crack with each hit.

Under the partial protection of the trees, the Magi watched in horror as Hutan and Zinawar struggled for their lives. The wood of their carts could be heard breaking with each hit of hail. Some of the men huddling under the trees stretched blankets over themselves and their animals to soften the blow of the falling hail stones, while the Magi took cover under a large piece of thick tree bark. Balthasar and Gaspar grasped the bark tightly, holding it above their heads as Melchoir stood between them.

Melchoir bent down to pick up a large piece of hail, comparing it to his clenched fist. The Magi looked at each other in amazement; Melchoir's fist and the hail stone were the same size. But they were not able to comment on their amazement, as the sound of the hail hitting around them was deafening and louder than their voices could carry. When one large piece of hail hit their bark, the bark was knocked from their hands, but still nothing could be heard but the smashing of the hail. Broken tree branches began falling around them and the ground was growing white with ice. What at first seemed to be an oddity and annoyance was causing great fear, with all that was happening around the men.

"If the hail does not kill us, the tree limbs will," shouted Balthasar.

"What shall we do?" shouted Melchoir.

"Pray!" shouted Gaspar and Balthasar in unison, screaming so their voices could combat the noise of the falling hail. The Magi got down on one knee as Balthasar and Gaspar tried to steady the remaining bark above their heads.

"Ahura Mazda, we have come too far to have this journey end because of falling ice. Please spare us and our animals," prayed Balthasar.

With the hail crashing around them, Melchoir and Gaspar did not hear a word of Balthasar's prayer. They prayed to themselves, asking Ahura Mazda to spare them. The three stayed on one knee as the hail bounced off the bark held above their heads and ice piled up around them. As they huddled praying, they noticed that the size of the hail began to shrink and, after a few minutes, the hail was replaced by heavy rain. The Magi stood and dropped their protective bark, watching as the rain slowed to a drizzle.

Gaspar left the protection of the trees and moved carefully through the hail that covered the ground. Afraid to lift his feet, he slid slowly through the ice clumps and motioned for Balthasar and Melchoir to join him. They walked beyond the trees to get a view of the clearing sky, where they saw that a magnificent double rainbow stretched across the sky to replace the rain clouds.

Seeing their men moving about, Balthasar shouted back to them, "Keep the animals still until some of the ice melts."

"It will be hours before it is safe to move the animals," grumbled Gaspar.

Hutan approached the Magi, cautious of his footing, and reported, "The boys are fine. The rest of us have many bruises, with a few cuts to heads and arms."

"And the animals?" asked Balthasar.

"I cannot be certain until we walk them. The horses caught in the open are badly bruised and cut by the ice. We will be lucky if they are able to walk, let alone healthy enough to pull a cart," Hutan answered.

Once the ice melted enough to provide safe movement, the men tested the animals. Balthasar and Gaspar watched as the injured horses and camels were led around in a circle. Hutan briefly shook his head from side to side and motioned for the men to stop the animals.

"They are not able to pull carts. Put some sap on those wounds so they do not get infected," Hutan ordered.

The men mixed tree sap with some dried plants they carried for this purpose, gently applying the mixture to the wounds in generous amounts, as their leader had ordered.

After applying the ointment and monitoring the horses briefly, Hutan again reported back to the Magi, "They are hurting and I fear that we will not even be able to get a blanket on them without causing pain."

"In that case, I suggest we spend the night in this place and take our time preparing for travel. We could all use some time to recover," responded Gaspar.

The men worked quietly for the remainder of the day, fixing their carts and caring for the injured animals. The men talked at length about the hail storm and they were quite upset about the experience and what happened. It was difficult for them to turn their thoughts to something else, since much of the ice remained on the ground, and the hail that collected in the shadow of the trees was even slower to melt.

The Magi conducted an Afrinagan that evening, during which many prayers of thanks were offered. When the prayers and songs ended, the Magi relaxed next to the fire. Melchoir scooped up a handful of ice, shaped it into a ball and held it lightly on top of his head. After a few minutes, he moved the ice to one of his shoulders.

Watching him tending to his sore limbs, Balthasar asked, "How are you feeling? Any relief from the swelling?"

"Ughhh!" grunted Melchoir.

"Would you like more ice?" Balthasar offered.

Melchoir raised his head and mumbled, "There is not enough ice to sooth this aching body."

After a few moments of silence, Gaspar stirred a stick around in the fire and spoke.

"If I had not witnessed what happened, I would not believe that a hail storm could be so violent. Have either of you ever seen such large hail?" he asked.

To sore to speak, Melchoir shook his head.

"I have been caught in a hail storm before, but never like the one today. How can one even explain such a thing?" asked Balthasar.

"Is it the work of Angra Mainyu?" asked a grimacing Melchoir.

"You told us that Angra Mainyu would put obstacles in our path. Do you believe the hail was the work of Angra Mainyu? This time of year… in this place… it must be common to see hail," answered Balthasar.

"Hail the size of my fist? That surely is not common to this place, or to any place. Trust me. There will be more problems. We should be cautious with every step until we reach Jerusalem," answered Melchoir as he held his head with both hands.

Balthasar turned to Gaspar for his reaction.

"Do not look to me for answers. What Melchoir suggests may be true. I am not saying that all of our problems are caused by Angra Mainyu. Consider the bandits who attacked us, for example. Did Angra Mainyu send them, or were we just a convenient target? Now, pummeled by great balls of ice… that is much harder to explain. It could be the work of Angra Mainyu. Perhaps Melchoir led him to us. We did not have these strange happenings until Melchoir joined us," Gaspar said with a smile.

Melchoir returned the dripping ice ball to his head and mumbled, "Laughter is good. I would join you if I was not so sore. I do not want to discourage anyone because that would please Angra Mainyu, but remember what I say: The most difficult part of our journey is yet to come." Melchior took one last sip of tu before tossing the remaining liquid from his cup.

The following morning, final repairs were made to the damaged carts before they were packed. Once ready, Balthasar placed two fingers in his mouth and blew a shrill whistle, the signal to start the caravan moving, but they moved slowly and rested frequently to accommodate the injured horses. During the ride, the men discussed the hail storm at length. With so many injured men and animals, the hail remained fresh in everyone's minds. There was also a growing fear among the men that there would be even more problems and, with that, more danger.

When the caravan stopped for an afternoon rest, Hutan spoke with Balthasar and Gaspar, relaying these concerns of the men.

"Our brave men are in fear because of an ice storm?" asked Gaspar.

"The hail was strange. When our caravan left the storm area, it was clear that the hail did not cover much land. It only fell around us! The men are frightened. They need an explanation," Hutan calmly replied.

"We will speak with them this evening. For now, tell the men that there is nothing to fear," Balthasar replied.

Hutan turned his horse and trotted toward the rear of the caravan while Gaspar spoke with Balthasar.

"I am relieved to hear that we have nothing to fear! What are you going to tell them?" Gaspar asked.

"Surely Ahura Mazda and the Hebrew god will deliver us safely in Jerusalem. It would be good for us to better know the Hebrew god. Perhaps Ethan can tell us if the Hebrew god will protect those who follow Ahura Mazda."

When the caravan came to rest, Balthasar asked Ethan to join him and Gaspar in speaking to the men after supper. The men began assembling before the Magi finished their supper.

Balthasar rose to speak and said, "Men, I know that this has been a difficult journey. We have been attacked by bandits, caught in a rock slide and battered by hail stones. And one of us continues to suffer from the lick of a ferocious tiger!"

This brought a quiet laugh and a few jeers to Vanghav, of whom Balthasar spoke.

Balthasar continued, "We have heard our Seres friends say that 'a gem is not polished without rubbing, nor a man perfected without trials.' Well, the trouble we have faced has made us better and wiser men. Remember, we have taken every precaution to keep our journey safe. Given the distance we have traveled and the dangers we have encountered, we have done quite well. Yet, there is always a risk of danger on a journey such as this. We cannot explain the hail storm. It was terrifying and beyond our understanding, but it is behind us now. We are no longer in danger. We lost a horse and suffered a few bumps and bruises, but we survived. Was it a coincidence that we happened upon our location just as nature unleashed its fury? Was it the work of Angra Mainyu, trying to discourage us from continuing on to Jerusalem?"

The men listened intently as Balthasar spoke of the matter that was on their minds.

"I do not know if Angra Mainyu has been at work in our misfortune. But I do know that Ahura Mazda has been with our every step. It may even be that the Hebrew god has helped save our skin. It is important to remember that we have overcome many challenges and suffered little damage, even when it appeared that we would suffer great harm," assured Balthasar.

Balthasar paused for a moment as he studied the men's faces and then continued in a reassuring voice, "When we were attacked by the bandits with Zheng's men hiding in the carts, we were heavily outnumbered.

We could have been butchered to pieces, but none of us received so much as a scratch. I am convinced that our good fortune is not a coincidence. You can decide for yourself about these things, but in my heart, I believe that we are being protected by the Hebrew god. For reasons I do not fully understand, I believe that the Hebrew god is among us and wants us to arrive in Jerusalem safely.

"Ethan knows far more about his god than I. I call upon Ethan to tell us about his god, so we might learn if his God helps those who seek him," Balthasar concluded, motioning Ethan to join him up front.

The men looked at each other in amazement. The Magi had never recognized another god in this way. Suggesting that another god could be protecting them was shocking news and it was more of a shock to hear this statement from their leader, a Magi. Gaspar and Melchoir did not say a word, only nodded in approval to Balthasar when he had finished speaking.

Ethan rose and took his position beside Balthasar. Before speaking, he jumped onto a nearby rock so he could be better seen and heard by the men.

Gaspar whispered to Balthasar, "What will Ethan say?"

"Ethan knows his god and he knows what troubles the men. Whatever he says will be the truth," whispered Balthasar.

"Soon after we began our journey, I spoke to you about our prophet Daniel. God had given him the power to interpret the King's dreams and to predict God's will," Ethan began.

The men nodded, indicating that they remembered the story of which Ethan spoke.

Ethan continued, "There is another story about Daniel in our scriptures that I will share. Daniel was a loyal and obedient servant to King Darius. The King rewarded Daniel by giving him great responsibilities, which he carried out with precision and honesty. The King had such great respect for Daniel that he planned to give him authority over the entire kingdom. But the satraps, the King's governors, became jealous of Daniel and schemed to trap him so they could bring charges against him. As hard as they tried, the satraps could find no corruption in Daniel because he was trustworthy. But knowing that Daniel was obedient to his God, the satraps asked the King to issue a written, unalterable edict declaring anyone who prays to any god or to any man except to the King, for thirty days, would be thrown into the lions' den. When Daniel learned about the decree, he prayed to his God, prompting the satraps to tell the King that Daniel still prayed to his God. When the King heard this, he was greatly distressed, but was compelled by law to throw Daniel into the lions' den, saying, 'May your god, whom you serve continually, rescue you!'"

Taking a moment to drink from his sheep skin, Ethan glanced at the faces of the men. He had their complete attention as he continued, "A stone was placed over the entrance of the den and the King sealed it with his ring, so that Daniel's situation could not be changed. But the next morning, when the King arrived at the lions' den, he called out, 'Daniel, servant of the living god, has your god, whom you serve continually, been able to rescue you from the lions?' Daniel answered, 'God sent his angel to shut the mouths of the lions.' Daniel explained that he was not hurt because he was innocent in God's sight and that he had never done any wrong to the

King. When the King heard this, he was overjoyed, giving orders to lift Daniel from the den. When Daniel reemerged, he was free from wounds, because he had trusted in God."

The men remained captivated by Ethan's story. When Ethan appeared to have finished speaking, Kanuka asked, "A great and powerful god who closes the mouths of hungry lions, why would he go to such trouble for one man?"

Ethan smiled, expecting one of the men to ask such a question, and said, "Each one of us is loved by my God as Daniel was loved by Him. You may not know my God, but He knows you."

Ethan continued, "There was even another time when God saved Daniel from great danger. On one occasion, God gave Daniel a magnificent vision lasting more than three weeks. God used the vision to show Daniel the future of God's people. Daniel became very weak while receiving the vision because he had little food and drink, so God's enemy, Satan, being a coward and an enemy of both God and Daniel, sought to attack him in his weakened condition. But God sent Michael, his powerful angel, to keep Daniel safe."

"Why do you think God sent his angel to protect Daniel from the lions and from Satan? God protected Daniel because he was obedient to God. He prayed and trusted his life to God," Ethan added.

Ethan paused again, searching for comforting words, and said, "I am a Jew. Daniel's God is my God. I joined you in this journey because I know in my heart that my God hung the star over Jerusalem for all people who seek him. If this were not true, you would not be able to see the star!"

Upon hearing this, the men began to talk among themselves. Were they being led away from Ahura Mazda? Ethan attempted to continue, but the men were in an uproar. Balthasar stood and, with his hands, pushed downward as a sign to be quiet.

Ethan began again. "There are many things that I do not understand about God. No man can know everything about God. I am not certain about what awaits us in Jerusalem, but I have faith in my Scriptures and I know that my God will protect the people who seek Him, just as he protected Daniel. We may have more problems on this journey, like bad weather, bandits, or perhaps Angra Mainyu himself will come after us! But take comfort in knowing that God will be with us!"

Ethan jumped off the rock and took his place among the men. The men, who moments ago were boisterous, were now silent and many wore smiles. The Magi knew that Ethan touched the men's hearts just as he had done to the Magi. When the prayers were given at the evening's Afrinagan, Ethan offered a prayer from one of his scriptures.

"Do not withhold your mercy from me, O Lord; may your love and your truth always protect me," sang Ethan to the accompaniment of the instruments.

Later in the evening, the Magi discussed Ethan's prayer. "Having Ethan pray to his god was not something we have included in the Afrinagan, but I could find no fault with it," offered Balthasar.

Melchoir and Gaspar nodded in approval and Gaspar responded, "The men accepted Ethan's prayer and song enthusiastically. We know in our hearts that he speaks the truth."

"I have never known an Afrinagan that includes homage to another god. Yet these are different times. The star is changing what we know as truth. What a remarkable star! What a remarkable time in which we live!" added Melchoir.

"Our fathers were wise and faithful men. Have you thought of how they would have considered this star and the god who sent it?" asked Balthasar.

"Our fathers would be doing as we do," answered Gaspar confidently.

The following morning, the caravan maneuvered over the winding road out of the mountains and within a few days, Ctesiphon was in sight. As they neared the city, the road was active with travelers. Militia groups, merchants and farmers were among those entering and leaving the city. Just outside the city, the caravan met a group of musicians and performers who prepared to enter the city with great fanfare. Balthasar's men were amused with the sight of the musicians and their brightly colored costumes. Ctesiphon promised to be an interesting place.

Chapter XII - Ctesiphon, City of Many Gods

Once inside the city, Balthasar's men were amazed at the sights. Merchants sold spices, perfumes, clothing and many other items that they had not seen before. Melchoir stopped at one merchant's tent to show his friends Egyptian breastplates that were used in battle. For several hours, the men visited the carts and tents of the merchants, sampling and buying unusual spices, fresh fruit and meat. At supper that evening, the men discussed what they had seen.
    Balthasar asked, "Hutan, what was it that you saw today that interested you?"
    Without hesitation, Hutan replied, "Why, the women, of course!"
    The men erupted in laughter until Balthasar asked, "Surely you have seen beautiful women before?"
    "It is the women who dance. I have never seen women dance in that way. Their stomachs roll to the music like water on a lake!" answered Hutan. The men whistled in agreement as Hutan continued, "So graceful, so exciting... so..."
    Balthasar interrupted, "Yes, the women are quite interesting."
    But hoping to change the subject, he moved to face Pulan and asked what his favorite part of the day entailed.
    Pulan responded, "The way in which the dancers threw their hair back and forth to the beat of the music. We were all put in a trance! It was fantastic!"
    Again there was a roar of laughter as Balthasar said, "I see that there is great interest in the women." He shook his head briefly and, with a smile, announced,

"Tomorrow, we will make our repairs and find supplies. Melchoir will help us replace our remaining horses with camels, so you will need to assist him when he calls upon you."

The men groaned after hearing the orders and a few of them begin to protest.

"We have enough camels!" one man shouted.

"I would rather walk!" shouted another.

But Balthasar dismissed their concerns, saying, "Once we leave Ctesiphon, you will be glad to have camels. The desert will devour our horses!" With that, the men realized they had no more say in the matter and accepted their defeat before falling asleep.

Ctesiphon was one of Persia's great cities. Built on the east bank of the mighty Tigris River, the city was home to a diverse group of people and an important trade center. It had also been home to many of Persia's rulers. Over the years, Ctesiphon had grown to cover a large area, making it one of the largest cities in this part of the world. Persian kings had always protected the city with a strong militia. Several hazarabams, each with more than one thousand men, were stationed there. Their leaders, the hazarapatish, could be seen moving about the city with their escorts.

The following morning, Melchoir instructed the men as he prepared two horses for trade. "If you are carrying heavy coats and blankets, this would be a good time to trade them. You will need light, loose fitting clothes for the desert. A light blanket or two will keep you warm at night. Do not weigh down our carts with things that are no longer needed."

Several of Balthasar's men accompanied Melchoir as he bargained with the merchants. As they made their way through the center of the city, they were distracted by several groups of men who were playing a game. Pulan, Ethan and several others squeezed in among the group where there was much shouting and cheering.

Not wanting to be delayed, Melchoir called out, "Stay away from there! Keep with me!"

Pulan glanced back as he raised his hand to signal that he heard Melchoir's call.

"We will be right there!" shouted Pulan as he and the others waded deeper into the crowd.

Melchoir shook his head and said to Nekdel and Rushad, "Do not mind them. We do not have time for such nonsense. Let us be on our way."

"We are not going to wait?" asked Nekdel.

"They will find us or they will find their way back to the caravan. They are not our concern," Melchoir snapped as he grabbed the boys by the arm and led them away from the crowd of shouting men.

Pulan and his companions were captivated with the site of men casting a handful of bones and wagering on how they would fall. Another group of men cast pieces of wood in the same manner. One of the men in Pulan's group attempted to join in the wagering, but Ethan grabbed his arm before he could toss in a coin.

"Time for us to go! This is not for us," Ethan said to his companions.

They maneuvered out of the crowd and along the row of merchants until they found Melchoir.

"Have you satisfied your curiosity?" he asked the men.

"It was quite fascinating… but not for us," replied Pulan.

"I hope it was not an expensive experience," said Melchoir.

"Oh, no, we did not wager," answered Ethan.

When the group returned to the caravan, Rushad and Nekdel told Balthasar about the men casting lots. Knowing that Nekdel was aware of the Magi's dislike of casting lots, Balthasar sensed concern in Nekdel's voice.

"Nekdel, the problem is not with the pieces of wood, stones, or bones. It is how they are used that becomes a problem. Back in Asdin, we sometimes cast lots when we need to choose someone for something. Lots are a way to keep the choosing fair. There is nothing wrong with casting lots in this way. But the men you saw today were wagering on the lots," explained Balthasar.

"Yes, and that is just the beginning of the problem with lots. Some men will cast lots to predict the future or will claim that the lots show them God's will. This is very dangerous and will surely bring trouble!" added Melchoir.

That evening, the men continued their conversations about the many activities in the city, but the Magi ignored the discussion until Melchoir observed Nekdel and Rushad listening intently. Melchoir stood to speak and the men became quiet to hear him.

"Women dancing wildly, casting lots for money, men using bones to tell the future: these are foreign customs that we do not need in Persia. I tell you that nothing good can come of such things," Melchoir warned.

"But *we* dance, *we* cast lots, *we* look for signs in the heavens that point to the future!" blurted Rushad in protest.

As the men laughed quietly, Melchoir smiled and replied, "Yes, we do all of these things. But as your uncle has told you, it is what we intend by our actions that is important. Unfortunately, the things you witnessed have become a common practice in Ctesiphon, and, I am sad to say, these shameful things are becoming popular in other parts of Persia as well. Persia will pay a steep price for this behavior!" But when Melchoir looked around at the men and saw that his cautions had had no impact, he continued in an attempt to clarify, "Tossing bones and pieces of wood can be harmless, but they can also be used for a darker purpose."

Melchoir looked among the men and then called, "Ethan! What do your Scriptures teach about casting lots?"

Ethan replied, "My scriptures teach that when men of God cast lots, it is done with God's purpose in mind. To be certain, there is nothing that happens by chance to any of us. Our Proverbs declare that the lot is cast into the lap, but its every decision is from the Lord."

One of the men called out to Ethan, "How does a man cast lots to serve God?"

Ethan shook his head and replied, "Let me explain. I am not saying that any of us should cast lots with the intent to determine God's purpose. But is has been done in this way. It is only when men place their faith and trust in God that it may further his purpose to have lots cast. Let me share this story from my scriptures."

Worried that the men would criticize him for telling another story about his god, Ethan paused before he began. But when there was no opposition, he spoke loud enough for all the men to hear and said, "There was a time when lots were cast to discover who had sinned, to avoid everyone suffering for the sins of one man. God saw to it that the guilty man drew the short lot. The

Scriptures record an occasion when lots revealed that a man called Achan had disobeyed God by stealing from the spoils of Jericho after its capture by the Israelites. Lots also showed that King Saul's son, Jonathan, had sinned against God by eating honey, after Saul swore an oath that his soldiers would fast until his enemies were defeated. And do you remember the story of Jonah, the man who was swallowed by a whale? The sailors on his ship made everyone cast lots to determine who was guilty of bringing the storm upon them. When the lot fell upon Jonah, he was thrown overboard. I tell you, God may choose to reveal his purpose to men who are obedient to Him. But when diviners cast lots, they do so to bring profit or glory to themselves. This does not bring honor to God. God commands us not to do as the diviners!" Ethan pointed to the men, who were still listening intently to his words.

 When Ethan finished, Melchoir placed his arm around him and, leading him away from the rest of the men, said, "Let us talk about the stars. As Magi, we have studied the heavens all our lives. For generations, Magi have watched for signs in the night sky that might hold important news for our kings and for Persia. We have been careful to use our knowledge wisely, but we know of men who study the stars for a darker purpose. It was a sad day for Persia when some of its sons began naming the stars and giving names to the images they formed in the night sky. Persians who do not know Ahura Mazda began worshipping the stars and making predictions for people based on the star under which they were born."

 Ethan nodded, understanding what Melchoir told him as things he had learned from stories and previous travels.

"You already know of that nonsense," Melchoir continued. "But it was not long before this evil practice spread to other lands. As you have seen here in Ctesiphon, our Greek friends have designed an elaborate story based on the stars. You have seen their charts! They imagine that their gods have origins in the stars. Believers of this false story are happy to persuade you that your futures are connected to the stars, but be warned: this wretched advice does not come free. You will be required to pay for this rubbish! The Greeks are not the only ones who follow this practice. The Romans and, I am sorry to say, some Egyptians, have fallen to worshipping the stars and the gods they have assigned to them."

When Ethan and Melchoir had finished speaking, the other Magi used this opportunity to satisfy their own curiosity.

"Ethan! It is your god who has placed the magnificent star in the heavens for us. What does your scripture teach about the stars?" asked Balthasar.

"Our Scriptures are clear; we are to worship God, not his creation. God made the stars as he has made all things and he warns that those who worship the stars will be judged by God! When the Israelites came into the Promised Land, they saw people worshipping the stars, telling fortunes and speaking with spirits. God told the Israelites that when they see the sun, the moon and the stars, they should not bow down to worship them. There is no doubt that God uses stars to get our attention, just as he has done with his star that we follow."

The Magi listened carefully, trying to understand this Hebrew god from the stories Ethan shared.

Ethan continued, "Our prophet Isaiah warns about those who study the stars to predict the future. He says that God's fire will burn them up like stubble. Our prophet Jeremiah commands us to ignore fortune tellers, dreamers, conjurers, or sorcerers, because their customs are a delusion. Not everyone abided by the words of our prophets. God destroyed the ten northern tribes of Israel because they bowed down to the stars and worshipped demons. God became so angry with Israel that He destroyed all of the tribes, except for the tribe of Judah. But when Judah also turned to these evil practices, God placed the people of Judah in bondage and exiled them to many different lands," replied Ethan.

Silence fell over the men as Ethan's closing words left his lips. The Magi had studied the stars and the signs of heaven and were revered greatly for this skill, but there was still more for them to learn.

Nekdel called to his father, "Do we anger Ethan's God by looking for signs in the heavens?"

"We do not worship the stars, we marvel at their beauty, just as we praise Ahura Mazda for all of his creation," responded Balthasar.

After pausing briefly to gather his thoughts, Balthasar continued, "We look for signs in the heavens, but not as the sorcerers do. We look for signs that we can share with our kings and for all of Persia, but not for our own benefit. My heart tells me that this is not displeasing to Ethan's god. If we displease him, he would not reveal his star to our Persian eyes."

When Balthasar sat, the men continued with their conversations. It was not long before the men were talking about different religions, some that they first learned of in Ctesiphon.

After listening to these discussions, Nekdel returned to his father and asked, "Father, today we saw people worshipping before altars and calling out to gods who seem quite strange to us. Who are these gods?"

"That is not an easy question, Nekdel. Some of the people you saw today were worshipping the gods of the Greeks and the Romans. They have many gods, too many for me to know. We have only one god: Ahura Mazda. For the Greeks, Zeus is their God of the Sky and ruler of all other gods. The Romans worship a supreme god they call Jupiter. The Greeks and Romans also have gods that rule the sea, the underworld and even war. But we have only one god: Ahura Mazda," answered Balthasar.

"What are the rest of their names? Are they powerful gods?" asked a persistent Nekdel.

Balthasar looked at Melchoir, who was listening to Nekdel's questions, and asked, "Perhaps Melchoir knows these gods?"

"Nekdel, it is all rubbish! Every bit of it rubbish! Yes, I have heard of their gods and they are many. The god who rules the sea for the Greeks is known as Poseidon. The Romans call upon their sea god, Neptune. And I know of their gods of war. The Romans also worship a god called Mars, while the Greeks bow down to Ares," instructed Melchoir.

"What god do the people worship in Egypt?" asked Nekdel.

"Many Egyptians worship the gods Isis and Osiris. Their story is a strange one. It is said that a god known as Re placed a curse on the goddess Nut, so she could not have children. But she was able to break the curse with the help of another god and had several children, including a son, Osiris, and a daughter, Isis. These brother and sister Gods were said to have married and they are the gods that many Egyptians worship today. You saw some

Egyptians in Ctesiphon today who are followers of Isis and Osiris. Does this religion seem strange to you?" asked Melchoir.

"Yes," nodded Nekdel, not quite sure if he was understanding what Melchoir was telling him.

"You are a smart boy. It is a very strange religion. It makes as much sense as worshipping a horse!" Melchoir said, letting out a small laugh.

With this, Balthasar decided to address his son on the matter, saying, "Many of our Persian friends who do not share our Magi beliefs have also adopted these foreign gods."

Before he could explain further, Melchoir cut in, adding, "Persians are too hasty in accepting foreign customs. It is one thing to wear their garments and eat the food of foreigners, but it is something quite different to worship many gods, to have many wives, to share the unnatural lust of the Greeks! Shall I go on?"

Sensing a captivated Melchoir, Gaspar stepped in, joining the conversation by saying, "Yes, Persians are embracing some dangerous customs, but our people continue to honor each other. We do not speak of those things that are unlawful. We take pride in saying the truth and we refrain from owing a debt. Unlike the foreigners who defile our land and water, we make great efforts to avoid such things. You will never see a Persian take a bath in a river like the foreigners. Who wants to drink from water that has been soiled? Perhaps our visitors will take some of our customs home with them!"

Nekdel followed every word and paused for a moment as he contemplated what had been said. With a puzzled look, he asked, "What about Ethan's god? We follow His star and we learn His teachings... do we anger Ahura Mazda?"

The men became silent after they heard Nekdel's question and turned to Balthasar for his response. Gaspar and Melchoir also looked to Balthasar for his response, but Balthasar just smiled at Nekdel and asked, "What does your heart say to you?"

Nekdel returned his father's smile and replied, "My heart tells me that Ahura Mazda is pleased with Ethan's god."

Balthasar nodded as he replied, "That is also what my heart says to me."

The men were pleased with this response and, a few moments later, several of the men walked into their circle, carrying trays of sweet cakes.

Everyone's eyes focused on the treats as Melchoir asked, "What is the occasion for this delight?"

Balthasar stood and announced in a loud voice, "It is my honor to be the first to congratulate Melchoir. Tomorrow is his birthday!" Quickly, the men congratulated Melchoir on his birthday before helping themselves to the cakes.

Balthasar held a cake high as he said, "One tradition that Persians honor faithfully is celebrating birthdays. You may not be able to tell by looking at him, but our good friend has celebrated a great many birthdays, far more than I; of this I am certain. We wish you well, good friend, and we pray that Ahura Mazda and Yahweh bless you with many more of these celebrations!"

In a brief moment, the cakes were gone.

The men were at peace this evening. Some of their contentment was the result of Melchoir's birthday celebration. But their recognition of the Hebrew God had eased the stirring in the heart that each man had struggled with for many months. There was much they did not yet understand, but there was enough to put their minds at ease.

On their final day in Ctesiphon, the men were busy organizing supplies, packing carts and tending to their animals. As some of the men prepared for travel, others got ready for the evening's feast in celebration of Melchoir's birthday. Persians observed birthdays as a celebration of life. During the course of the journey, each man's birthday was honored by his companions. Since Melchoir was their guest, his birthday was an even more special occasion. Melchoir accompanied Balthasar and Gaspar early in the morning to acquire an ox that would be the main course and the men took the ox back to their camp to kill it. A small tree was chopped down and fashioned into a pole to serve as a giant skewer, on which the ox was baked whole, all day, over a large pit. The men worked in shifts, turning the ox and fueling the fire, and as the aroma of the baking ox filled the air, the chore of packing the carts was made much easier this day with something exciting to look forward to in the evening.

When evening arrived, Balthasar began the celebration by raising his cup of wine, honoring his friend as he said, "To our brother, may God bless you and keep you in good health."

The men cheered as they drank their wine, and Melchoir accepted a freshly sharpened sword from Gaspar for carving the first piece of ox. He carefully carved a generous slice of juicy meat, still steaming from the heat of the fire.

Balthasar held a large plate to receive the first slab, and as Melchoir placed the sizzling meat on the plate, he announced, "Men! This piece is for you to share! The rest is mine!"

The laughter that erupted from Melchoir's joke carried for many hours while the men played their instruments and sang as the wine flowed and the men had their fill of food. It was much more than a birthday celebration; it was the last time to relax before returning to the road. It was also an intense spiritual time for them, as they came to realize that it was the Hebrew god who called them to Jerusalem.

Chapter XIII – Mercy in the Desert

All was quiet in the camp the morning the men departed from Ctesiphon. The evening's fire smoldered in the pit as a lone bird chirped to greet the new day. Nekdel and Rushad were the first to emerge from the tents, and after bringing a flame to the fire, they placed two large pots of water nearby before returning to the tents to wake their companions, who struggled to awaken as a result of last night's wine. After some prodding by the boys, the men finally assembled outside their tents, but were moving slowly and still not speaking above a strained whisper.

Rushad nudged Nekdel and said in a voice low enough for only the other boy to hear, "It is good that we are a small caravan. If there were many more birthday celebrations, we would never reach Jerusalem."

The boys giggled as they watched the painful expressions on their friends' faces as they readied themselves for the day.

The caravan usually departed within an hour of dawn, but this morning the men were moving a bit slower than usual. It was mid-morning when the caravan was finally packed and ready to move. Balthasar mounted his camel and led the caravan west out of Cresiphon toward the Euphrates River. They left the city without a military escort and Balthasar hoped they would be able to join other caravans along the way. They planned to follow the great river for two months until they reached their next destination, the oasis of Palmyra. There would even be times when their route would take them into the desert, but the men were prepared and growing more anxious by the day to reach their star. The men soon adjusted to their camels and, on their second day of travel, joined another caravan for a few days.

It was during their second week of travel when the road led the caravan into the desert, on a more direct route to Palmyra. They were only half a day's ride from the river, maneuvering around sand dunes, trying to keep their camels to the level areas, when Hutan first noticed the dark sky to the south and immediately alerted Balthasar.

"Look at the southern sky! If you can see through the haze, you will see dark clouds. A storm is approaching!" announced an alarmed Hutan.

The Magi watched the storm for a moment and then surveyed their surroundings.

"How bad is it?" Balthasar asked Melchoir, who used Hutan's shoulder to steady himself as he stood on his camel to get a better look.

"It is quite large and it is moving in our direction," replied Melchoir as he strained to see the storm through the glare of the desert.

Gaspar added, "I see flashes of light, but how bad can it be? We have been through severe thunderstorms before."

"But have you been through a storm in the desert?" asked Melchoir.

Before Gaspar could respond, Melchoir continued, "There will be sand! The greater the wind, the worse the sand!"

"There is no wind upon us now," said Balthasar, observing the still sand below his camel's feet.

"No, but it is coming," Melchoir said as he steadied himself again with a hand on Hutan's shoulder. He shielded the sun from his eyes with his other hand for a better view of the approaching storm. Dropping his hand from his eyes, he shook his head and mumbled as he lowered himself back onto his camel and said, "My eyes must deceive me, for it appears to be Angra Mainya himself."

Melchoir turned his camel around to face Balthasar and Gaspar. Pointing to the clouds on the horizon, he said, "Look at those clouds closely. See how the dark cloud in front does not rise as high as the lighter clouds behind it?"

"Yes, what does it mean?" asked Balthasar.

"A large sand storm leads the storm, a great wall of sand coming in our direction. I have seen them before… but none as large as this one!"

"Can we turn toward the river and out run it?" asked Gaspar.

"No, I estimate that we have about half of an hour before it is upon us. I suggest that we ride to the larger dunes ahead and take our position on the side with the wind, so we do not get buried. The sand will collect on the other side, but we need to hurry. Once the wind begins kicking up the sand, the camels may go crazy. They know when these things are coming before we do!" replied a worried, but excited Melchoir.

Hutan passed the word to the others and the caravan hurried toward the dunes. As they rode, Gaspar looked back several times to check on the position of the storm.

"Are you looking for the storm or for Angra Mainyu? I tell you, he is in there somewhere!" shouted Melchoir.

They reached the dune just as the wind began and it quickly gained speed mere seconds later. The men grimaced from the stinging sand, and when Balthasar and Melchoir reached the dune, they jumped from their camels and began directing the other men into position. As the wind increased, the camels bleated as they are stung by the sand. Melchoir caught a glimpse of one camel breaking out of line, running toward the east.

He shouted to Balthasar, "I am going after one of your men; he lost control of his camel," as he climbed onto his camel and began the chase. Balthasar grabbed Nekdel and Rushad and helped them under his cart as two-by-two, the men led their camels to spaces between the carts and tied them together to help protect the men from the stinging sand. Gaspar greeted each man with a water jar he held in one hand and a small jar of cooking oil in the other.

The men quickly dropped pieces of cloth into the water jar and wet their fingers with the oil, rubbing the insides of their noses to keep them moist from the sand and covering their faces with the wet cloth. Once under the carts, the men locked their arms to avoid being separated during the storm, but there was no way of knowing if the sand would blow for minutes, hours, or longer.

As Melchoir rode toward the runaway camel, he saw the rider kicking his camel and pulling hard on the reins in an effort to turn him. But this made the camel run faster, preventing Melchoir from gaining any ground. When the runaway began climbing a dune, Melchoir rode around the dune and was able to reach the rider and his frantic camel as they came down the other side.

Riding at full speed, Melchoir shouted at the rider, "Stop pulling on the reins! You will tear out his nose!" As ordered, the rider loosened the reins, but the camel kept running. "Hold on! He will slow down!" shouted Melchoir, and within moments, the camel had slowed to a trot.

"Hand me your reins! I will lead you back!" Melchoir shouted as he reached for the reins with one hand.

Turning into the blowing sand, Melchoir covered his face with cloth, leaving only small slits for his eyes. He kept his head down, only looking to ensure he was staying on course. When they returned to their dune, Melchoir tied the camels to the others before joining his rescued companion, whom he now recognized as Zinawar, under the carts. The men under the carts had also covered themselves with a piece of tent canvas, and when Melchoir and Zinawar also squeezed in underneath, one of the men handed them a wet cloth that they immediately placed over their noses and mouths. Linking arms with the others, they began praying for Ahura Mazda and Yahweh to save them.

The minutes turned into hours as the men lay covered, listening to the wind-blown sand hit the carts, their camels and themselves. Darkened from the sand, the sky lost its light, making the storm even more terrifying. As the hours passed, the men felt the sand piling up around them, and every few minutes, one of the men broke the arm link briefly to stretch, trying to bring relief to a cramp or shake feeling into a numb arm or leg.

It must be evening now. Perhaps the night will weaken the storm, Melchior thought.

It was a terrifying night as the men hid from the storm in complete darkness, half buried in sand. The storm produced deafening blasts of thunder and bolts of lightning, adding to the terror. Balthasar lay under his cart with Nekdel and Rushad under his arms. Every so often, Balthasar bumped the boys on the head with his elbow and waited for a bump back, reassuring him that the boys were still breathing.

It was late afternoon the following day when the wind lost its fury and the sky began to brighten. Balthasar slowly got on his hands and knees and called for his companions to begin digging out. Slowly, the men staggered to their feet. Sore from lying on their stomachs all night, the men groaned and complained as they stretched their stiff bodies. When Gaspar got to his feet, he moved slowly through the loose sand, calling out names to make sure all were present. The men shook the sand from their clothes and beards, and brushed the sand from each other's backs.

"You found us a good place to hide from the storm. We would not be alive if not for your help," Balthasar shouted as he turned to face to Melchoir. But when Balthasar did look north, where his friend stood, he was startled by what he saw. Ahead of them were newly formed dunes stretching for miles.

Melchoir's legs wobbled and nearly gave way as he took in the sight and replied, "Great waves on a lake... they are enormous! From where on this good earth could all of this sand have come?"

Gaspar shook his head and said, "Those dunes are higher than the one that saved us. We would have been buried alive, hidden forever had we tried to outrun the storm."

After several minutes of surveying the scene in disbelief, the men began working. Hutan and a few men tended to the camels while the others began digging out the cart wheels that were half covered in sand. Once the wheels were free, they began digging out the cargo, which was covered by more than two feet of sand.

Once everything was free of sand, the Magi brought the men together for prayer. Melchoir began with a quivering voice, "Great God in the heavens, be you Ahura Mazda or Yahweh of the Jews, we thank you from the deepest places of our hearts for saving us from destruction. We know that we could have been gone in an instant, buried forever, if you had not shown us mercy. Continue to protect us for we know that Angra Mainyu desires to end our journey and to bring an end to us."

Others offered prayers of thanks, but it was Melchoir's prayer that captured everyone's attention. It was this prayer that all would remember as the first time that one of the Magi called upon Ethan's god, the god of the Jews. The Magi had discussed the Hebrew god, but this was the first time that they had called upon Him in prayer. God's true identity was something that the Magi had been contemplating since each had first seen the star, and the men were also struggling with his identity. As they came to know Ethan's god, they were confused about their god, the god of their ancestors. The Magi could not have contemplated a time when any of them would call upon another god, certainly not in the presence of their companions. But there it was, out in the open and coming from the Magi most intolerant of other beliefs. Once said, it did not seem wrong or disrespectful to Ahura Mazda. It seemed to be a natural response to their circumstances. No one asked for an explanation and everyone was at peace within their own hearts.

There was a connection, a growing bond between them and the god whose star they sought. Anyone with doubts about the authority of this god only had to consider the star, for the idea that the star was not revealed to everyone was enough reason to pay homage to this god. As students of nature, the Magi were quite aware that what they were experiencing is God's direct intervention into their world. God was reaching into their lives in a way that they could have never imagined and, even now, could not fully explain. After their prayers, when the tents were erected and supper finished, the men prepared for a more restful night.

It was now that Melchoir said to his Magi friends, "About my prayer this evening, I praised the Hebrew..."

"There is no need to explain. God has revealed himself!" Balthasar interrupted.

Gaspar nodded in agreement and with a shrug said, "The truth is the truth!"

When the caravan was underway the next morning, it was slow going as the men led the camels carefully through the mounds of loose sand to avoid toppling the carts. It was the noon hour when Hutan noticed a piece of wood protruding from the sand and, leading his camel out of the line, jumped off so he could give the piece of wood a kick. Expecting the kick to free the wood, he was surprised when it did not budge. Hutan dropped to his knees and began digging with his hands around the wood so he could pull it from the sand. After several minutes of digging, Hutan noticed that one edge was connected to another piece of wood. He stopped digging and sat back on his knees to rest for a moment, considering whether he should bother any longer with the wood.

"What is the problem?" shouted Gaspar who trailed the last of the carts.

"I am not sure what this is; a box discarded by a caravan?" asked Hutan.

Gaspar motioned for two men to join him in helping Hutan dig out the box.

"Let us do this quickly so we do not fall behind," Gaspar said as he dropped to his knees with a small shovel in his hands that he retrieved from a cart.

After a few minutes of digging, one of the men uncovered the top of a wheel. "Oh no, when we began uncovering wood, I was afraid that it was an abandoned cart. Keep digging," Gaspar said as he directed the men and then rose to his feet. He placed his fingers in his mouth and lets out a shrill whistle, bringing the caravan to a stop.

In a moment, Balthasar arrived on his camel and asked, "Is there a problem?"

"Hutan found a cart buried in the sand. Normally, I would not bother with it. But after the storm, who knows what might lie with it," responded Gaspar who was back on his knees, digging with his hands.

Balthasar thought for a moment and then replied, "Let us put everyone to work so we can finish quickly."

Within minutes, all of the men were digging in the area next to the cart. And a few minutes later, someone shouted, "Something else here, another cart perhaps!"

Soon, the digging had uncovered three carts, and crates of supplies and other items, within a few feet of each other.

"This is not good. Perhaps the owners unhitched their camels, abandoned their carts and tried to outrun the storm… or perhaps they perished in the storm," Melchoir said as he looked at a folded tent lying in the bed of one of the carts.

But Melchoir's thoughts were interrupted by a scream from one of his men. Rushing over, all anyone could see was a hand that had been uncovered.

"Horrible! Buried alive, what could be worse?" Melchoir said as he motioned the men to keep digging.

When the men finished digging, they had uncovered the bodies of four men.

"What do you make of it?" Gaspar asked Melchoir.

"Who can be sure? The camels might have run away in the storm, or perhaps there were others who tried to outrun it. We may never know. Unfortunately, with no large dunes in this area, they had no place to take cover. No large dunes in this area. Looks as if this whole area is covered by several feet of new sand," answered Melchoir, observing his surroundings.

Gaspar shook his head and said to Balthasar, "That could be us buried beneath the sand. As quickly as the storm was upon us, there was no time to seek a safe place. Had we been a little further away from the dunes, we would have suffered the same fate."

"We should be thankful that we were spared, not troubled that it could have been us! Let us say prayers for these unfortunate men, provide them with a proper burial and be on our way," Balthasar replied.

Balthasar directed his men to lay out the four bodies on top of the sand so the hot sun would cook the flesh off of their bones and a few short prayers were offered. As the Magi discussed with their Mede friends, Persians would not defile the earth by placing a body into the ground.

They were within a week's journey of Palmyra, named for the city's many palm trees. They saw few caravans on the desert trail, but the number of travelers began to grow as they edged closer to Palmyra. It was late afternoon when the Magi found a small oasis to provide some relief from the sun and it was here that they discussed whether they should spend the night beneath the palms or push on towards Palmyra. As they talked, Melchoir rose to his feet, shielded his eyes with his hands and scanned the southern horizon.

"What is it?" asked Balthasar.

"Many riders come from the south. The breeze picks up their sand," Melchoir answered.

"How many?" a surprised Balthasar asked, not even sure as to how Melchoir could sense such things.

"A hundred riders, perhaps more," Melchoir answered in a tone that seemed to question his response.

Gaspar jumped to his feet and asked in disbelief, "A hundred riders… here?"

Balthasar joined his friends in straining to see who was coming their way. "Who could be traveling in such numbers… in the middle of the desert?" asked Balthasar with a puzzled look.

"Persian or Roman soldiers," replied Melchoir.

"Romans? Here?" asked a bewildered Gaspar.

"Palmyra has become a popular place. The Romans like its location near the mouths of the two great rivers. If they gain control of the region, they will control trade. They know the value of what passes through here because much of it finds its way to Rome!" Melchoir replied with a laugh.

"But this is Persia! Where is the Persian militia?" asked Gaspar.

"Oh, the Persians are here, too! Although they paid little attention to Palmyra until the Romans came visiting," Melchoir retorted.

"Since we are not sure if our visitors are friend or foe, I suggest we leave here quickly," Balthasar said as he took a drink from his sheep skin.

"A wise suggestion. That many men – out here – there are too few of us and our cargo is too valuable to take the chance. We have a quarter of an hour to get ourselves out of sight. On the other hand, most Romans will recognize Magi as ambassadors and will not interfere with our affairs," answered Melchoir with a worried look.

"We cannot take the risk! Nothing has been unpacked. All that needs to be done is to tie the carts to the camels," Balthasar said as he ordered the men to move.

Balthasar led the caravan toward several large dunes they maneuvered around to hide from view. Melchoir trailed the caravan at a distance with Hutan. They decided to watch the arrival of the riders from a distance to make sure they were not followed.

Perched on top of a dune, the two noticed that the caravan was out of sight behind them when the first of the riders came into view. Hutan began counting them as they arrived.

"There is no need to count them. We should know in a moment if there are many or few, and if they will rest or come after us," Melchoir instructed.

Two by two, the riders on camels arrived; some of the camels pulled carts, others were heavily packed.

"Well, look at that, some of those men are on foot, walking through the blazing sand! They are either very rugged men or are out of their minds," Melchoir said to Hutan in a whisper.

"Why are you whispering? They cannot hear us," Hutan replied.

"The wind carries sound a great distance in the desert, and we can never be too careful."

The two watched as the riders settled in around the palms.

"Oh no, it looks like they have found our tracks," Hutan said in a barely audible whisper.

"The first soldiers to reach the palms saw our tracks, but no one seems anxious to follow after us. And why do you whisper so quietly? They are not going to hear you if I cannot."

But it was not until Melchoir was certain that the Romans had no interest in pursuing their caravan that he tapped Hutan on the shoulder and they crawled down the hidden side of the dune.

When they reached their waiting camels, Hutan asked, "Are we safe? Perhaps we should watch a little longer."

"If we wait much longer, we may not find the caravan. I am not certain in which direction Balthasar has taken them and if the wind becomes much stronger, their tracks may disappear," cautioned Melchoir.

"Then let us get moving," Hutan said as he pulled down on the reins of his camel and gave the command for the camel to sit.

The two lost the caravan's tracks a few times, but, after searching, were once again able to locate them. As they reached the top of one dune, the tracks completely disappeared. The two circled in opposite directions, hoping to pick up the tracks again. When they met, they were quite concerned about their situation.

"I do not understand. The wind has not been strong enough to cover so many tracks so quickly!" Hutan said, his voice quivering.

Melchoir looked at the sand beneath his camel and said a prayer. When he raised his head, he turned to the west and smiled. Melchoir nodded to Hutan and said softly, "There they are."

Hutan looked to the west and saw the silhouette of their caravan climbing a dune in the setting sun with the star shining brightly above them.

"And right where they should be," shouted a relieved Hutan, holding his arms in the air above his head.

Melchoir held his index finger to his lips and made a "Shhhhh" sound to Hutan, to which Hutan chuckled and asked, "Are you worried about a few Romans?"

Melchoir, choosing not to answer Hutan's question, gave his camel a kick and said, "Let us go before we lose them again!"

Off they rode toward their friends, the setting sun and the star that called to them.

It was nightfall when they finally reached the caravan after several hours of trailing them. The men were gathered around a small fire burning between the tents.

Balthasar greeted his friends, "We were ready to give up on you."

"Were you trying to lose us?" Melchoir replied with a smile.

"We did not want to take any chances, and we knew that God would lead you to us," answered Balthasar as he welcomed his friends with an embrace, happy that they had returned to the group.

"You did the right thing. A great number of Romans took our places among the palms just moments after you were out of sight. We are fortunate they did not come looking for us," replied Melchoir.

"How many?" asked Balthasar.

"A hundred or more. A 'maniple' is what I believe they call units of that size. Some on camels, a few on foot, but it is hard to say where they came. They must be exhausted, otherwise they would have sent some men after us. It was obvious that we left the area in a hurry," answered Melchoir.

"Is it not unusual for that many Romans to be out here in the desert?" asked Balthasar.

"Perhaps, but Palmyra is an unusual place. To be safe, we should post extra guards this evening so we have some notice if they come for a visit. Hutan and I were fortunate to find you. I doubt that the Romans will find us here, but I suppose they could stumble upon our tracks. To be cautious, we should leave at first light," Melchoir answered as he sat to remove his boots.

After supper, Balthasar explained the situation to the men. They did not know much about the Romans and did not want to be surprised by a large force who could have been their enemy.

Although still several days away, Palmyra was of great interest to the men and their arrival distracted the men from the threat of any invaders.

Melchoir had been to Palmyra many times and this evening as he described the city, he told the men, "Palmyra is unlike any place you have ever been or will ever visit. 'The Bride of the Desert' is what she is called."

"How much of a threat are the Romans to Palmyra?" asked Gaspar.

"They are very much a threat, but fortunately for Palmyra, the Romans are a long way from home. When I was a boy, the Romans tried to capture the city but failed," Melchoir responded.

"Was there a great battle?" asked Nekdel.

"There was no great battle. The people of Palmyra ran away, escaping across the Euphrates River, only to return once the Romans departed," Melchoir answered with a laugh.

Melchoir paused for a moment and then continued, "The Romans will be back in Palmyra in greater numbers. The wealth and power of this place is hard to resist."

Melchoir motioned with his hand for Nekdel to sit next to him and then Melchoir asked Ethan, "When we reach Palmyra, we will be have three months travel to Jerusalem. Do your scriptures speak of Palmyra? The land of the great rivers holds much for everyone."

"Our scriptures speak to this great city, but we give it the name of 'Tadmor.' At one time it was ruled by our King Solomon. He built great walls around the city to protect it, as well as a great stone chamber with large columns on its outside. Perhaps these still stand today," Ethan replied.

Melchoir nodded and said, "Perhaps they do. There are many interesting things about this place, but what amazes me is that, in an instant, we will go from desolate land, such as where we sit, to the fullness of green plants and trees, running waters and many delicious markets. Ah… the smell of the sweet cakes baking and the fresh fish smoking. I can taste the juicy fruit picked ripe from the trees!"

There was laughter and talk among the men about what awaited them in Palmyra.

Balthasar clapped his hands to get everyone's attention and cautioned, "Let us not get ahead of ourselves. We have several more days of travel in store for us before we reach Palmyra. Let us get an early start in the morning. Check in with Hutan for your guard duty. Stay alert... perhaps the Romans are on their way!"

Each day the road became more level as the caravan moved closer to Palmyra. It was late afternoon on the day Palmyra was first seen on the horizon. The men were in good spirits and, to celebrate the occasion and give thanks for their safe travel, the Magi prepared for an Afrinagan by building the Adar, the sacramental fire.

To prepare the fire, Melchoir began by retrieving a barsom from his cart. A barsom was a bundle of twigs the Magi used for the sacramental fires. When traveling through the desert, the Magi only carried a small number of barsoms with them. There was plenty of camel dung to be collected and used as fuel for cooking. Only wood was used in the ceremonial fires.

Balthasar and Gaspar assisted Melchoir by arranging the sticks on the ground, assorting them by size. Melchoir then picked up the twigs and began placing them in a rectangular shape, with the end of each twig placed on top of the other. Once the twigs were in place, Melchoir ignited a twig with a spark from his flint rock and blew on the glowing ember until the fire Adar was burning.

The men gathered around the Adar as Melchoir put on the Sudre-Kusti, the sacred shirt and girdle.

Melchoir also wore the padan, a white cloth mask that was used by the Magi to keep their breath from touching the fire. Melchior was performing the most important part of the ceremony when a group of Roman soldiers approached on camels. They were riding away from Palmyra when they turned off the road and rode into Balthasar's camp. It was not a large number of men, only twelve, and no one was threatened by their presence. Balthasar raised his right arm as a signal to stop the ceremony so he could greet the visitors, but the Romans ignored his welcome. Instead, the Romans continued riding until they reached Melchoir and the men gathered around the Adar. The Roman leader surveyed the scene for a moment, shouted something in a language that no man in the caravan understood and then spat on the ground.

The Roman leader then surveyed the scene and motioned with his hand for his group to follow him as he turned his camel back toward the road.

To everyone's great surprise, Melchoir gave out a great shout, "Dew! Dew! Riman!" Mede words, "Dew" meaning demon, and "Riman" used as an insult. They were meant to convey that the Romans were polluted from contact with something dead.

While Balthasar's men were disturbed by the Roman leader spitting, they were shocked by Melchoir's outburst. The Romans stopped in their tracks and looked back to see Melchoir pick up the sacramental knife, the Kaplo. With the Kaplo in his right hand, Melchoir motioned with both hands for the men to spread apart, making it seem as if Melchoir was about to charge the Roman leader with knife in hand. Seeing, but not believing what was unfolding before him, Gaspar lunged at Melchoir, tackling him to the ground. Gaspar and Hutan restrained Melchoir while the others looked to the Romans for their reaction; their leader had a confused look on his face. He shrugged his shoulders and gave the signal for his men to follow him back to the road. Once the Romans were well on their way, Gaspar and Hutan let go of their friend.

Balthasar reached his hand out to Melchoir to pull him to his feet and said, "What was that all about? Does he owe you a debt?"

Having some time to think about his behavior, Melchoir knew how foolish he has behaved. "I am sorry. I could not help myself... he interrupted our sacred ceremony only to call us 'animals' and 'fire worshippers!' Can you imagine that? A vile Roman calling us those things! Fire worshippers!"

"Is that what he said? I thought they wanted to stay for supper," snapped back an agitated Balthasar.

"I know enough of their language to know what he said and I wanted him to know it," replied a still agitated Melchoir.

"Oh, I think he heard your greeting, but we are fortunate he did not lose his temper. Look, good friend, no one likes insults and it is all the more hurtful when our beliefs are ridiculed. But you need to remember the purpose of our mission and it does not involve starting fights with Romans. You put us at risk… all of us… over a few words that you alone understood," scolded Balthasar.

Melchoir fell to his knees with his head down, ashamed of his behavior. Balthasar motioned to the men to come close as Balthasar offered a prayer.

"Great God in Heaven, we thank you for sparing us from trouble this day and we are grateful for you bringing us so far without loss of life or serious injury. You know that we are tired, weary from this journey and worn from the heat and dryness of the sand. Give us strength and guide us on our way," he said, with each of his men listening.

As the men broke from the prayer, Balthasar shouted, "Let this be a lesson to all of us. At the first sign of approaching strangers… hide all knives and sharp things from Melchoir!"

With this, whatever tension was created over Melchoir's behavior quickly dissipated. The men were excited about Palmyra and this bit of excitement got everyone's blood flowing again. Some men were satisfied that Melchoir took such offense to the Roman insults. No one but Melchoir knew much about the Romans, so naturally, the men were curious about them. The fact that there were not many who could produce such an emotional reaction from a man like Melchoir, a thoughtful, wise, and disciplined Magi, interested the rest of the men in learning more about these Roman warriors.

Chapter XIV- On to Damascus, and Warnings of Danger

The next morning, the great palms of Palmyra could be seen and, by the afternoon, the caravan arrived in the city. Riding together as they entered the city, the men quickly found the city to be everything that Melchoir had described to them.

"I expected to see walls surrounding the city or at least gates through which we would pass, but the entrance to the city opens wide for us. Magnificent palms everywhere... look at the size of these palms! Such an oasis! It extends as far as we can see!" Balthasar shouted.

"Is it not marvelous? And this is only a small part of the city. Let us keep riding; there is so much to see," replied Melchoir.

As they moved through the city, Melchoir pointed out an area to Balthasar and said, "There is a good place to station ourselves, for there are plenty of trees and water. We can keep to ourselves here."

Within a few minutes, the caravan was at rest and the camels were released from their carts and led to water. Several of the men began unpacking a cart and were stopped by Gaspar.

"The carts can wait. Would you not prefer to lay in the shade of these great trees and pour cool water over your head?" Gaspar said with a grin. A spontaneous cheer erupted as the men removed most of their clothes and became more comfortable than they had been for many months.

That evening, they celebrated with prayers, music and plenty of food. The Magi discussed their situation over supper.

"I do not believe that I have seen the men this excited," Gaspar said as he nodded his head in the direction of the men, his hands busy holding a large piece of lamb.

"And I do not believe that any of us could be happier. Jerusalem is finally within reach and we are able to rest in this place of great beauty!" replied Balthasar.

"Indeed, this is a wonderful place, but we need to be careful. Not everyone here is our friend and once beyond this city, we will continue to be in danger," added Melchoir.

"You have been troubled about our safety since we left Ecbatana. Why do you have such fear?" asked Balthasar.

Melchoir was quiet for a moment before replying, "When we leave this city, we leave Persia. Life will become more complicated for us. We will no longer be able to rely on the Persian militia to protect us. You saw the city today: Romans, Greeks, Jews, Egyptians… why I even saw people here from the Sātavāhana Empire. Yes, most are quite friendly, but some would not hesitate to slit our throats while we slept if they knew the value of our cargo."

"Do not worry, friend. We have not taken unnecessary risks and nothing has changed," replied Balthasar.

The next morning, Balthasar said to the men, "One reason that Palmyra is so interesting is that many different people come and go from here. This is Persia's gateway to the rest of the world. There are merchants, traders, militia and farmers among us… and also bandits and murderers. I know little about this city and even less about what lies beyond. Fortunately for us, Melchoir knows much about these things. He is good to remind us that we should trust no one with information about the valuables we carry or our plans for travel. Those who may appear to be our friends could mean trouble for us."

"Continue to be cautious with your words and diligent with your guard duty. Over the next few days, we will be replacing camels, obtaining supplies and deciding on a route for the remainder of our journey. Hopefully, we will benefit from the safety of other caravans when we leave here, but we must continue to use caution and be prepared to defend ourselves. Now that is the end of my speech, which is not meant to alarm, only to remind that danger will never be far," Melchoir said in closing.

Over the next several days, the Magi prepared for the trip to Jerusalem. They spoke with caravan drivers and militia groups arriving from the west to learn about their routes.

When they were finalizing their plans, Balthasar asked Melchoir, "Considering all that we have heard, have you decided on a route?"

"Northwest until Damascus… then follow the King's Highway south. God went to great lengths to create the beauty along this smooth, wide road. You will love the King's Highway. We will pass through magnificent forests and fertile fields that seem to go on forever, but will later give way to deep ravines as we descend close to the desert."

"Why is it called the King's Highway? Is it named for a king?" asked Balthasar.

"I have asked that question myself. I was told that the Jews gave the road its name."

"How far from Damascus do we travel on this Highway?" asked Balthasar.

"At some point we will have to move west and cross over the Jordan River. I have not crossed the Jordan in this area, but I know there is a road near Rabbah-ammon. It will not be a problem for us," Melchoir replied confidently.

After five days in Palmyra, the preparations were made and the caravan was ready to depart the palm city for Damascus. They estimated it would take two weeks. From there to Jerusalem could have taken another two weeks. Balthasar's men departed Palmyra with several Greek caravans and, much to the dismay of Melchoir, their escorts were Roman soldiers. The Magi were uncomfortable with their escorts, but they believed there was safety in being part of a large procession. They placed their caravan at the end of the line and did their best to keep to themselves. They offered food and drink to the Romans, but divulged no details as to the purpose of their trip. As far as anyone outside of Balthasar's caravan knew, Damascus was their final destination.

The men asked Melchoir many questions about their next destination and he told them, "We will be riding from one patch of desert to another for the next several days. When we reach Damascus, you will see that it, too, is a beautiful oasis, yet is different from any other place. It also has a rich history and has been of interest to foreigners… and their militias. Control of the city has been passed to many nations. Jews have played an important role in its history."

He paused for a moment and looked among the men until his eyes focused on Ethan.

"Ethan, what do your scriptures record about Damascus?" asked Melchoir as he motioned for Ethan to sit next to him on the back of his cart.

"Our Scriptures call this area the gateway of the Garden of Eden because of its richness in land and water," Ethan replied.

"Whose garden?" asked Nekdel.

"The Garden of Eden, the place where God created the first man and woman, a beautiful garden where nothing died or decayed. It was the beginning of a perfect world until the man and woman sinned against God at the urging of Satan," Ethan shared with the men.

After a moment, when Ethan saw that he still had the attention of the men, he continued, "Our King David conquered Damascus and placed his governors there. David gained much of his power by controlling the King's Highway. But Israel did not always hold Damascus; it fell from their hands when Solomon was King. It was not long after this time that Damascus became the capital of the Aram Damascus kingdom, in place for five hundred years until the Assyrians destroyed it. But not all of the Jews who came to Damascus with King David left the city, as Aramean king Ben-Hadad permitted our merchants to stay. I have heard that there are many Jews in Damascus to this day. In many ways, the history of Damascus is similar to Palmyra. Many nations have fought for control of it and it was not long after the Assyrians took control that Israel's King Jeroboam captured the city. The trade that passed through it made it very prosperous. Our Scriptures tell us that the richness of the land also supplied the oasis with great wealth from its trade in delicious wine, fine wool and fruit that is beyond compare."

Ethan looked in Melchoir's direction and continued, "We hear you speak of the King's Highway, a road that we may take to Jerusalem. It was paved with black stone by King Solomon who kept his roads in good order in case the Jews needed to flee in a hurry. When the roads were built, they were to be forty-eight feet wide and were to have bridges and sign-posts to mark the way. Melchoir, did you find the road as the scriptures describe?" Ethan asked.

"Yes! You are right! Your Solomon lived a long time ago, but much of his road remains as you say: wide, black, smooth and paid for by tolls, although much of the road is worn and needs repair. The Romans control all of the roads and they keep them clear of trees and debris. You see, they too want to make sure they can move quickly when necessary. Once you leave the Highway, the roads are narrow, perhaps five feet wide in places," Melchoir replied, in amazement at the accuracy of Ethan's description of a road he had never seen.

Ethan, after listening to Melchoir, said, "Long before Solomon paved the King's Highway, our great prophet Moses used the road to lead his people north through the land of Edom. Before Moses, the road was the route taken by four kings from the north who marched their troops to battle against the five kings of the Cities of the Plain, including the wicked cities of Sodom and Gomorrah. Our prophet Abraham chased the invading kings up the highway, through Damascus, and did not stop until he rescued his nephew, named Lot. The roads leading out of Damascus are important links to Jerusalem and Egypt to the south and the Great Sea to the west. The city was an attractive target for Alexander when he marched through here. And while Persia has fought Rome for control, it has been in Roman hands for most of the past 300 years. I do not doubt that one day, Persia will wake up and challenge the Romans for control of this great oasis."

With this, the men cheered for Persia and grumbled about the Romans. Balthasar took this opportunity to close the discussion.

"After hearing the history of the King's Highway, it seems most appropriate that we take this road to meet the Messiah," he said.

As the caravan neared Damascus, they passed militia groups from Persia and Rome, caravans and bands of riders. The Magi felt unprepared for the number of potential threats they encountered, so Balthasar kept his carts close to other caravans also traveling to Damascus. There was a growing uneasiness over the many militia groups and heavily armed riders they saw moving through the desert. Although a long trip to Palmyra, there was a sense they were close to danger, and the caravan was relieved when they finally arrived, safe in the city. Although Magi, who had been coming to this city for many generations, were known as Persian ambassadors, there was no way of knowing what would happen if the caravan encountered Roman soldiers in a remote area.

After two days in Damascus, most of their concerns faded as the men became comfortable in their new surroundings. In accordance with their practice, the men were not permitted to leave the caravan alone, and even when the men did leave in small groups, they first had to coordinate their movement with Hutan. One afternoon in Damascus, Ethan reported to Hutan that he would visit a temple for an hour. Since Ethan's request was of a personal nature, Hutan did not require he take a companion. Several hours later, Hutan reported to Balthasar that Ethan had not returned. The men knew that plans could change quickly for the caravan, so it was unusual for any of the men to disregard the rules. Both Balthasar and Hutan, worried for their friend, decided that a search group had to be organized. But just as they began to organize the search effort, Ethan returned to the camp, bringing with him a stranger.

Balthasar wasted no time letting Ethan know of his displeasure. "Explain yourself!" he shouted.

"I am sorry that I am late. I visited a Jewish temple where I met this man, Simcha. He is a rabbi, a Jewish teacher. I encouraged him to return with me so you could hear what he has to say," replied Ethan, troubled because he had never before displeased the Magi.

Not wanting to embarrass Ethan in front of his guest, Balthasar asked "Will you leave your guest for a moment and walk with me?"

Ethan walked with Balthasar for a short distance until Balthasar stopped to speak.

"Ethan, you are a good man, but you have broken our rules. You departed here alone, you are late in returning and you bring a stranger into our midst without approval," he said.

"I ask that you trust me on Simcha. I have spent much time speaking with him and I know that God is with him. What he has to say about the Romans and their leader in Jerusalem is something you should hear," Ethan pleaded.

Balthasar thought for a moment, nodded in approval, and said, "My trust in you is not in doubt. If you believe this man's words are important to us, then we should hear from him. Let us ask him to join us for supper and then have him speak to us. But first, I want your word that, in the future, you will abide by the rules."

"You have my word," Ethan replied as he embraced Balthasar.

When supper was finished, Balthasar asked Ethan to introduce his friend to the rest of the men.

Ethan stood and says to the men, "While in the city today, I visited a temple where I met this man who sits beside me. His name is Simcha. He is a Jewish teacher and knows a great deal about Jerusalem and its rulers. He has agreed to speak to us about things that will keep us safe during our journey and even after we arrive."

Ethan helped his friend step up on to a cart, so he could be heard, and torches were placed around him so he could be seen. He was old, frail and short in height. His back was bent with age, causing him to stoop. When Ethan asked Simcha to visit the caravan, Ethan intended for Simcha to speak only with the Magi; he was uncertain of whether or not Simcha could be heard by all of the men who had gathered, but Simcha did not seem to mind, wearing a broad smile as he began to speak.

"Good evening friends!" he said in a thunderous deep voice, startling everyone. Immediately there was laughter as the men spread themselves out, moving back from the cart. "I can tell that you are surprised to hear such a loud voice coming from such an old, broken body. Yes, my body is old and worn, but I thank God for every day he gives me life and the strength to speak. My name is Simcha, which means Happiness and Joy," Simcha began, immediately capturing everyone's attention.

The men chuckled as they listened to their guest, who spoke in short, yet clear sentences. Simcha continued, "I am a Jew and I have lived most of my life in

Jerusalem. What I am about to tell you is not a pleasant story. You need to hear my words for your own safety. These are troubled times for Jews and for all people in this region. The Romans have broken the spirit and the will of many. Their ruler in Jerusalem is dangerous and cannot be trusted. I speak of King Herod. Perhaps you have heard of him. He is not to be trusted. Herod is ambitious and evil."

Ethan offered Simcha some water, but Simcha shook his head and continued speaking. "There are things you should know about Herod. He came from humble beginnings. His father, Antipater, was from Edom, a stretch of desert near Jerusalem. His mother, Kupros, was an Ishmaelite, desert people who trade spices. Herod's father became a trusted procurator of Judaea and won the friendship of Hyrcanus, the King of Judaea. The King was from the Hasmoneans family, a well respected Jewish family whose members have served as priests and kings for many generations. Antipater used his friendship with the King to secure good jobs for his sons, Phasael and Herod. Phasael was made Prefect of Jerusalem. Herod was given the job of Military Prefect of Galilee."

The men were unsure where Simcha's story would lead, but they were nonetheless captivated by this animated old man and his words, which were clearly full of purpose and reason. "But Herod is ambitious and was not content with that position. To win the King's favor, Herod divorced his wife and married the King's granddaughter, Mariamne. The Jewish leaders, the Sanhedrin, had come to know Herod as violent and hot tempered. The Sanhedrin went to Hycranus and accused Herod of violating the laws by putting men to death without first consulting the Sanhedrin. But the King protected Herod from being sentenced to death and helped Herod escape to this place, Damascus," he said, stunning the men with a reference to the city they had found so safe and enjoyable in recent days. "Herod hid here until the Parthians invaded the region and captured Jerusalem. Herod then traveled to Rome, where he convinced the authorities to give him the title of 'King of the Jews,' pledging to return and take Judaea back for Rome. By this time, the Parthians had put their own king in place, King Antigonus."

Simcha paused for a moment to catch his breath and could see in the faces of the men that they were following his words closely, so he continued. "When Herod returned with his newly acquired power, he began his military conquests. First taking Galilee and then capturing King Antigonus, Herod took control of the kingdom in just three years. Once in control, he had all but one member of that Sanhedrin killed. Although Hycrannus had helped Herod and was no longer a threat, Herod had him murdered as well.

"Trying to win favor with the Jews, Herod began rebuilding the temple, which had been destroyed in war. He started new towns and built harbors to improve shipping. He used his military power to add neighboring regions to his kingdom. They must love Herod in Rome, but he has never been liked by the Jews. He worships as a Jew, but no Jew believes him to be sincere. The Jews never forgave him for removing Antigonus from the thrown. Herod thought that he would be respected by the Jews because his wife Mariamne was also from the Hasmonean family. But the Jews saw through his schemes and never trusted him. Some reasonable people in positions of power might have recognized their limits and relinquished power to someone less objectionable, but Herod chose a different path. His rejection by the people has caused him to become evil and murderous," Simcha said, taking a breath, and was interrupted by Gaspar.

"Is that not what rulers do? Protect their positions and authority so they can stay in power?"

"You must hear the rest of the story. Then you can decide if Herod is like other rulers," answered Simcha.

Gaspar took his seat and Simcha continued. "Herod began to distrust everyone, even those closest to him. It was on his orders that the high priest, his brother-in-law Aristobulus, was executed. Then he killed his uncle Joseph because he wrongly believed that Joseph desired Mariamne. Poor Mariamne, she kept her distance from Herod, but she too was murdered."

Gaspar interrupted again, "I understand your fear of Herod, but we pose no threat to him."

Simcha shook his head and then warned, "Perhaps you will not draw Herod's attention, but you should still hear more. Herod became very sick from his guilt and sadness. It appeared to those closest to him that he was near death. Expecting Herod's death would come soon, Mariamne's mother, Alexandria, took steps to put Alexander and Aristobulus into power, the children of Mariamne and Herod. But what do you think happened to Mariamne's mother when Herod heard of her plan? Murder! There are also stories, which are likely true, that Herod also gave the orders to have two of his sons starved to death. A horrible fate for even the most vicious of animals... let alone his innocent sons."

The men listened to Simcha in disbelief and were beginning to understand why Melchoir harbored resentment for the Romans.

In a softer but firm voice, Simcha said, "I tell you these things because they are true. Herod and Rome have brought much grief and pain to many Jews who have suffered at their hands. For some, the burden has been too much to bear. It is not only physical pain – the Romans also demand heavy taxes.

"They call upon us for ground poll taxes on all other property and income. Everyone is required to pay: young children, old women; everyone. Taxes come to all those who use the highways and bridges, and they track our population numbers to make sure everyone pays. At one time, Jews only paid tribute to God, but now we are forced to pay tribute to the Emperor. To humiliate us further, the Romans do not even collect these taxes themselves. No, that would require them to look us in the face. They use slaves and other desperate people to come calling for their payments. And as if their taxes are not high enough, many Romans scheme to overvalue our property, making our taxes more of a burden."

Simcha paused briefly, overcome by emotion, but continued, "Jews who work the land are forced to produce more each year in order to pay, and if there is bad weather and the land does not produce, the land is forfeited to Rome. Those who resist the Romans and their rule are dealt with harshly. The worst offenders, those who hold their ground or attempt to lead others against the Romans, are crucified. If you are not familiar with that horrible torture, the unfortunate victim is nailed to a tree and left to bleed to death!"

Troubled by Simcha's report, the men shared their fear with each other. Seeing the reaction his words had stirred in the men, Simcha paused for another moment in the hopes that the men's emotions would calm enough for him to continue. When they did settle down, he said, "You must wonder why I tell you all of these things; you are only passing through this land. I tell you so that you will know that the Romans have no heart. Many Jews have lost everything; their homes, their belongings and their families! Rather than rely on their faith in God to see them through this cruelty, many Jews have given into their hate and have become bandits, seeking revenge against all who cross their path. They have become bandits and thieves because they believe there are no other options. Some have been taxed so heavily by Herod that they were forced to sell everything they own, including their land. It has been said that 'conquerors are kings, the beaten are bandits.' That is what has happened to us. Perhaps the bandits will come together one day and rise up against Rome, but for now, they may be satisfied attacking wealthy foreigners traveling across their path, foreigners like you."

Melchoir took this opportunity to step in first before the other men started asking questions. "What he said is true! Whenever I am in this region, I take every precaution because I have seen the remains of those whom have been laid to waste on the road," spoke Melchoir, who, until now, had kept silent.

Simcha nodded and continued. "The bandits will not stop to ask where your allegiances lie. They are desperate men seeking revenge. They are interested in one thing: what you carry in your carts! My message is a warning. Protect yourself from bandits on your way to Jerusalem, avoid trouble with the Romans and keep clear of Herod. I have one final message. When I spoke with Ethan this afternoon, he said that he travels with Magi. I know something about the Magi," Simcha said as he nodded his head in approval and focused his eyes on the three men. In a loud whisper, Simcha continued, "I know that you come from a place quite far from here. I know that you study the stars. And I know that you are men of great knowledge and wisdom. Knowing these things about you, I have concluded why you have traveled such a distance."

Simcha had everyone's attention as he inched to the edge of the cart to whisper, "The star has brought you here, I am sure of it. Many Jews in Damascus see the star, but we do not discuss it outside of our family for fear of the Romans. Jews have waited a long time for the one who will defeat our enemies and free us from oppression. I have not heard whether this warrior is already among us, but I pray that his time has come. Oh, how we have prayed for the Messiah, a great military leader like Joshua who can return our land to us and rule as King David. Perhaps you will meet him! I pray that you will return to this place to share your story with me."

"We know little of this messiah, but we are certain that only a man in God's favor would have his presence marked in the sky with a star," replied Balthasar.

"Simcha! You must come with us to Jerusalem and see for yourself!" Gaspar shouted.

"No, I am too old. I will be fortunate to find my way home this night. A trip to Jerusalem is not possible for me, but I will pray that God delivers you safely to the Messiah," Simcha replied with a smile.

Ethan helped Simcha down from the cart and Gaspar asked the men to prepare a camel that could carry Simcha home.

"No need for a camel, but it would be good to have someone walk with me. My eyes are of little good in the night," responded Simcha.

"You can ride on my camel and we will walk to your home together. First, join us in prayer," answered Balthasar.

Both men prayed. Balthasar asked God to guide the caravan safely to Jerusalem, while Simcha prayed for God to help the Messiah free the Jews from Herod and the Romans. Soon, Balthasar had escorted Simcha back to his home and returned to camp to prepare for the next day and to rest.

The following afternoon, the three Magi were talking among themselves as they crossed a road near the market place, as a voice called to them, "Look out! Out of the way!"

The Magi looked up just in time to see two galloping horses charging at them. Balthasar grabbed each of his friends as the horses and their lone rider brushed by them at full speed.

"We could have been killed!" shouted Balthasar at the driver who was just now bringing the horses under control.

"That was close. It must be Angra Mainyu," added Gaspar, still holding on to Balthasar's arm.

"Quite the contrary! It is one of God's angels," blurted Melchoir.

"What are you mumbling about angels? That driver nearly killed us!" Balthasar replied.

Melchoir was now walking toward the horses and driver that nearly ran them over as he turned his head to speak to his friends. "Did you not see her? She is incredible!"

Balthasar and Gaspar watched as Melchoir helped a woman down from one of the horses. The two of them spoke for several minutes before Melchoir returned to his friends.

"The most amazing woman I have ever met. She is wonderful. Did you see how she handled those horses?" Melchoir asked his friends.

"Are you serious? She nearly killed us!" answered Gaspar, still confused by Melchoir's behavior.

"No! She saved us! The horses do not belong to her. They are runaways! She leaped from a camel to bring them under control. I shall go with her now to find the owners. She is a caravan driver. Can you believe it?" asked an overjoyed Melchoir.

Balthasar and Gaspar were speechless as they watched their friend disappear up the road with the woman who nearly ended their lives.

"Perhaps he has found the woman who can tame him. She did a fine job bringing those horses under control!" Balthasar half jokingly said to Gaspar.

"Such a match could only be made in Heaven!" laughed Gaspar.

Hours later, when Melchoir returned to the caravan, Balthasar asked Melchoir, "Did you learn anything this afternoon?"

"Yes, I learned many things. Her name is Desta, which means 'happiness.' Damascus is her home. She has never married…"

Balthasar interrupted, "Melchoir, I was asking you about caravans moving south."

"Oh! Yes, I did learn something about that as well. Egyptian traders will soon be taking their caravan south on the King's Highway in the company of Roman soldiers. I do not know any of these men, but from one Egyptian to another, they gave me their word that they will provide us protection if there is trouble," replied Melchoir.

"I thought that you were Ethiopian?" Balthasar asked with a smile.

"Shh!" Melchoir whispered, holding his index finger to his lips. "For the next few days, I am a full blooded Egyptian... and one who was known to Queen Cleopatra."

"You knew Cleopatra?" Balthasar asked with a laugh.

Melchoir shrugged his shoulders. "For purposes of our trip south with our new friends, I knew the Queen. It is not as if they will be able to prove me wrong, she killed herself years ago. Besides, I actually did see the Queen once."

"You saw Cleopatra?"

"Yes! It was from a distance, of course, there was a large crowd and I did not have the best vantage point, but everyone was shouting greetings to the Queen! I was quite young at the time," replied a smiling Melchoir.

"It sounds as if you knew her quite well," Balthasar laughed as he bowed to Melchoir. Balthasar paused for a moment and, in a serious tone, asked, "Can these Egyptians be trusted? We will be at their mercy if they are many in number."

"I suppose they can be trusted... as much as any trader can be trusted," Melchoir responded with a shrug.

"That does not put my mind at ease. What do you know about these people?" asked Balthasar in an irritated voice.

"Well, they have a reputation for being fair... that is, fair for traders. The merchants do not speak poorly of them and it does not appear that any of them are wanted by the authorities, as much as I can determine," Melchoir replied in a serious tone, recognizing that Balthasar is challenging his judgment.

Balthasar stood frozen in silence with his head slightly cocked, his arms outstretched and his hands open, as if waiting to hear more from Melchoir.

"What else can I tell you? Do they hate Persians? I cannot say that they will be our friends, but I am certain that they will do us no harm. They travel this route for a living. That is what they do. There is no future for them in robbing their companions. I do know that they hate the Romans. Everyone hates the Romans. Egyptians would like to have their country back, just as the Jews would like to have their country returned. If we offer the Egyptians something of value for escorting us south, we will have nothing to fear from them. Remember, it will only be for a week or so, just as long as it takes to find a suitable crossing over the Jordan River. What we do then for protection, I do not know," answered Melchoir.

"Your plan is as reliable as any we have had on this journey. Besides, we know that God will be with us, but we do not want to make his task any more difficult than necessary," Balthasar answered with a smile.

Balthasar now understood that Melchoir had given serious thought to his plan and had used his best judgment in arranging travel with the Egyptians, so he conceded in pairing his own caravan with that of Egyptian travelers.

Chapter XV - Jerusalem: Herod Appears and the Star Vanishes

Three days later, on the morning of the Jewish Sabbath, Balthasar led the caravan to join the Egyptians and their escort of Roman soldiers.

Once the procession was moving, Balthasar asked Melchoir, "Can we trust our Roman friends?"

"They know us as ambassadors of Persia, but they do not know the purpose of our journey. It might be best if we keep our purpose to ourselves," answered Melchoir.

As the procession moved south along the King's Highway, Balthasar and his men encountered many travelers. There were many conversations with travelers coming from Jerusalem and from as far away as Egypt. One evening, the Magi shared supper with Jews who had come from Jerusalem.

Balthasar shared with them the purpose of their journey, saying, "We have come a great distance to pay homage to the Messiah who has come to the Jews. We follow His star!"

Their guests were indifferent to this news of the Messiah. One guest replied, "A messiah has come? I hope that he does not meet the same fate as the others!"

"Other messiahs have come to the Jews?" asked Balthasar.

Another guest replied, "Many have claimed to be the messiah. Not in our lives, but we have heard of them. In our father's generation, there was a man of great size and strength known as Simon. He claimed to be the messiah and he was beheaded! Later, there was another giant of a man, Athronges. He also claimed to be the messiah before he was killed. If you believe another messiah awaits you in Jerusalem, you should hurry to see him before he meets the same fate!"

When their guests departed, Balthasar spoke to his fellow Magi. "That was a discouraging conversation. They have come from Jerusalem and have not heard of the Messiah. The only messiahs known to them are dead ones!"

"Do not be discouraged! It is obvious that they have not seen the star shining just beyond us. Their eyes have not been opened to the star, nor to the Messiah it heralds. Do not forget that we have also met others who do not see," Gaspar replied.

"You are right. We know what we see and what has been placed in our hearts. Our guests must be the mistaken ones," added Melchoir.

Their Roman escorts also showed little interest in the Magi. Although not part of their original plan, the Magi felt comfortable discussing the purpose of their visit freely with other travelers because they were anxious to learn news of the Messiah. Unfortunately, no one they met had heard of the Messiah and no one was even aware of the star, even though it shone brightly before them. Although frustrating for the Magi, they were confident that all would be revealed when they arrived in Jerusalem.

On their twelfth day of travel from Damascus, they left their Egyptian friends and their Roman escorts and turned west at Philadelphia. This route would take them across the Jordan River, through Jericho and on to Jerusalem. Their safety was now their own responsibility. They had no trouble crossing the river and, later the same day, they rode through Jericho.

It was early afternoon the following day when they could see Jerusalem on the horizon with God's star shining above it.

It was Hutan who first alerted his companions with a loud, "Jerusalem!"

The caravan came to a stop as the men joined together briefly for prayer and song.

"We can reach the city before the sun sets! Jerusalem! Jerusalem!" shouted Balthasar.

As they rode, the chatter among the men was non-stop. Conversation was interrupted briefly at times when the men erupted into more shouts of, "Jerusalem!"

After one such outburst, Gaspar asked Ethan, "What does it mean?"

Ethan turned to Gaspar with a puzzled look on his face and Gaspar clarified his question, asking, "Jerusalem! What is the meaning of its name?"

"It means 'founded by Shalem,' and is also called Beth-Shalem, or 'House of Shalem.' In ancient times, 'Shalem' was the Canaanite god of Twilight," answered Ethan.

"Interesting that we should be coming to her at twilight," Gaspar nodded in appreciation for Ethan's explanation.

Before they passed through the city's gates, people were already taking notice of Balthasar's caravan. Some recognized them as Magi, others were unsure of the caravan's origin, but knew the men had come a great distance. The appearance of the men was quite different from the residents of Jerusalem; the Magi and their men drew attention because of their fine clothes, the craftsmanship of their carts and the quality of their animals. It was apparent to the people in Jerusalem that the Magi were men of wealth.

The caravan moved slowly through the city and the Magi asked many people, "Where is He who has been born King of the Jews? We saw His star in the east and have come to worship Him."

Their inquiries drew much attention, causing a stir among the people. Stopping at an intersection near the center of Jerusalem, the Magi walked together, their camels tied to carts behind them, looking for anyone who could help them find who they had traveled so far to see.

"How can this be? No one here knows anything about the Messiah. They look at us as if we have lost our minds," Balthasar shared with the other Magi.

"I cannot explain it. Are you sure that we are in Jerusalem?" asked Gaspar with a puzzled look.

"It gets worse!" Melchoir said. Holding his clenched fist in front of his chest, Melchoir pointed his index finger upward and said, "It is gone!"

Melchoir and Gaspar tilted their heads back and turned in place searching the sky.

"Incredible! I cannot believe it. When did we lose it?" asked Balthasar.

"I just noticed," replied Melchoir, shaking his head in disbelief.

Gaspar, also confounded, asked, "How can the star be with us night and day for more than a year and then as soon as we step foot in the place where it led us, it is gone?"

As the Magi discussed their dilemma, they were unaware that King Herod had already posted spies among the people in Jerusalem so he could learn of any plans made against him. When one of those spies learned that the Magi were asking about the Messiah, the authorities were notified and it was not long before several Roman soldiers approached on horseback, leading more horses without riders behind them.

"It appears that we will receive an official welcome!" Melchoir said as the Magi turn their attention to the soldiers.

When the soldiers stopped, their leader inspected the Magi from his horse and said, "Welcome to Jerusalem. Identify yourselves so that we may be of service to you."

"We are Magi from a distant kingdom in Persia," replied Balthasar, unsure of how much detail to provide as to the purpose of their trip.

"King Herod would like to welcome you personally to Jerusalem," replied the soldier.

Turning toward his fellow Magi so his face could not be seen by the soldiers, Balthasar grimaced briefly to Gaspar and Melchoir.

Balthasar turned to the soldier and replied, "That is a kind and most generous gesture, but we do not want to trouble the King with our presence. He must have more important business than greeting our humble group."

"The King insists," responded the soldier, curt and unwilling to compromise.

"There are many of us and we have much to attend to," Balthasar began to reply before he was cut short by the soldier.

"The King does not want to see all of you, just the Magi," he said in a louder voice, making it known that he was growing impatient.

"Oh, I see. Let me have a moment to share this news with my men so they may find a place for our caravan," Balthasar replied with a nod to the soldier. Balthasar turned to Gaspar and Melchoir and whispered, "Any thoughts?"

"We have no choice," replied Gaspar.

"We will tell the King why we are here. We are no threat to him," Melchoir replied.

The caravan was placed under Hutan's command and the Magi were led on horseback by the soldiers.

While traveling to the King, Melchoir pointed to a large building and asked one of the soldiers, "Is that not the King's palace?"

"Yes, but we take a different route," replied the soldier.

The Magi thought to themselves as they were being led in a roundabout way to the palace. They wondered what was happening to them, and if they were being summoned by the King, why were they being led through dark streets, away from the palace?

In a few minutes, they arrived at a side entrance to the palace. As the Magi dismounted from their horses, Melchoir whispered under his breath to Balthasar, "Quite a welcome for us… this must be the servants' entrance!"

The Magi were escorted through narrow hallways, up staircases and finally into a large room where they were told to wait until the King called for them. The Magi were left to themselves while guards waited outside of their room.

Gaspar said to Balthasar, "You should speak for all of us."

"Yes, I agree, you should speak, but please be careful to not offend the King," Melchoir added with a smile as he ran his index finger quickly across his throat.

"Friends, I know what you are thinking. You are reminded of Simcha's stories. But remember, the King knows that we pose no threat to him with our small band of men. It is an honor to be seen by the King," replied Balthasar, trying to both calm his friends and himself.

A soldier opened the door to their room, motioned with his hand and called to the Magi, "The King will see you now."

As the Magi were led down a grand hallway, they saw the King sitting on his throne in a great hall. Many men surrounded the King, and some held parchments and scrolls. When the Magi were introduced, a number of heads turned to them as they entered the hall. The King motioned to the group of men with his hand and they quickly collected their things and departed the room, leaving one soldier with the King. As the Magi approached the King, he had a look of concern, but forced a smile. The Magi did not bow or kneel to the King, but instead offered their traditional embrace and kiss to the cheek. The King warmly greeted the Magi by quickly returning the embrace and kiss.

The King then asked, "Tell me Magi, what area of Persia is your home?"

Balthasar explained, "Gaspar and I come from kingdoms near the Caspian Sea. Melchoir's home is every place between Ecbatana and Egypt."

"I see… how fascinating. You have traveled a great distance. A difficult and dangerous journey!" replied the King.

Herod motioned with his hand to the soldier, who immediately summoned servants. Moments later, the servants entered the room carrying trays of food and drink.

"Please, sit with me, you must be very tired," said the King as he led the men to a table.

"A glass of wine to celebrate your arrival?" asked the King as he picked up a silver cup from the servant's tray and handed it to Balthasar. When each man held a cup, Herod offered a toast, "Welcome to Jerusalem! May your stay with us be enjoyable and prosperous!"

After the men drank, the King said, "I am told that you have been asking for the one who has been born King of the Jews. That you saw his star in the east and have come to worship Him. Have I heard correctly?" asked the King.

"Yes, you have heard correctly. That is why we have come to Jerusalem. I am surprised that you learned of us so quickly. We have only been in Jerusalem a short time," responded Balthasar as he glanced at the faces of his companions.

"Why, you are important visitors, of course! Word of your arrival came to me quickly," replied the King as he lifted his cup into the air once more in honor of his guests.

After drinking from their cups again, the King asked, "So you are from Persia… you saw a star over Jerusalem. When was the exact time the star first appeared?"

"I believe it has been a year since we first saw the star. Fourteen months perhaps," Balthasar replied with Gaspar and Melchoir nodding in agreement.

"The star has been in the sky for that long? Fascinating!" replied the King.

The King took another drink from his cup and then said, "My priests and scribes tell me that the Messiah is prophesized to be born in Bethlehem. Do you know that place? It is not far from here. May I suggest that you go and search carefully for the child and when you have found him, report to me, so that I too may come and worship him?"

The excited King placed his cup on the tray of the waiting servant and the Magi did the same, taking this as a sign that there meeting with the king had ended. The King embraced each Magi again, then nodded to one of his soldiers.

"I will not keep you. I know that you are anxious to return to your men, but be sure to report back to me right away when you have found the child!" King Herod said.

With that, the King departed the great hall while the Magi were escorted back to the street by the King's soldiers in the same manner in which they arrived.

The Magi were soon riding with their escorts in the direction of the caravan. They kept silent until they reached the caravan and returned their horses to the soldiers.

"You did well Balthasar; we still have our heads!" Melchoir said with a laugh.

"We have survived until now," Gaspar added.

"The King was gracious enough, but there is something troubling about him. Perhaps I was reminded of Simcha's stories," Balthasar replied.

"That appeared to be quite a meeting that the King was in the midst of when we arrived. Is it not amazing that none of them mentioned seeing the star, nor have any of them seen or know the exact location of the Messiah? And why were we taken to the palace out of the sight of the people?" asked a troubled Melchoir.

"I do not have answers to your questions, but I agree that it was quite strange. Did you see the look on his face when we told him that we search for the King of the Jews? His face became red and I thought that the vein on his forehead was going to burst. Do not forget that he has a reputation for taking vengeance and committing murder. Let us not test him!" replied Balthasar.

"It is unfortunate that we were the ones who had to break the news of the Messiah to Herod. I assumed that all of Jerusalem would be celebrating the Messiah when we arrived," added Gaspar.

"If you ask me, that murderous King cannot be trusted. He is planning something," Melchoir mumbled.

"You may be right, but I see no choice but to honor his request," said Balthasar.

"He means nothing to us! Why not ignore him?" Melchoir asked.

Looking around them as if he were looking for bandits among the rocks, Balthasar sternly answered, "The King knew about our every movement once we entered the city. He will likely have us followed to Bethlehem. What happens to us if he learns that we did not honor his request? Murdering Magi along the highway is not a troublesome task for someone who murdered his own family!"

"We do not know if we will find the child. We no longer have the star! We may have no reason at all to report to Herod if it never happens," Gaspar added.

Hutan and the others quickly gathered around the Magi to hear about the trip to the palace.

"How was your meeting with the King?" asked Hutan.

"Our meeting went well. The King wants us to send him word once we find the Messiah," replied Balthasar as he tried to comfort an anxious Hutan and the men.

But there was no response from Hutan or the others, only looks of concern on their faces.

"How have things gone for you here? Has anyone been helpful to you with the location of the Messiah?" Balthasar asked.

The men looked at one another in silence, until a nervous Hutan replied, "No one knows anything about the Messiah, but many people have warned us about troubling the King with such news. The people are fearful that the King will be threatened by the news of the Messiah and will take his vengeance on them. It might be a good idea for us to move from this place soon!"

"Well, I am afraid that we may have already put the King on alert!" answered Balthasar. Looking to Gaspar, Balthasar said, "Jerusalem does not hold the answers that we had expected. We must speak with Ethan before we plan our next move."

With that, Hutan was asked to retrieve Ethan so he and the Magi may talk by the fire and consider their options that would be least likely to upset the King.

Chapter XVI - God Lights the Path to Bethlehem

When Ethan found the Magi, he told that he had also been speaking to people in the streets of Jerusalem and that he, too, was troubled by what he had heard of Herod's likely response to news of the Messiah.

"King Herod told us that his chief priests and scribes say that the Messiah is to be born in Bethlehem. Remind us what your Scriptures teach?" Balthasar asked Ethan.

Ethan thought for a moment and then replied, "Micah the prophet said that, 'Out of Bethlehem of Judah shall come a ruler, and he shall rule my people Israel.'"

Balthasar turned to his fellow Magi. "Then let us go on to Bethlehem as the Scriptures prophesize. That is where Herod believes the Messiah can be found. Should we spend the night in Jerusalem and make our way to Bethlehem tomorrow? I do not see a need for us to leave Jerusalem this night, but Ethan and Hutan are saying that we have stirred up the city with our presence."

"I am tired, but I do not want to stay in Jerusalem if it will put our men in danger," replied Gaspar.

Melchoir placed one hand on the shoulder of his two friends and urged, "We should leave this place quickly. I do not trust Herod."

"Ethan, do you believe that we are in danger if we stay in Jerusalem tonight?" asked Balthasar.

"There is always the possibility that we are the ones who will bear the King's fury. I spoke with people who told me that it was not long ago that some Pharisees, Jewish priests, predicted that God decreed Herod's government and property would end. So the King has been burdened with seemingly endless bad news. We need to remember that Herod is a foreigner to these people. He became their King by force and he eliminates any who threaten him. So I am afraid that our arrival may have him believing that the prophecy is being fulfilled!" answered Ethan.

"I do not need to hear any more. Hutan, give the order for us to move," directed Balthasar.

"In what direction? We rest at a cross road," said Hutan.

"In the direction of Bethlehem!" Balthasar shouted.

The Magi and their men were discouraged as they left Jerusalem.

Gaspar asked Balthasar as they began to ride, "I do not mean to add to our woes, but how will we discover the Messiah? Conduct a search of Bethlehem?"

"That is a good question, but let us depart the city before we begin worrying about that problem!" Balthasar replied.

The Magi led their caravan south in the direction of Bethlehem.

"Once we leave the city, it will be difficult to see. Are we sure that we know our way?" asked Gaspar.

Hutan, who was riding just behind the Magi with Ethan, answered, "We were told that Bethlehem is about five or six miles from here, to the southwest. We will be climbing hills into the mountains and Bethlehem sits at the summit."

"Five or six miles? Up the hill? Our camels are tired, but I believe that they will manage. Let us not lose our way in the darkness," Balthasar replied.

Gaspar then asked Ethan, "What can you tell us about Bethlehem? What is the meaning of its name?

"It is a small city, home of Boaz and Ruth, whose story is told in Hebrew Scripture. It was also the home of King David. Bethlehem in Hebrew means 'House of Bread,' and our scriptures tell us that bread gives life. In our Persian tongue, 'lehem' means 'flesh…' 'House of Flesh.' Some interpret the meaning of Bethlehem as the place that will provide the bread that gives life to the flesh!" replied Ethan, happy to share his knowledge of Hebrew tradition.

As they pass through Jerusalem's gates, Nekdel and Rushad ride on the same camel and move alongside Balthasar.

Nekdel, sitting on the front of the camel, asked, "How will our ride be this night?" but he was interrupted by a sharp jab to his side by Rushad. Nekdel began to turn his head back toward Rushad when Rushad's out stretched arm brushed by Nekdel's face and he shouted, "Look! Look!"

The caravan came to a stop. All was silent as the men dismounted from their animals and watched in amazement as the star took form in front of them. The men cheered wildly at the sight, embracing each other and slapping each other on the back.

"It is the most amazing thing I have ever seen!" shouted Gaspar.

"It is larger, brighter and closer! It is as if we can reach out and touch it!" Melchoir shouted.

After wiping the tears from his eyes, a speechless Balthasar put an arm around Gaspar and Melchoir as he stared at the star.

"You have yet to say anything, is it not beautiful?" asked Gaspar.

"It moved!" replied Balthasar, keeping his eyes fixed on the star.

"No it is still there, in front of us!" Melchoir said, confused by what his friend has just said.

Balthasar brought his arms together, bringing his friends against his body, and said in a voice cracking with emotion, "No, no! It has changed its position. It is no longer over Jerusalem! It is leading us south to Bethlehem! My God! Your star goes before us, lighting our path!"

With Balthasar's statement, all of the men fell to their knees on the road. They said prayers of thanks and sang praises to God for not abandoning them.

Balthasar held his hand outstretched before him and, looking at the ground, said to the other Magi, "Look at this! My hand casts a shadow in the light of the star! A few moments ago, I could not even see my hand in front of my face."

Gaspar, now sitting on his camel, moved closer to a mesmerized Balthasar, gave him a gentle nudge with his foot and said, "It is time to go, friend. You can watch the star from your camel."

Balthasar shook his head briefly, as if waking from a dream, then leaped onto his camel, gave it a kick and joined the other Magi as the caravan began climbing the hill toward Bethlehem. The men rode in silence as they watched the star.

Out of reverence and a sense of wonder, Balthasar whispered to his friends, "Do you see that it moves ahead of us? It does not stay in one place for us to find our own way... it leads us! How is this possible?"

There was no response; the men knew that God was among them, but they cannot explain it.

Gaspar asked, "Ethan, what do you think is happening?"

"Shechinah!" shouted Ethan.

"What is it you are saying?" asked Gaspar.

"It is not a star that leads us… no star can disappear, reappear and move in this way! It must be the Shechinah Glory Cloud!" blurted an excited Ethan.

Gaspar laughed and requested, "Please explain this Glory Cloud of which you speak."

Ethan moved his camel next to Gaspar so the Magi could hear him speak. "Our scriptures tell us that there were times when God would shine His light on His people. It would come in the form of a light, a fire and sometimes a cloud. A fantastic pillar of fire, the Shechinah Glory Cloud stood in the camp by night and led the Hebrew slaves out of Egypt. God's glory light also filled the tabernacle and temple. This must be what goes before us! What else could it be?" Ethan said to the Magi.

At this moment, the Magi brought their camels to a stop while they spoke.

"Surely what Ethan says is true! The Hebrew God has led us all these months with his star to this place, just as he has led his people!" said Balthasar.

Gaspar's eyes were wide open as he asked, "This God has revealed His star and Himself to us. Why are we deserving of this miracle?"

"The best is yet to come! God is leading us to the Messiah, the one who God himself has chosen! This is happening to us now! And it will soon be upon us: the Messiah, the one who is born to fulfill God's prophecy!" added Melchoir.

At Melchoir's words, the three Magi began to tremble in their excitement and in their fear of being in

God's presence. The rest of the men now surrounded the Magi; they, too, feel God's presence. Filled with intense emotion, a feeling of great joy that was tempered by the trembling fear that came from being in the presence of God himself, the men were silenced by the great power that surrounded them, guiding and protecting.

Balthasar broke the silence by asking what he had been asking himself, "What is expected of us now? How do we properly honor the Messiah when we find him? What could we possibly present to him that would be enough?"

"We offer him what we have!" replied Melchoir.

Balthasar addressed Melchoir and Gaspar, saying, "Of the treasures we carry, we need to prepare the most precious of these for the Messiah. Gold, frankincense and myrrh, are these suitable gifts?"

Gaspar, nodding approval, said, "These are the best of what we carry."

The Magi looked to Ethan for a response. "These things are acceptable to God. Gold, presented to kings and a symbol of royalty, is a most appropriate gift for our new king. We even use gold to honor God in our temple worship. Frankincense is also used in our worship, burned at the altar of our holy place. The intense fragrance of myrrh is used in our burial ceremonies, reminding us of the shortness of our lives and of the immortality of God," Ethan replies.

After speaking, Ethan thought for a moment and then continued, "These items also remind me of those things contained in God's Ark of the Covenant. Gold can be thought of as manna, the frankincense as the tablets of the Ten Commandments and the myrrh as a symbol Aaron's rod," Ethan explained.

After hearing this, Balthasar said to the other Magi, "Let us quickly prepare these things now, so that we can give them to the Messiah."

The Magi went into their carts and removed these valuable items so they would have them when they reached the Messiah. The gold was acquired by Melchoir in his travel in Egypt, while Balthasar traded for the frankincense; like gold, it, too, was costly, made by distilling the resin of the fragrant gum that came from the bark of the Arbor thuris tree. Finally, Gaspar provided the Myrrh, which meant "bitterness," and came from a thorny tree grown in Persia and Egypt. It was used in perfumes and incense and was known to strengthen sick children.

Following the star that lit their path, the caravan climbed the hill toward Bethlehem. They rode in silence, the air is still, and all that could be heard was the feet of the camels and an occasional squeak of a cart wheel.

The Magi led the procession with Balthasar riding in between his two friends. Each of them was in deep thought about what they were experiencing.

In a whisper, Gaspar asked, "Are we dreaming?"

Melchoir answered with a whisper, "We are in the presence of God… our God," Melchoir answered with another whisper.

With that statement, Balthasar reached out to touch both of his friends. Tears flowed from their eyes as they came to realize that, at this moment, they had become followers and believers in the Hebrew God. The God who revealed the star to them those many months ago was about to complete their transformation by revealing the Messiah to them in a most personal way.

With tears still flowing, Gaspar turned to speak to his good friend Balthasar, but the words did not come.

Balthasar nodded in agreement and said, "There are no words."

When the caravan reached the summit, the men saw Bethlehem ahead of them. As they moved toward the town, Melchoir called out, "The star! It will only be a minute more until we reach our destination."

Balthasar gave his camel the command to sit so he could dismount. "Let us walk from here," he spoke softly to the others.

"Hutan, when we come to the place of the Messiah, continue up the road to a suitable location to spend the night that is big enough for all our men. We will come to you when we have finished," spoke Balthasar.

When they came to the small house sitting beneath the star, Melchoir said, "Can this be the place?"

Noticing a mark on the door, Gaspar whispered, "This is the house of a carpenter."

Balthasar knocked once on the door and immediately it opens. Balthasar was about to introduce himself and his companions, but the door opened wide to reveal the Messiah, a young boy, perhaps one year of age, sitting on his mother's lap. The man holding the door motioned for the Magi to come into the house and then he said in Hebrew, "I am Joseph and this is my wife Mary."

God's presence was overwhelming. The Magi fell down, their bodies flat on the floor. They worshipped the Messiah with their prayers. The Magi bowed in reverence as they presented their gifts to the boy's mother.

Melchoir first presented his gift of gold at her feet and quietly said, "Nothing that we possess is worthy as a gift."

Next, Balthasar placed his jar of frankincense by the gold. Gaspar followed with his gift of myrrh.

When they finished worshipping and rose to their feet, Joseph asked the Magi, "Will you stay with us this night?"

Without hesitating, Balthasar replied, "Yes! It would be an honor. I will tell our men that we will stay with you tonight."

When they reached the caravan, the Magi shared the news about staying the evening in the house of the Messiah.

Hutan directed the men to erect the tents and asked Balthasar, "We know it is quite late, but we were also hoping to worship the Messiah."

Balthasar paused for a moment and replied, "If Joseph gives his permission, I will motion for you to come. If permission is granted, it can only be for a moment."

Hutan thanked Balthasar and gathered the men so they could move to the house quickly. When the Magi returned to the house, Balthasar spoke briefly to Joseph and then waved for Hutan and the others to join them.

The men walked to the house quietly and when they reached the door, Nekdel and Rushad were placed in front so they were able to see. When the door opened, they dropped to the ground, worshipping the Messiah from outside because of the little space inside. When the men returned to their tents, they prayed to the Messiah and to the Hebrew God, softly singing praises to him, unable to believe that after months of travel, they had finally found the Messiah beneath the star.

Chapter XVII - Home by Another Road

The Magi settled into their small room in the house of Mary and Joseph. Although exhausted from their long day of travel, they were too excited to sleep. They had already forgotten about their troubling experience with Herod and were overwhelmed with thoughts of the Messiah and their encounter with God Himself. They lied in their room, speaking softly to each other.

"I never imagined our visit with the Messiah would be like this. I thought we would be in a king's palace with many other people, paying our respects. We have been led by God to the Messiah who He has sent! It is incredible!" whispered Balthasar.

"When we entered Jerusalem and learned that no one knew anything of the Messiah and then our star disappeared, I feared that our journey was a failure. And now this! We are with God!" added Gaspar.

"What is God's plan for the Messiah? We never discussed how long we would stay in Jerusalem. I would like to stay in this place, here in Bethlehem, for I do not have family waiting for me," spoke Melchoir.

"We would all like to stay in this place. Perhaps we can serve the Messiah in some way!" replied Gaspar.

"There is much to consider. We will discuss this tomorrow. We will also need to let Herod know that we have found the Messiah. We do not want him to come looking for us," answered Balthasar.

"We should discuss this Herod matter tomorrow. I worry about sharing the news of this boy and his parents with such an evil person," whispered Melchoir.

"If Herod sees the Messiah with his own eyes… and feels God's presence as we do… perhaps he will worship him," Balthasar replied with some hesitancy, as if awaiting confirmation on his statement, but hoping it held some truth.

"Perhaps he will not honor him as we do! Remember, he has not seen the star, he had not heard the news of the Messiah's arrival and he is a murderer. Can he ever be trusted?" asked Melchoir.

The Magi contemplated all of these things as they drifted off to sleep, but no resolve was offered.

The next morning, the light of dawn was brightening the sky when Melchoir was the first to awaken. As his eyes opened, he sat up quickly and gasped for air, startled out of his sleep by a nightmare.

He shouted to his friends, "Wake up! Hurry!" nudging them to awaken from their slumber.

Gaspar, quite startled, reached for his sword before realizing that his sword was with the caravan, but within seconds, the other two were quickly on their feet, fully awake.

"I had a terrible dream, at least I believe it was a dream. It was as if God was speaking to me! He warned us!" spoke Melchoir, as if disbelieving his own words.

"I also had such a dream. God commanded us to leave this place quickly and to not return to Herod!" replied Gaspar.

"God came to all of us! The same dream also came to me!" added a wide awake Balthasar.

"We must tell Joseph!" responded Melchoir.

At that moment, Joseph appeared in their doorway, asking, "Is everything good with you?"

"God came to us in a dream and told us to not return to Herod, but to instead return to our country on a different road! You should leave this place quickly," replied Balthasar.

In a calm voice, Joseph replied, "You must do what God has told you, but we will wait for God to reveal his plans for us."

"God has told us to return to our countries and that is what we will do!" answered Balthasar.

For a few moments, the Magi prayed with Mary and Joseph, thanking God for His warning and asking for God's continued protection. When the Magi reached the caravan, they woke their men and directed them to pack the carts. Balthasar's men were shocked to hear of God's warning to flee Herod and Bethlehem, but no questions were asked as the men hurried to pack, heeding God's warning.

When the caravan was packed and the men were mounting their camels, Balthasar asked Melchoir, "If we are to go home by another road, do you have any suggestions?"

"I suggest that we take the road east to Jericho. We will avoid Jerusalem and be on our way to the King's Highway, and then north to Damascus. We should be well on our way before Herod realizes that we will not be returning," answered Melchoir.

Gaspar joined his friends and, seeing that they were ready to travel, raised his hand to set the caravan in motion.

As they began to move, Gaspar said, "Let us pray that we can put enough distance between ourselves and Herod."

"Once we reach the highway, we will join a caravan moving north and blend in so we do not draw attention to ourselves," offered Melchoir.

"God told us to move with haste. There can be no delays. We need to keep everyone moving," Balthasar said as he turned to check on his men.

"Melchoir, I thought that when our time in Jerusalem was through, you would return to Egypt," Gaspar commented.

"That was my plan, but everything has changed. I must stay with you until God tells me something different," Melchoir answered without hesitation, Gaspar nodding in approval.

"Perhaps God intends for me to see Desta again in Damascus," Melchoir said with a smile.

But Melchoir's smile soon faded and his face instead showed concern as he asked his friends, "What about the Messiah? Should his parents travel with us? We can offer protection to them. If we are not safe in this place, surely they are in great danger!"

Balthasar nodded in agreement and said, "We are all worried about the Messiah, but we heard Joseph. They will wait until they hear from God. God delivered us to this place from our far away homes, he will have no trouble keeping the Messiah and his family safe," Balthasar confidently replied.

The two other Magi nodded in agreement, silently contemplating their last twenty-four hours and speaking very infrequently as Bethlehem faded in the distance behind them. Melchoir led the caravan east for most of the day and it was early evening when the caravan came to rest within sight of Jericho. The men remained quiet as they continued to contemplate all that they had experienced and considered what else awaited them on their trip home.

Balthasar led the men in prayer and song, and the joy in their hearts surpassed any fear of reprisal from Herod. Each man knew that his life had been forever changed, and although a full day's ride from Bethlehem, God's presence among them remained as strong this evening as it was in Bethlehem.

After the prayers were offered and the songs sung in praise of Yahweh, Balthasar said to the men, "We have seen our way through many difficulties and we have witnessed many wonders. Yet nothing compares to what we have experienced in the past few hours. Last night, we met the Messiah and were in the presence of God Himself, a presence that continues on with us. After our long journey, I never imagined that we would reach our destination only to flee quickly from it to save our lives. What is more remarkable is that we flee with great joy in our hearts and a satisfaction that comes to few men.

"When we worshipped the Messiah, we presented him with our gifts, which we thought to be of great value. Yet we have been given a gift worth far more! God revealed Himself to us through His star and through the Messiah, who has come to all men. May God stay with us!" Balthasar shouted.

Before Balthasar could continue, the men fell to their knees in praise of Yahweh, tears flowing before the men were back to their feet, sharing embraces.

When the men were calm once more, Balthasar continued, "Our hearts tell us that God has provided us with this knowledge and comfort so we will share it with others. I cannot say for certain where God will lead us now, but wherever we are led, we will share the news of the Messiah."

Hearing these words, Melchoir jumped to his feet and shouted, "Our journey is not over! It is only beginning!"

The rest of the men joined Melchoir, raising and lifting their voices in cheers and praises of God. Nekdel and Rushad climbed onto the shoulders of Hutan and Pulan and joined the celebration.

Balthasar put an arm around Gaspar and Melchoir and asked, "Friends, now that we are well rested, are you ready for the trip home?"

The men laughed as Gaspar replied, "I cannot imagine a better way to spend our days than riding through Persia sharing our news!"

And with that, the men looked forward to the many more months ahead that they would spend spreading the news of the Messiah to those they met, knowing that they would never forget the wondrous site they saw – and the powerful presence of God they felt – when the door was opened to them in the little town of Bethlehem.

Byron Anderson

Made in the USA
San Bernardino, CA
10 December 2014